SALTY DOGS

"BOOT"

Bro. Harris Alexander

Dedication

To the US Navy and the men and women worldwide who answer the call and serve their country through military service; whether in times of peace or times of conflict.

Contents

Chapter One

1. Abrupt Departure

11:45am. April 1988. Messenger County Federal Courthouse. Four young men stand before a judge as the Assistant DA reads a list of charges and suggests to the judge that the young men be taken into custody immediately and be held until the investigation of a shooting wraps. The judge agrees with the Assistant DA when one of the young men speaks, "Excuse me, your honor. I was told by Captain O'Bryan of the Beach City Police Department that if I enlisted in the military, then I wouldn't be tried for any of this."

The judge looks at the young man, "Well, mister um... Trevion Louis Carson, did you enlist?" Trevion takes a moment to reflect on how he got to this position. Invited to an out-of-town party by a friend of a friend. A group of guys show up and gunfire quickly follows. Trevion is crouching behind a car with the two guys he came with as a full-fledged shootout is going on. They need to get across the street to their car, but they're pinned down. Trevion looks over and sees that the friend of the friend of a friend has a gun, but is almost soiling his boxers in fear.

"If you're not going to get us out of here, give me that strap, punk!" Gun in hand, Trevion moves to the rear of the car and sees one of the shooters. Two shots to his right knee, and he goes down. Trevion creeps out a bit further and sees another shooter ducking behind the

1

car that they need to get to. Aim. Fire. The target moves. Instead of hitting him in the rear end, it's a body shot. "Let's go!" he yells, as the three dash to the Cutlass Supreme and make their escape.

"Yes sir, your honor, I joined the Navy; here are my orders." A bailiff walks over and takes the paperwork from Trevion and brings it to the judge. As the judge reads the orders, Trevion remembers the deal that Captain O'Bryan gave him two months ago. Trevion was playing basketball when he was picked up by detectives and brought in for questioning.

Trevion knew that there is no way they have any evidence on him. The gun was a revolver so there were no leftover shells. He kept the gun, much to the dismay of its previous owner, and destroyed it. Neither of the two guys that he was with knew his real name, they only knew him by his nickname; Sloppy.

As Trevion sits in the shorts and tank top that he came in wearing, a detective walks into the interrogation room and removes Trevion's restraints. "Young man, I just read your file, and I just need to ask, were you there on the night of the shooting?" Trevion denies being there. "See, I'm not in the business of ruining someone's future if they actually have potential. Those cops out there, they don't care if you were there or not, as long as they lock up as many of you as they can. If you get caught up in this, it's over for you. Your school records are impressive; good grades, good attendance, and what good-looking, athletic kid joins the chess club? Do us both a favor and join the service, boy. Do something with yourself, and I'll make sure that you ain't involved in any of this mess."

The judge hands the paperwork back to the bailiff. "Mr. Williams, any objections to this arrangement?" The assistant DA looks over at Trevion, "No, your honor, if he's headed to boot camp, then the people decline to object and wish him well on his pending service. Just a question; why the Navy, son?"

Trevion thinks for a moment. "I was going to go to the Army until I saw a commercial talking about how they do more before 4am than most people do all day. And, I'm not really a morning person." The judge bursts into laughter then dismisses Trevion.

2.   A Lesson in Trust

Trevion was never a troublesome kid, quite the contrary. He has always been a very polite and intelligent young man. Sweet to the point of gullibility at times. His father was a gun enthusiast who owned his own small gun store, so Trevion grew up shooting. He listened very closely in court to hear if anyone died that night, but they just kept calling it a shooting, so he's still not sure.

As he rides the bus home from the courthouse, he reads his orders which have him going to boot camp in San Diego and then to Logistics school in Mississippi; the latter would not be happening if it were not for the random sailor who walked up to him during his two-day testing period.

Trevion had passed the written portion of the test with a high score and had just completed the physical portion when he was sent to a Petty Officer sitting behind a desk. The Personnelman Petty Officer Second-Class, or PN2, offered Trevion what is called Apprenticeship Training, where he'll be able to see every job on the ship and choose which department he wants to work with.

This sounded good, and Trevion was ready to sign when the PN2 looked at his watch then said to return after lunch. "Here you go, son. Sign your life away," an older serviceman says as Trevion walks to the cafeteria. Trevion picked up the pen and wrote his name then signed. The serviceman thought the joke was a winner because he repeated it to everyone who entered the cafeteria. Trevion sat there, looking at the pitiful food on his tray before deciding to walk down to a burger joint that he saw when his recruiter dropped him off.

There, the random sailor, who was dressed in full uniform, asked if he could sit with Trevion. "I saw you in the MEPS station, what did they offer you?" After hearing what Trevion was offered, the Petty Officer informs him that he's being undersold. "If you scored an 87, then you pretty much have your pick of jobs anyway. Apprenticeship is for the people who score too low to qualify for those other jobs."

Trevion returns to the PN2's desk armed with information and demanding a guaranteed 'A-School'. The PN2 is taken aback by the suddenly informed young man and pretends to make a phone call. "Sorry kid, all of the slots are taken. But you can still go to Apprenticeship Training, then once a school opens up, you could get in."

Trevion remembers what the sailor told him back at the burger joint, "Ok, thanks very much for your time. Could you please call my recruiter and tell him to come and pick me up?"

The PN2 pretends to make another phone call then looks up something on the computer. "Which school did you want?"

Trevion pauses as he's suddenly out of information. He remembered that the sailor was in logistics and he mentioned something called a West Pac. "I want a guaranteed logistics school and a guaranteed West Pac."

The PN2 looks at his computer. "You mean Storekeeper? The only way is if you leave this Tuesday." Trevion agrees since the summons that he received two weeks ago in the mail demanded he appear that Monday. Trevion's pager goes off, snapping him out of the flashback. It's his ex-girlfriend's best friend. Trevion considers staying on the bus for three extra stops to go and visit her. "What the hell?" he thinks.

4

3. Basic Training

"What the hell are you doing here?" Trevion says as he looks in the mirror, which draws laughter from the six men who are also cleaning the bathroom area.

Quincy, another recruit, says, "It's almost over, Carson, where are you headed after we're done with Boot Camp?" Trevion tells him Meridian, MS. "Yo, ain't that where that movie Mississippi Burning happened?"

Trevion thinks for a second, "No shit, and they pulled the sailors from the nearby base to help with the search."

They all pause, then Quincy says, "So, I think that you'd better stay your dark-brown ass on the base!" They all laugh and continue cleaning and chatting until they hear "Company 1116, attention on deck!"

Everyone stops what they're doing and stands at attention as the Company Commander walks in. He goes around looking at the berthing area before making his way back to the showers. "Good job men, wrap this up then you can write letters and shoot the shit until Taps. Tomorrow morning, most of you will be headed to the Galley where you'll do whatever you're told and you'll do it at the highest possible level. Eleven – Sixteen is the best company on this base, and I fully expect everybody here to demonstrate that during Detail Week! You're all targets, other companies want to take your spot at the top. Don't do anything that will let us all down!" The grizzled Senior Chief Petty Officer looks around for a moment then yells 'Carry on!' as he exits.

Detail Week is a six-day assignment away from the berthing area that had become the recruits' home over the course of boot camp. Detail Week comes towards the end of basic training and involves the recruits being assigned to different areas around the base to work. Many of the recruits are excited about doing something other than training all day, while others would rather not work in the Galley all day.

The Company Officers, who are recruits that have been given leadership positions, will be getting much better assignments than the rest of the recruits. Trevion is one of the Company Officers, he is what's called the Master-At-Arms. His responsibility is to lead the recruits whenever they are inside of any building. Only thing is, he's been assigned to the Galley as well.

The others poke at him about it, especially the Company Secretary who will be assigned to the Processing Center where he'll get to boss around the newcomers in the same way that they were all bossed around when they arrived. "You're a man of the people, right Carson? Don't you want to get your hands dirty with the other blue collars?"

Trevion scoffs, "Dumb-ass, we're all blue collars. You have on the same blue shirt that we all have on. Those sock-cocks, fresh off of the bus and scared shitless, will think you're someone important; but we'll all know that you're just a dweeb who became Secretary because you were the only one of us who knew how to type."

The Secretary smiles, "Yep, you'll know that while you're sweating your balls off in the Galley. Coming back here smelling like Pine-Sol and French fries. "

4.   First Liberty

The Galley is a beast. Three different dining areas with two kitchens in the center and six dish-washing stations. Those assigned to the kitchen spend their time running around following the orders of the kitchen staff, who are unnecessarily mean and bossy. Those assigned to the dish-washing station receive the endless stream of eating trays and dishes filled with leftover food.

The unlucky pull garbage detail, which takes the longest at the end of the day and sends the recruits back to the berthing area later than anyone else. Trevion, being his company's Master-At-Arms, is assigned the role of Floor Warden and floats around the Galley with a clipboard making sure that everyone is doing their jobs.

Two-thirds of the Galley is for the recruits. They're herded in, told where to sit, and have a certain amount of time to finish their meals before the Company Commanders bangs their fists on the table and order them to "Pop tall!", signaling the end of their dining experience. The line leading to any of the dish-washing stations on the recruit side always moves slowly as recruits try to finish their meals before surrendering their trays to the 'scrub crew', who would spray their trays and dishes before loading them into an extremely hot dish-washing machine.

"Hey, Carson! Come over here for a second," the other Floor Warden calls out from across the dining area.

Trevion strolls over, "What's up, Graham?" He tells Trevion a plan to leave the recruit side of the base and go to the McDonald's that's located on the Apprenticeship side.

"Most of us will be staying here after graduation," Graham explains. "I know that you're going to A-School like me so, since we won't be seen here again, here's what I have in mind."

Graham tells Trevion that while the recruits are all doing the Detail Week assignment, they're not wearing the white leggings and green duty belt that distinguishes recruits from apprentices; and that they could just walk over to have lunch at McDonald's and no one would know. Trevion thinks about what his Company Commander told him about his company being the best and that no one had better tarnish that reputation, but the prospect of a McRib Value Pack is too much for him to resist.

So, the next day, he makes his usual rounds throughout the Galley, checking in with Graham every so often. At 10:30am, Graham signals Trevion, and the two hide their clipboards in the office and casually stroll out of the Galley.

They walk from the recruit side to the Apprentice side is a short one. Trevion is so focused on eating McDonald's that he's not at all nervous about the trip; Graham, on the other hand, lost his confidence the moment the two left the Recruit side of the base. "Alright, Carson, we've walked on the wild side. Let's go back now."

Trevion looks over at Graham in shock. "Isn't this your master plan? Look, I can see those golden arches from here. Look, the place is right in front of us, a hundred yards tops. You honestly want to back?"

Graham needs a bit more convincing before they're able to continue on; and a bit more once they reach the restaurant; and even more in order to go inside. The place is very crowded, filled with apprentices, Petty Officers, and Chiefs, so Trevion uses this fact to ease Graham's concerns that the two will be spotted. As they eat their meals, three female apprentices approach their booth asking if they can join them. Graham relaxes around the ladies and they have a nice time talking with them. The two recruits return to the Galley and resume their responsibilities unnoticed.

5.   McDonald's Girls

With basic training over, all that's left for the recruits is graduation. Their Company Commanders are basking in the glow of having the best company of recruits in this class, being a 'Color Company' having earned every commendation, competitive award, and the highest test scores in quite a while. Trevion and his company enjoy the final week of basic training mostly unsupervised. They wake themselves up, do morning exercises, and march to the Galley on their own. The CCs only stop by first thing in the morning, just before Reveille, and at night right before Taps. The same applies to Graham's company.

While having lunch, the two talk and decide to take a trip over to the Apprentice side of the base later to hang out with the females they had met during Service Week. The apprentices are having a small gathering in the berthing rec room as many of them have received their orders and are heading off to join the fleet.

Trevion and Quincy wait until their CC finishes his evening visit and the company is either laying in their bunks or at the Centerboard table writing loved ones before making their exit. They must make it to the Apprentice side before taps and, since there are only two of them, by rule they must double-time; which means jog. Halfway there, they are joined by Graham and two recruits from his company. "Dude," Quincy says as they jog across the marching area called the Grinder, "I'm going to be all sweaty once we get there!" As they approach the path that leads to the Apprentice side, they stop jogging, and Graham pulls out a small duffel bag from inside of his shirt. The five recruits remove their duty belts and leggings and put them inside of the bag as they stroll to the berthing area recreation room.

6. A Lesson in Quick Action

Trevion was never a big drinker. In fact, he's not had many drinks as he is only eighteen and wasn't a huge fan of beer, which was the drink of choice with his friends back home. The punch that the apprentices were serving was delicious but, unbeknownst to Trevion, very strong. As he dances with the girl that he met during Service Week, he mentions that he'd rather be somewhere more private with her.

The female sailor invites Trevion and his friends over to her room to hang out with her and her fellow apprentices. Normally this would be out of the question, Trevion knows that they need to be back to their bunks before Reveille, but the alcohol in that tasty punch has convinced him that the best thing to do is to gather his buddies and leave with these girls.

Trevion takes a deep breath and opens his eyes, squinting at the sunshine filling the room. "Holy mother of God!" he screams, waking up his bedmate. Trevion looks around the room and sees Graham jumping out of bed in a panic. The two get dressed and rush into an adjacent room to get the rest of the recruits, and they all make a mad dash off the Apprentice side of the base. "What time is it?" Quincy's question brings another wave of panic over the recruits as they make it back to the recruit side and begin putting their gear back on.

"I don't know, that may have been worth it if we get caught."

Trevion looks back at Graham, "Maybe to you, I can't wash out, or I'm headed to jail, so how about we do less talking bullshit and more hustling back!" Trevion and Quincy make it back to their berthing area and slip in through the side entrance only to find the whole company sitting on the floor in the meeting area.

"Welcome back, boys," sings the Company Secretary in a loud enough voice to alert the CC. "Where did you guys run off to so early in the morning?"

The CC exits his office and walks towards the two sweaty recruits. Trevion replies, "That's exactly where we went; running. Just like we do every morning before you pussies wake up. Why is everybody sitting in here anyway?"

The Company Commander walks over to Trevion. "Did you clear that action up the chain of command, recruit?"

Trevion stands up straight and says, "Yes, sir. You gave us standing orders to 'maintain our excellence' until graduation. We all know that you go for a run every morning before getting here, so we decided to go for a run every morning before you get here. Sir! This morning, we did a blow-out run, and it took longer than we anticipated. It was my idea to do it so the fault lies with me, sir, I should have had us back before the kids woke up."

The smirk on the Secretary's face melts away as the CC accepts the explanation, then relieves Trevion and Quincy from morning marching practice. "Get showered, get some chow, then meet us on the Grinder at nine-hundred hours; understood? Good! Now, as for the rest of you pussies, fall out and get into ranks!"

7. Off to A-School

Standing at the airport in his dress blues or Cracker Jack uniform, Trevion feels great as he realizes how much attention he's receiving from the pretty girls around him. He tries his best to stand like the iconic painting of the Lone Sailor that he had seen back in boot camp. Upon graduation, he, along with a few graduating recruits, went out to celebrate before they all went their separate ways. It was their first official liberty night, so they went to as many bars and strip clubs as they could before they had to be back to the base.

Trevion takes a long look at his tickets, which will take him from San Diego, CA to Atlanta, GA, and then on to Meridian, MS. Before long, Trevion is joined by two other recent graduates, also dressed in their blue uniforms. The trio enjoy the VIP treatment from the flight crew, and when Trevion mentions that this will be his very first time flying, the sailors are bumped to first class on their flight to Atlanta.

They arrive in Atlanta and meet up with several other sailors who are headed to the logistics school. The group of young men and women stand near Gate 24, waiting for their flight to begin boarding. 'Flight number 4345 to Meridian, MS is now boarding at Gate 24' The group walk over to the gate door and wait for the flight attendant to open it.

"Oh, you all can just go right through that door," says the young lady standing at the ticket counter. Trevion opens the door and is immediately greeted by a gust of heat that felt as if he had just opened a hot oven.

He looks through the door and sees a portable stairway leading down to the runway. He looks back at the number on the door and then at his boarding pass. "I'm sorry, is this correct?"

The young lady behind the counter chuckles and tells the group that their plane is on the runway. "It's the white plane with the two blue stripes, it has 4345 on the tail." Trevion looks down onto the hot runway and can see a small, two-engine plane about one-hundred yards away.

"You mean the crop duster? The plane with the propellers?"

The sailors make their way down the metal stairway and across the airport runway which has been heated by the hot Atlanta sun. By the time they make it to the small plane, they're all dripping sweat. "Yeah, these heavy, wool uniforms don't seem like such a swell idea anymore," Trevion jokes as the group begins taking their seats. The plane has only one aisle with two seats on one side and a single seat on the other. This is a far cry from the first-class luxury that Trevion had just experienced, and his anxiety over flying returns. There are a few other people on the flight, businessmen mostly, who acknowledge the guys for being in the military.

The plane shutters as the engines turn on, the young lady from the ticket counter walks onto the plane and pulls out a small megaphone. She begins to give the mandatory safety speech. 'Really, a megaphone?' Trevion thinks to himself as he tries to calm his nerves. The plane begins taxiing down the runway. Trevion looks over at the other side of the plane and can see the propeller spinning, then looks out of the window on his own side and sees that the propeller is not spinning.

He watches it for a few moments, waiting for it to kick in, when the plane begins picking up speed. "Um," he nervously says, "is there any reason why this propeller isn't spinning?" The flight attendant assures Trevion that there's nothing wrong, but her words do nothing for his anxiety. Finally, just before liftoff, the propeller comes to life, and the plane is on its way.

8. And so, it Begins

The passengers all exit the plane and walk into the luggage claim area of the very small airport. They range from pretty tipsy to fully drunk from all of the in-flight drinks that they'd consumed. When the flight attendant came by taking drink orders, Trevion tried to order a Tequila Sunrise to calm his nerves. "I'm going to have to see your ID, sugar," the attendant said, to which Trevion presents his brand-new military ID. She apologizes and says that he can't drink because he's not yet twenty-one.

"Let that young man have a drink!" demands one of the passengers. "If he's old enough to die for our country, then he's old enough to have a drink!" yells another passenger. The flight attendant consults with the plane's pilot and Trevion is allowed to buy drinks; only he never actually buys one because the passengers buy him and the other sailors all the drinks that they want.

A chute opens up and all of their luggage comes sliding then crashing down to the end of a ramp. "Are you kidding me?" Trevion asks in disgust. "That's how they treat our luggage out here?" The group erupt into laughter and begin to say their goodbyes.

One gentleman hands Trevion a business card, "If you ever make your way out to Jackson, look me up. We can have a few drinks."

Trevion takes the card, "You got it, buddy. If they give me some liberty over here, I'll give you a call."

The cab ride to the base was long, almost an hour long. The two other students in the cab with Trevion begin to get nervous as they draw closer to the base. Trevion has never been this tipsy before and has the power of liquid courage on his side. They get to the base and are greeted by two servicemen who process them in. Once they've been assigned their rooms, the servicemen give the new students the standing orders and base rules.

One of them concludes by asking, "Are there any questions? Good, your class will start next Monday. There's still a few more students heading in. Until then, you'll report to Building 4 every morning at 0900. Got it?"

"Yeah," Trevion responds.

The serviceman looks at Trevion, "Yeah?"

Trevion looks back at him, "Yes." Folding his arms, the serviceman warns Trevion of his attitude.

"So, my Company Commanders in Boot Camp told me that I'm only supposed to call officers sir, and you're rocking the dungarees so…" The other new students begin snickering at Trevion's comment.

"Great, we got a bunch of fun-guys. We'll change that real quick. Grab your shit and get to your bunks, Taps is in two hours which gives you plenty of time to get your beds made."

9.   Mid-Terms

A-School was a breeze, most of what Trevion is being taught has to do with numbers and accounting, which comes easy to him due to his summers working in his dad's store. Inventory, budgeting, part numbers, the stuff that he grew sick of his dad drilling him on is exactly what's being taught. Trevion makes sure to call home and thank his dad for those summers because now he spends far less time studying than the other guys in his room.

The dorms are set up with a large common area and four bedrooms called tacks because you give your room number as *'Building G, Room 14 tack 2' or 'Building D, Room 21 tack 4'* with the tack being a dash and the number following it being which bedroom you were in. The tacks each had four beds and a bathroom. The common area has only sofas and coffee tables so the guys in Trevion's room all pitched in and rented a full entertainment center set; which made the room one of the more popular hangout spots.

The base cafeteria was something of legend, being staffed with civilian cooks from Meridian and the nearby cities who bring their southern touch to all of the food. Students would be out in town, then take the very long cab ride back to the base just to catch dinner in the cafeteria, only to take the long cab ride back to finish enjoying their liberty.

As Trevion sits on the sofa watching TV with his roommates, he takes a moment to reflect on things. How disappointed his father would have been if Trevion had procrastinated any longer and not enlisted, then ended up going to jail with the others following that court date. How he'd be sitting in a jail cell rather than watching an episode of COPS in a college-style military dorm.

"Alright, ladies, Taps is in ten minutes, so kill this zombie box and go to your tacks!" The room lead is the highest-ranking sailor in the room and has the responsibility of keeping order. Sitting from his bed inside of his tack, he yells orders and cracks very inappropriate jokes. "And make sure you make your fucking beds in the morning! If Chief Sheldon chews me out again about you pussies leaving your bunks out of order, I swear, you will not like it." Trevion makes his way to his tack along with his only tack-mate, Brenner.

Brenner is from a small town in Wyoming and considered himself anti-racist while most of his friends and family were not. At all. But, boot camp and now A-School is testing that stance as he's, for the first time, surrounded by other nationalities and feeling pretty uncomfortable about it. Trevion is helping ease the transition with his willingness to speak honestly and without prejudice.

Being from Beach City, where the population is pretty evenly mixed and most schools were fully integrated, Trevion grew up with many nationalities and is only prejudiced towards racists; of any nationality, including his own.

"Trey, let me borrow your notes on the mid-term."

Trevion laughs, "Dude, relax. You know this shit; you'll do just fine. You actually need to focus on this weekend and the New Orleans trip. That package that we bought is out of this world, man! I'm telling you, we're about to have a ball."

Brenner slips into his bunk, "You ever been there?"

"Once, when I was about eleven or twelve. My mom's family is from out there so I went with my grandmother during Spring vacation. But I don't remember shit. Well, other than some weird shit, but we have really nice rooms, and I have family out there to point us to the best spots. Dream of all that Louisiana tail that we'll be chasing and stop worrying about a test that you're never going to fail."

The two lay in their bunks for a while before Brenner asks, "What weird shit?"

Trevion tells him about a day that he was out playing with the other kids and there was this guy sitting on a recliner. "He was there every day! In the morning, he'd go to work; then he'd come home and take a shower then sit in that chair watching TV."

Brenner asks what's so weird about that, to which Trevion says, "Because I was in the back yard and my aunties were back there grilling ribs or something. One of my aunts said that she buried that guy's underwear somewhere in the backyard, that's why he's just sitting there watching TV and not hanging out with his friends like he used to." There is a silence, then Trevion says, "Voodoo, man! They put some kind of spell on him and he wasn't able to leave the house."

Brenner turns over in his bunk. "I would be pissed at you right now for sending me to sleep with a fucking boogieman story, but I did ask."

10. Blown Away

Once A-School students take their final exam they're given their orders based on their final score; which consists of their overall grades, their mid-term score, and their final exam score. Everyone fills out a wish list of places they'd like to be stationed, and the students with the highest final scores get orders based on their wish list, while the rest get assigned by the needs of the Navy. Trevion and Brenner are amongst the top students and both aced their mid-terms, so the chances of them receiving orders from their wish list is pretty high.

The two, along with many other students from the base, set off for a weekend trip to New Orleans with a package offered by the base at an incredible discount. The group will be staying at a hotel located on the world-famous Bourbon Street and each received a coupon book giving incredible discounts to many of the city's attractions and restaurants.

Trevion was never a ladies man; his natural personality always gets in the way of trying to be suave. But standing next to Brenner, Trevion is a pimp. The others in the group of seven young sailors all come from various places across the US, and they're all in awe of downtown New Orleans. Brenner, being a natural leader, has everyone following him as he follows Trevion, but always has the final word on whatever Trevion suggests. This works out well as he allows a bit of hijinks on Friday but vetoes all outdoor activities on Saturday when the weather turns.

Brenner suggests that everyone just hang out at the hotel until the sudden rainstorm subsides, which turns out to be a good choice as they receive notice that due to weather they're returning early. Anyone not in the hotel during the announcement will have to hope the weather isn't too bad for the regular bus to travel.

The group pack up and hop on the early bus back to the base. "A hurricane, awesome!" Brenner exclaims.

Trevion looks over at him in horror "What? Awesome? Exactly what the hell is so awesome about the roof dislodging from the barracks and flinging us all into the sky?" Brenner laughs, but he laughs alone.

Everyone is very nervous about the hurricane that's heading in. "You guys watch too much TV, we'll be nice and safe in Meridian and only will catch the tail end of a swirl at best." One of the group asks if Brenner is a meteorologist, which brings the tense group to laughter.

Three and a half hours is how long the bus ride back was, but it felt like an eternity as the rain would pour and then stop and then pour and then stop.

Brenner is the only one fascinated by the pattern, pointing out of the window and explaining the cloud formations. They arrive back at the base and the weather has calmed. A few of the female students from the bus say they'd like to go to shoot pool at the base club and ask Trevion and Brenner if they'd like to join them. It's a few hours still until dinner will be served at the cafeteria so they decide to go.

On their way back, it gets very cold. "Do you want my jacket?" Trevion asks Crawford, one of the female students.

"No, but we can walk closer together." Trevion puts his arm around her and the two chat as they walk through the quarter-mile of woods leading back from the base club. As they approach the back side of the cafeteria, it abruptly begins to hail. Everyone runs to take cover in a doorway, except for one of the female students.

"I've never seen hail before! Oh my God, it's so cool. Ice is really falling from the sky! Ow!" She picks up the large hail stone that hit her in the head. "Look at the size of this thing! Ow! Ow, ow, ow!!" The group laughs hysterically as she runs towards them while being pelted with marble-size hail. The five students stand there waiting until the hail turns into rain, then make a dash to the cafeteria to enjoy the first-rate food.

"Listen up!" Everyone in the cafeteria stops eating and looks over at the Petty Officer standing with his hand up. "We are officially on shutdown, which means no one is allowed to exit whichever structure they're in. Please finish up so that the staff can do their jobs then everyone move to this area over here. Once we get word, we'll start letting folks out."

Everyone watches through the window as the storm gets worse and worse. Trees begin falling over from the very high winds, and the rain is flooding everything. The decorative notches around the windows suddenly make sense as panels are attached and secured into place. Repeated pleas to let everyone leave are answered with rejection as the doors are locked and no one is allowed to exit. Brenner is the only one fascinated by the storm, everyone else is quite frightened.

Then the power goes out, and suddenly Brenner isn't so fascinated anymore. Trevion sits with Crawford, trying to comfort her even though he's completely freaking out inside. Lightning and thunder add to the tension as the storm begins to grow in strength when suddenly the Petty Officer says, "Alright, we can't order the kitchen staff to stay here and they've chosen to go home. So, everyone exit! There will be staff outside to direct you to safety."

Brenner explodes, "You've got to be shitting me! We had a chance to get out of here when it wasn't Armageddon outside and you wouldn't let us go, but now that shit is flying around and trees are falling over, you're pushing us out? What kind of horse shit is that?" The Petty Officer frowns and orders Brenner and everyone else out.

It usually takes about seven minutes to walk from the cafeteria, but seven minutes out in this weather is six and a half minutes too long as they have to stand close to walls in order to not be blown over by the very strong winds. A few of the teaching staff are outside directing people into the first available rooms, which are filling up as everyone takes shelter from the storm. "This way!" one of them yells as Trevion runs towards him with Crawford clutching the back of his jacket. The five of them are pushed into an empty room to sit and wait out the storm.

After a while, a member of the teaching staff comes in with a plastic bag full of blankets and pillows, "You guys are lucky, this is an empty room. Everybody that was in here graduated already. Find a bunk and rack out, this storm is going to only get stronger throughout the night. Ladies in one tack and guys in another. We'll bring food in the morning if it's still too dangerous to go to the cafeteria."

The students divvy up the beddings and find a room. There are only three females and two males so, Trevion and Brenner volunteer to share a tack so that the ladies can have their own space, which the ladies unanimously shoot down. They all sleep in one tack with Trevion and his new friend sharing a bunk.

11.   Sliding Into Home Plate

The storm was timed perfectly. A large portion of the students had recently graduated while an influx of new students were arriving, just in time to assist with the cleanup. All of the students who signed their names as responsible for the entertainment center inside of Trevion and Brenner's room had all received their orders and were gone, everyone except for Trevion, who now had total responsibility for the bill. The bill which had been neglected and was past due.

Trevion calls his dad to ask for help, his dad suggests that Trevion roll the entertainment center into his tack and just pay it off. "It'll help grow your credit and I'll pay for it to get shipped here when you leave." Half of what his dad is saying is meant to help Trevion while the other half will benefit his dad who will get a new entertainment center for his den. Trevion knows this but doesn't mention it since he's asking for money at the moment. Paying for the entertainment center reduces the extra cash that Trevion has, but it's offset by the fact that he's now dating a much older Crawford who helps him out with whatever he needs.

The tack, which only had Trevion and Brenner in it, is now at its capacity with the arrival of new students and a new room lead, BM3. The BM3 took the Apprenticeship route and served three years on a ship before making Petty Officer and being able to attend A-School. The old lead was tough, but this one is simply an ass. He's not at all likable and speaks down to everyone. When Trevion complains to Crawford about him, she seems to tilt towards BM3's point of view.

It doesn't take long before Crawford leaves Trevion and begins dating the unsavory new lead, who rubs it in Trevion's face by repeating, "I have too many Cs. Car. Crow. Cash. Charisma. You didn't stand a chance, schoolboy." BM3 tries to take charge of the entertainment system when it's in the common area, which makes Trevion leave it in his tack. This gives BM3 more ammo to use against Trevion to turn the students in the room against him.

12. Speed Bump

Crawford was rather beautiful, which earned her a following around the base. When she left Trevion, many of the girls that she hung with wanted to be there to pick up the pieces. Trevion wasn't interested in any of them, or any woman on the base for that matter. Being dumped is one thing, it happens to the best of them. To be dumped for another person, that stings. Considerably. Torture is when the one who took the person that dumped you not only lives with you, but has authority over you and uses that to constantly chastise you. Constantly belittle you. Constantly bully you.

Brenner wants to beat BM3 up, but Trevion says no. "Bro, we only have four weeks left here then it will be off to a different adventure. Right now, we're studs. Top of our class, known around the base, still in our teens. Both of them are already in their late-twenties and getting desperate. Let them have each other, we're kings of the fresh-out-of-high schoolers." The two decide to rent a car and drive to nearby

Jackson to get away from the so-called 'service skirts'.

Jackson is nothing like Hollywood, so Trevion isn't impressed, but he knows that he's jaded by being from a real big city so he tries not to rain on Brenner's excitement over being there. "Hey, I know a guy out here!" Trevion says as he pulls a business card from his wallet.

They go to a pay phone and call up Vick, the guy that Trevion had met on the flight into Meridian. "Trevion, how the hell are you, boyo?" Vick yells over the phone. Trevion tells him that he and a friend are in Jackson and asks where the hot spots are. "Where are you guys? I'll come pick you up and bring you to my brother's hotel; he works downtown and can get you the best rooms at the cheapest prices. Then, we'll go from there."

Vick brings the young sailors to a very expensive hotel where they meet his brother who says, "Tell you guys what, I need a place to throw a little kick-back tonight so, I'll give you guys one of the family suites and only charge you for a single room; but you have to get it for two nights and tonight, you have to let me host a wine tasting in it. What do you say?"

The two agree and spend the evening rubbing shoulders with the young, up-and-coming elite of Mississippi as Vick introduces them to everyone; addressing Trevion as his 'buddy in the military'. Trevion knows that Vick is just using him as cool-cred around the more prominent members of the wine club, but he doesn't mind.

He even talks up his relationship with Vick to help him out and co-signs Vick's exaggerated story of their flight into Meridian. At around midnight, the party dies out and everyone goes home, Trevion and Brenner are left with a huge, two-room suite for the rest of their visit and a bunch of wine that the party left behind.

The next day, while shopping in the downtown area, Brenner meets a young woman who is there with a friend. Brenner summons the courage to suggest that the four of them have drinks later on, then tries to contain his glee when she agrees. Running back over to Trevion he exclaims, "Alright, now it's time for you to be my wingman. You can demonstrate all of those skills that you've been trying to teach me. We have a date tonight with those two over there."

He points to the two ladies exiting the store. "Not bad, rookie!" Trevion exclaims while patting Brenner on the back. "What are their names, and where are we meeting them?" Brenner's triumphant smile quickly fades, then he runs out of the shop after the two.

Later that night, the four do an abbreviated bar crawl, meaning they went to whichever bar would serve to a minor who was in the military. Surprisingly, there were quite a few. Being a good wingman means that Trevion needed to pull the tag-along away from target often, in order to give Brenner time alone with her. This wasn't very difficult for Trevion because the tag-along was quite attractive. They all ended the crawl with wine back at Trevion and Brenner's hotel room.

The next morning, the two couples sit and enjoy the complimentary continental breakfast offered by the hotel. Trevion and the tag-along sit together chatting, "You're really only eighteen?" she asks. Trevion pulls out his military ID and shows it to her, to which she pulls out her driver's license and shows it to him.

"You just turned twenty-one, Miss Yolanda Gates. Any relation to Nathanial Gates?" Trevion and Brenner chuckle at the question, but both girls freeze then look at each other before excusing themselves. Brenner tries to figure out what happened as the two kiss the boys then rush off.

"What the hell did you say, wingman?" Brenner asks, but Trevion is still trying to come up with any other conclusion than the obvious one. Nathanial Gates or, more precisely, Chief Nathanial Gates is the head instructor back at their A-School. "Bro, I think they're Chief Gates' daughters or something." Trevion's fears became a reality the following day in class when Chief Gates walks in and begins speaking to Trevion and Brenner's instructor. Chief Gates gives Brenner a very hard look as he walks out of the classroom.

"Alright," the instructor yells out, "looks like Chief Gates needs a permanent work detail consisting of students who have less than a month remaining. You'll need to report to the Admin Office every morning at 0600 hours, then you'll have class, then you'll report back to the Admin Office every evening at 1800 hours. Chief Gates' staff will give you further instructions. From my class he has selected Brenner and Carson, you start today so be at the Admin Office at 1800."

Brenner raises his hand, "What will we be..." the instructor cuts him off and says that he has no details then continues with the lesson.

13. Aloha

Last day and everyone is hugging each other and promising to stay in touch. Brenner and Trevion have endured three and a half weeks of extra duty at the hands of a very vengeful Chief Gates; who had the two doing everything from standing 'Toilet Watch' to cleaning the tires on the garbage trucks. The two had no days off, even on the weekends when class was out.

They had to report at 6am and 6pm every day. It didn't stop until three days ago when Brenner found Chief Gates' home phone number in the Admin Office and called when he knew that Chief Gates would be still in traffic, speaking to the girls and pleading with them for mercy.

Trevion looks at his orders, San Francisco. He wanted to be away from home but not too far. "Where are you headed, Brenner?"

"Honolulu," Brenner replies with a devilish grin. "I got top of my wish list. What about you?"

"Frisco. San Diego was my number one, but I'll settle for number two." The two laugh and gloat as they exit the dorm full of mid-termers. They hop a cab to the airport and discover along the way that they're both flying to Honolulu. Trevion will meet his ship there while Brenner has a base assignment.

In the airport, they stand chatting when Crawford walks up and asks if she could speak to Trevion. Brenner looks at Trevion with 'Hell no' in his eyes but Trevion pulls her to the side. Crawford apologizes to Trevion for what happened, saying that her time with the other guy was terrible compared to what she had with Trevion. She asks if they could have lunch together during the Atlanta layover, Trevion agrees. Brenner is beside himself with anger over Trevion's decision, but that fury turns into amusement once Trevion explains what he's going to do.

As they fly to Atlanta, Trevion convinces Crawford to go into the bathroom with him so that they can both qualify for the Mile-High Club. The flight to Atlanta afforded two trips to the bathroom, just to be sure they qualified. Once the plane lands in Atlanta, Trevion tells Crawford to freshen up and meet him outside of the restrooms.

As soon as she walks into the ladies' room, he and Brenner leave the airport to explore Atlanta since their flight to Honolulu won't leave for another seven hours. The two laugh and joke in the cab leaving the airport, but Trevion actually feels really bad about what he did. He wants to go back and spend Crawford's two-hour layover with her, but Brenner's relentless verbal assault against her keeps him firm.

"She only wants you because that slime ball ditched her a week ago. She thought she'd have somebody to write to while she's wasting away in Tehran. What a shit detail," Brenner teases. "Her final score must have been terrible to get sent to Tehran, Iran!" The two sailors take in the city then return to the airport to fly to Hawaii, sleeping the entire flight then awakening to a beautiful island with pleasant weather. Brenner checks in with the Base Logistics Command while Trevion, along with three others who arrived on the same day, gets assigned as clerks to an office inside of a bungalow on the base until their respective ships arrive.

14. Home, Jeeves.

Trevion spends his first day making McDonald's runs for the office staff and cleaning the fallen fruit from the enormous apple tree just outside of the bungalow. He spends his first night with Brenner walking along the beach, flirting with girls and sampling the food. "Damn man, you're stationed here for the next three years! That's epic!"

Brenner smiles and puts Trevion in a headlock, "Thanks to you, bubba. You kept me up to snuff in A-School."

They hang out and explore the area into the wee hours then head back to the base. The next morning, Trevion is walking back from McDonald's with coffee and breakfast sandwiches for the office staff when he notices a very beautiful convertible Cadillac parked outside with flags on both sides of the grill. He walks in to distribute the order and overhears that an admiral needs a driver.

"Listen up," a sailor in a white uniform says to the staff, "Vice Admiral Unger is retiring, he's already had his retirement ceremony and his award presentation. He has a few weeks left before he goes home and his driver just received his transfer orders. Which one of you has a driver's license?"

Trevion is the only one of the clerks to raise his hand, which he knows is bullshit because he saw one of the clerks renting a car from the airport just yesterday. Trevion realizes that he didn't hear whatever the conversation was before he walked in, which is probably why he's the only jerk with his hand in the air. "Perfect, Seaman Recruit Carson, come with me."

In an hour's time, Trevion finds himself standing outside of the motor pool dressed in his Service Whites, with a gold cord looping from his right shoulder and a white cap, which looks suspiciously like the ones reserved for only female officers and female chief petty officers. "Well, get a load of her. Looking good darling!" the guys inside of the garage tease as they whistle at and make fun of Trevion. A mechanic pulls up in the Cadillac and tells Trevion not to pay attention to the guys in the service station then hands him the keys.

Trevion drives to the other side of the base and finds that it looks like a beautiful neighborhood; complete with houses, corner convenience stores and a park. He finds the address written on the orders, it's a very large and beautiful house with a well-manicured lawn and flower beds lining the walkway. As Trevion is walking towards the door the Vice Admiral emerges. "Alright, you must be my new driver. My name is Dan but in front of anyone its Vice Admiral Unger or sir, you know the drill. Come on, I'm late for a lunch in my honor so I hope you can drive fast."

Trevion runs to the car and opens the door, "Yes I can, sir. I'm from California so I know how to dip."

Dan pauses before getting in, "Where in California?" Trevion tells him that he's born and raised in Beach City. "Get the fuck out of here, which school did you go to?"

Trevion holds up two fingers on each hand, "Richard Nixon High." Dan also holds up two fingers on each hand and the two recite the Nixon War Chant together.

Dan claps his hands and says, "Perfect, let's go!"

Trevion spends his days driving Dan around as he ties up loose ends and attend lunches and dinners hosted by his many protégés and admirers. On days that Dan has nothing to do, he opens his door and waves Trevion off then gives a phone sign meaning he'll call the phone inside of the Cadillac if he needs a ride anywhere. This usually happens if Dan brings home a female guest. On those days, Trevion is free to change into civilian cloths and take the Cadillac off-base.

On a Thursday morning, Trevion is waiting outside of Dan's house, rubbing the Cadillac with a cloth when Dan comes out. He's still in his pajamas and robe. "Carson, I'm taking off for the weekend to approve the crap that they're doing to my condo back home. My flight returns on Sunday at 6:45pm, make sure to be there. Oh, and I have these passes to a luau tomorrow night, and I obviously won't be able to make it. The passes are for me plus one and it comes with a room at the hotel that's hosting the luau along with a bunch of other crap that I didn't pay attention to because I don't really want. Anyway, here's the packet. Get whatever you can and keep it all; have fun but be at the airport to pick me up on Sunday."

With the day off, Trevion has time to scout the hotel and ask Brenner if he wants to come with. While wearing his bright, white uniform, Trevion is able to convince the Maître D' at the hotel to give him a tour. "The admiral is considering having his international friends come and experience your luau," Trevion tells the middle-aged hotel head. "I'm not really into the whole luau thing and the admiral knows that I'm not so, if I'm impressed…"

"Let me stop you right there, sir. If this tour hasn't impressed you then that's actually great. Because our luxury suites coupled with our luau experience is world class, and it will make a believer out of you. I'll have everything arranged, so you can check in tomorrow at any time, but I suggest you check in very early because the complete experience begins at 10:00am. And, since technically you're scouting our hotel to give a review, I'll comp any and all meals delivered from our gourmet kitchen to your room."

Brenner said that he was in but, no way he'll be able to be at the hotel that early. Friday on the base and everyone will be grinding to make sure their weekend liberty isn't trampled by unfinished work, so he'll have to meet Trevion at the hotel once he's finally on liberty. Trevion returns to the base and changes into his civilian clothes then takes the Cadillac to the shop to be serviced and detailed.

The same guys who mocked Trevion's white uniform are there when he drops the car off. "The admiral made a comment about how much noise the engine has been making lately. I just started driving it recently, so I'm not sure what he's hearing but just wanted to warn you guys. I'll be back to pick the car up in the morning, 0800." He walks away knowing that now the mechanics will need to perform a full preventative maintenance package on the car, which would take around three extra hours.

15. Island Girl Vol. 1

The morning portion of the all-day luau consisted of a story of how the ancestral Hawaiians came to the island, illustrated by several hula dancers and two large men digging a hole. The food, native Hawaiian cuisine, was different but very delicious. Trevion along with the other guests watch as a fire is started inside of the hole dug by the two natives, and the dancers begin moving around the fire. The festivities conclude with an enormous pig which had been gutted, cleaned, and impaled on a stick is carried out and placed into the hole where smoke has replaced the fire once burning within. The two large natives place palm tree leaves atop the pig then bury it in the sand. Trevion watches the entire ceremony and thinks that it feels kind of like some sort of ritualistic sacrifice or something.

Afterwards, Trevion walks out of the hotel's main entrance to sightsee and do some light shopping. His ship will port soon, and he wants to make sure he remembers this place in case he never returns. As he's contemplating a necklace made of colorful polished rocks, a young Hawaiian walks into the booth and looks at a necklace there. Trevion recognizes her from the luau, she's one of the dancers.

"Hello, I really enjoyed the show." The girl turns to look at Trevion and every ounce of courage runs right down his leg as he stares at the most beautiful girl that he's ever seen. His inner voice is yelling at him not to stare too hard, not to say anything stupid, to close his mouth, to stand up straight, not to say anything stupid, don't look at her cleavage even though she's wearing a skirt and bikini top, and for God's sake not to say anything stupid.

"Thank you, I hope you enjoy the rest of the luau, I know the tickets cost a fortune." Before he can think he blurts out that he didn't pay for the tickets, that his boss gave them to him; which makes his inner voice go berserk and a bit of sweat begin to emerge from his forehead. "Oh wow, that's really cool of him," she says with a sweet smile that swells Trevion's tongue and suspends his brain cells.

"Yeah, there's no way that I'd ever be able to afford anything like this, I'm just starting out in the Navy so I'm pretty broke." *Oh yeah, tell the beautiful girl that you're a broke idiot!* Trevion's inner voice yells at him, making him perspire a bit more.

The girl touches Trevion's face as she walks away, "Honesty is very sexy, enjoy your time here."

31

At 4:00pm Brenner arrives and can't believe the level of luxury that the room has. The two suddenly wish that they didn't have the 'No Service Chicks' rule so they could call up a couple of girls from the base to hang out with. Trevion shrugs his shoulders and says, "Oh well, we can go and watch some hula dancers to take our minds off of it. The best part is starting now so, let's go."

The back of the hotel leads directly to the beach, where the luau is in full swing. Trevion sees the beautiful island girl standing off to the side with the other dancers and musters his courage. "Wish me luck bro, I'm after the mythical unicorn on this one." Brenner watches as Trevion walks over to the dancers. He sees Trevion speak briefly to one of the girls then hand her a small bag before walking back.

"What did you give her?" he asks.

Before Trevion can answer, an announcer calls the guests to their assigned places as the sunset ceremony is about to begin. The guys walk up to the prime spot in the front that was assigned to Trevion. "Well?" Brenner demands as they sit.

Trevion looks over at the girl and smiles, "It's around her neck." Brenner sees a colorful necklace just hidden beneath the rows of flower leis around her neck. As the show begins, Trevion tells the story of how he clumsily made a fool of himself earlier when he saw her and how she was looking at that necklace. The dancer notices Trevion looking at her and blows him a kiss.

16. I Love the Navy

The show ended with another dance-illustrated story and the two large men digging the now-cooked pig from the sand and preparing it to be served. The guys are in awe of how tender and delicious the meat is. While they're eating, the hula girl walks over with a few other performers. Trevion quickly stands and puts out his hand to shake hers, which she sidesteps and gives him a hug. "Thank you for the very thoughtful gift, but would you mind if I gave it to my mother? She's who I was shopping for."

Trevion clears his throat and tries not to sound too pathetic, "Of course I don't mind, it's like two gifts in one." His inner voice lambastes him for such a corny remark.

Brenner clears his throat which makes Trevion say, "Oh, my name is Trevion by the way, and this is my friend B." The girl introduces herself as Lani then introduces her coworkers. They all chat as they enjoy the Hawaiian music and watch the tourists dancing and having fun. Trevion is in disbelief as it seems that Lani is not only spending time with him, but is acting as if she's actually into him. He keeps reminding himself that this could all be an act that she plays on horny tourists, but enjoys dancing and drinking with the very lovely girl.

Trevion drives them all home at the end of the evening and receives a big kiss from Lani as a reward. He and Brenner drive back to the hotel congratulating each other as if they had just scored with supermodels, even though they both only received goodnight kisses. The next morning, Trevion is awakened by the phone ringing. The front desk called to inform him that his stay has been extended by the hotel manager and that his new checkout will be Monday morning. Two more days enjoying the lavish accommodations and free room service.

He calls Lani to tell her and tries to convince her to come and hang out with him, and to his surprise she agrees and asks if they could come and pick her and her friend up. Brenner is beside himself wishing he had brought his camera, "My friends back home will never believe this, I need photographic evidence!"

On the way there, Trevion stops and buys a few disposable cameras. "You're not the only one who will have trouble convincing people about all of this." They drive back to Lani's house, and her mother invites them in to have lunch before they go.

The guys enjoy being catered to by the house full of beautiful native women; until it suddenly gets dark in the living room as several rather large native men enter the house through the open front door. "Yo, who is this?" one of them asks. Lani's mother enters the living room and hands the men beers, then returns to the kitchen.

The largest of the young men looks at Trevion, "T-shirt, khakis, and Chucks? Where you from, fool?" Trevion knows very well what that question means. He grew up in a gang neighborhood and was courted on in Jr. high school. "I'm from Beach City, Cali," he nervously says.

The Hawaiian takes a step closer to the two, "No, I mean where you from?"

This is a no-win situation and Trevion knows it as the other young men begin to stand around the couch. He looks over at Brenner who is sitting very stiff with his eyes bulging out of his head. Trevion takes a deep breath and says "Deuce Mafia" while holding up two fingers and his thumb. "Oh! You a Cripster?"

That question, coming from the six-foot, six-inch, three-hundred-pound mountain of a man caused Trevion's body to go weak as he imagined him and Brenner trying to break through the offensive line that stood between them and the front door; and then the mad dash down the hill to their parked car.

"Yeah, Mafioso Crip." The feeling of terror is replaced with a wave of relief as the young men all cheer and introduce themselves. This is a family of Hawaiian Crips and Trevion, being from a California Crip neighborhood, is welcomed. Lani and her friend Gale come from the kitchen with plates of food for everyone, and they all eat and swap stories.

Afterward, the two couples return to the hotel area to sightsee. Trevion feels like the man as he walks down the beach with such an amazingly beautiful girl on his elbow. The night ends with the two making out on the balcony of the hotel room. The ladies have such a great time that they want to do it again the next day, but Brenner has to be back to stand his duty day. So, in the morning, Trevion goes alone to pick up Lani.

Towards the end of the afternoon she asks to go back to Trevion's room, and the two begin fooling around in bed. "Maybe I'll spend the night with you tonight?" she whispers to him. "We would have to leave really early in the morning because…" Trevion freezes, a feeling of dread washes over his body. "Oh, my Lord! What time is it?" 6:30pm and he needs to be at the airport by 6:45pm. Impossible. Trevion jumps up in a panic but is calmed by Lani and her idea.

At the airport, Dan waits with his buddy from back home. He looks at his watch, 7:22pm. His friend jokes "I thought you said this guy was one-in-a-million?" Dan sees the convertible pulling up and is ready to scream at Trevion, until he sees the hula girls in the car with him. The girls jump out of the car and put flower leis on the two men's necks then perform a short dance routine around them which draws a small crowd. Trevion quietly puts their luggage into the trunk then stands by the door trying to read Dan's mood.

Dan and his friend are both smiling very brightly as the girls finish their dance routine to a round of applause from the onlookers, then escort the two gentlemen to the back seat, sitting on their laps as Lani gets in the front seat and Trevion drives off. He brings the two to the hotel room, which he had housekeeping clean in preparation. They all hang out until the wee hours then Trevion drives Dan back to the base, dropping Lani off at her house along the way. "Not bad, son. And I almost thought you let me down back there."

Trevion says 'Never, sir!' as he drives Dan home.

17. This is the Navy?

Trevion has been in Hawaii now for almost three weeks, and life is good. He has a dream assignment driving around a retiree who regifts him all sorts of expensive things and gift certificates, he's seeing a gorgeous girl who hates when he spends money on her, and his base-buddy works in the warehouse so he gets coveralls and expensive pilot's boots almost free. It's a beautiful Sunday evening, and Trevion has the day off, so he's in Maui with Lani using one of the weekend getaway certificates that Dave handed him.

The two lay in bed discussing what they're going to do for the rest of the night and how early they'll have to wake up in order to catch the first boat that leaves in the morning. "Have you ever thought about leaving the islands?" he asks her. Lani laughs and says that she'd never move away. Trevion asks "What if you met someone who wanted to marry you, and that person lived in, I don't know… say California, for example. Would you move to be with him?"

Lani stops smiling then climbs on top of Trevion, "We have a really fun time together. You're a really nice, very funny guy, and I love being with you. But…"

The pause after that word is only a second, but to Trevion it's an eternity. His inner voice is strangely silent as if every part, every ounce, every bit of him wanted to hear this response. "But… I'm already engaged to someone. He's gone for a while, a long while, but he's going to come back, and I belong to him." Trevion can't think of a single thing to say. "I'm really sorry Trey, I just thought that we were having fun. You never talked about anything serious and neither did I… wait, were you just trying to ask me to marry you?"

And there it is, the *Out*. A quick response here would save face, save the rest of the night, and save the possibility of more sex from this goddess. Trevion's inner voice is repeating exactly what he should say, but it still comes out as "I didn't know that you were engaged." Lani tries to roll off of Trevion but he stops her, "Hey, I'm not upset. I'm just glad you told me before I started having so much fun with you that I started feeling something." That's what the inner voice told him to say, and it works. Lani begins kissing Trevion and the two spend the rest of Sunday in bed.

The next day, Trevion is in the shower almost in tears over a second beautiful woman choosing another person over him. Although he spent last night having a great time with Lani, he was hurting the whole time. The kiss he gave her when he dropped her off was, to him, a kiss goodbye as he plans to stop seeing her. He thinks *how could this possibly get any worse* when the phone in his room starts ringing.

He walks out of the shower and answers, it's the Admin office letting him know that his ship pulled in late last night and that he's to report there immediately. That works out for Trevion who is very eager to get away from the beautiful heart-breaker roaming the island, but anxiety starts slowly setting in as he realizes that he's about to finally go to his ship. He calls Dan to let him know, Dan orders him to swing by his place before taking the car back so that he can give him a few things and a bit of at-sea advice.

Trevion puts on his blue working uniform and visits Dan for the last time, telling him what happened with Lani. "Ha! Dude, you got a free ride with a *Get Out of Jail Free* card. What the hell are you all gloomy about? Trust me, young man, you didn't want to marry that one. You had fun, you took pictures, you now have a great story of the time you spent with a Hawaiian hula dancer, backed up with photo evidence! Believe me, one day you'll be really glad it went this way." Trevion acts like the talk pepped him up, but it didn't. They say their goodbyes, then he brings the car and special driver's gear back to the motor pool.

A mechanic drives Trevion to his ship, which is on the other side of the island at the Naval Weapons Magazine. "Damn, Carson! Why is your ship way over here?"

Trevion looks at his orders, "I don't know, USS Mt. Wilson AE-42."

The mechanic lets out an *Oh, ok* and explains to Trevion that his ship is an ammunition ship. "Yeah, it carries bombs and missiles and shit to the fleet."

Trevion thinks to himself *So, the next three and a half years on a ship loaded with bombs and missiles? Wonderful. Oh, and let's not forget about the shit! He said bombs, missiles, and shit!*

Trevion can see the ship as they turn to enter the base, the mechanic drops him off close to the pier then wishes him luck before driving off. Trevion looks up at the large, gray ship and the sailors tending to it both on the pier and topside. He looks at the long stairway leading from the pier to the ship's quarterdeck, then down at the three large bags that he's going to have to bring up. He straps the bags on and begins to climb. Once he reaches the top a sailor smiles at him and says, "Damn, not bad Boot Camp! Are you in Deck Department?"

Trevion takes a deep breath, "I don't know, I'm an SK." The three men on the quarterdeck let out a disappointed groan then tells him to drop his bags for inspection. The three men consist of the Officer of the Deck, which is a Chief Petty Officer or above; the Petty Officer of the Watch, which is, as the name suggests, a Petty Officer or E-4 to E-6; and last is the Messenger of the Watch, who is an E-3 or below. The Officer of the Deck instructs the Messenger to help Trevion bring his things up to the Personnel Office for processing then down to the Supply Berthing Area.

"Hey, Carson!" One of the clerks from the Hawaii office is in the Personnel Office.

"Oh, hey Wong, I didn't know you were waiting for this ship too."
Wong shakes Trevion's hand, "Yeah, I came aboard last night. They said that you were on assignment from the Vice Admiral, what did he have you doing?"

Trevion laughs, "He ordered me to use one of his three-day passes to a private resort in Maui."

Wong punches him in the shoulder and calls him a lucky S.O.B., then talks to him while his paperwork is being completed. "Make sure you lock up your stuff, then somebody will come and get you from the berthing area to join your division. Good luck."

The Messenger helps Trevion bring his things to Supply Berthing, where the Supply Department sleeps. "There you go, Boot Camp, I would say *Enjoy your stay* but, you won't." Trevion looks at the Messenger as he laughs and exits. The bunks are three deep and it looks as if all of the middle bunks are taken. None of the top bunks are taken and there's one bottom bunk which has no sheets or locks on the casket-styled locker attached to the bunk. The room is very cramped, as if they tried to squeeze as many of the triple-bunks as they could into the space.

There is a wall-mounted television and a table that's welded to the floor. Aside from the bunks, there are lockers with corresponding numbers. Trevion takes a moment to look around and absorb his surroundings, since this will be his home for years to come, and decides on the last available bottom bunk since there must be a reason why all of the top bunks are still empty.

Last night, he slept in a king-sized bed next to an insanely beautiful hula girl in a 5-Star resort on a private beach. Tonight, it will be in a cramped bunk on a 2" mattress surrounded by potentially snoring dudes. He takes a deep breath, "So, this is the Navy, huh?"

Chapter Two

1.   I Hate the Navy

An SK, which means Storekeeper, comes to the berthing area and instructs Trevion to put away his things quickly then leads him down one deck level to his work area; General Store Keeping or GSK, which is a large, open area made into a storeroom with an office in the front. The office area consists of three rows of four desks along with an area with computer stations and two very large printers.

"There's my guy!" the Chief Storekeeper or SKC says as the two enter the office. "Tell me something, why can't we order parts starting with the part number 9842?" Everyone in the office pauses and looks at Trevion, who replies that the number is reserved for special weapons or presidential supplies. SKC claps his hands while the other sailors in the room groan and return to work. "They told me I was getting a hot shot; hope you live up to that."

The rest of the day, Trevion spends following guys around and doing whatever he's told. He can tell that the SKs who work there aren't too enthused by his arrival. They're all very prickly and passive-aggressive towards him. None of them took the time to tell Trevion how to get to the mess decks to eat or what the schedule was for anything. Trevion felt as if perhaps it was some sort of hazing ritual or something because these guys were SKs like him, right? Shouldn't they be making sure that he, at least, knew the basics?

"Hey, Boot Camp!" the SK2 yells from the rear of the storeroom area. "Get the dry mop and start back here, I want the entire deck swept before you leave here today." Trevion looks at his watch, 2:55pm or 1455 and everyone's off work at 3:00pm or 1500. "I'm on it." Everyone walks out snickering and making comments as Trevion grabs the dry mop and begins to do the floors.

One of the SKs is still sitting at his desk, SKSN Dean "Monster" Parker who had duty and couldn't leave the ship. "Yo, Boot, pick up whatever pile you have right now and get out of here."

Trevion walks up to put away the dry mop and thanks Monster, who says, "Don't sweat it, youngster. You're the only SK down here who went to A-School aside from the chief and he's been rubbing that shit in for the past month and a half, *We're getting a A-School SK down here; Oh, I just heard he's in the top of his class; Our new guy is waiting for us in Hawaii; He's not here to help us bring up these endless fucking pallets of supplies from the pier because he's finishing an assignment from Vice Adm. Unger.* We're already sick of you. By the time you finally made it down here, all the hard work was done."

Trevion apologizes but Monster shakes his head, "Not your fault, little brother. You can go." Trevion decides to stay and avoid the others as they showered and got dressed to go out on liberty. Monster, called that because he stood 6'3" tall and was built like a professional power lifter, explains to Trevion what he needs to be paying attention to, and that he's in a really tough position because the Chief is going to be using him against the rest of the team.

"You may not have done yourself a favor by being so good in school, I bet he's going to give you the Returnable/Reparable area. That's a bitch and a half, nobody can get that shit right." Trevion asks what he should do, to which Monster advises that he study the procedure manual in his free time so he'll be ready for the enormous job.

42

Three other sailors come down the stairwell making a bunch of noise and laughing. "Yo, Monster!" says a slim, Italian man. "Where's your Boot Camp? We need to give him the Welcome Aboard treatment."

Monster says "Ha! Too late for that, big mouth. This is him."

The three introduce themselves, the young Italian guy is a Gunner's Mate named GMSN Frank Buono. Everyone calls him Franky. Next is a very dark-skinned guy from New York named Tyrone Moore, everyone calls him Moorish because he's heavy into the African History and equality movements.

Moorish is in Deck Department like Franky, but works with the Boatswain's Mates or BMs. Ysidro Fernandez is from Texas, he's also working with the BMs but is doing what's called Striking. Striking is when you have no rate so you spend your free or approved time working with another department so that you can take the advancement test and become that rate.

Everyone who goes through Apprenticeship Training after boot camp goes to their first assignment without a rate. On a ship, they're either assigned to Deck Department to work with the Boatswain's Mates or Gunner's Mates, or to Engineering Department to work with the Boiler Technicians or Machinist's Mates.

"A Salaam Aleichem, my brother," Moorish says to Trevion, who responds with 'Aleichem Salaam'.

Monster shakes his head, "Here we go, Martin Malcolm Garvey over here is about to start recruiting again."

Moorish tells Trevion to ignore Monster and begins asking how 'awake' Trevion is. "My dad told me that only a very few of you Black Power guys are real about what they say, the rest are either cowards who can't stand for what they really believe in or fuck-ups who want to blame the White Man for his own failures."

The guys all give a collective 'Ooohhhh!!' Fernandez suggests that Trevion get a tryout to be in their clique, Moorish seconds it saying that Trevion is 'Playing chess while most youngsters are stuck on checkers'.

"We'll see about that," Monster remarks. "We need to take him out tomorrow night to make sure he won't be a liability out there. We'll take him to the Coconut Cup and see how he handles himself. SKC put him in Duty Section 4 so we got two nights out to test him."

The guys agree. Trevion doesn't feel honored in any way, these guys seem pretty lame and corny to him. Maybe their little clique consists of the misfits, which is why they're so quick to recruit him. *This is high school all over again*, Trevion thinks to himself.

That night, laying in his tiny, bottom bunk, Trevion is looking through his pictures. Brenner was a total shutterbug, taking pictures all the time so Trevion has a large number of photos of himself and Lani. He stares very hard at the picture of them kissing on the beach, remembering how in love with her he was at that point then remembering that she didn't feel that way about him, at all.

He decides to walk down to the pier and call her to say goodbye. They talk for a long time before Trevion reveals that he's being taken to a place called the Coconut Cup. Lani tells him that she knows the place and to be careful, '*The girls in there are aggressive and they love sailors, especially young cute ones,*' she laughs. They say goodnight, and Trevion walks back up to the quarterdeck then back to his bunk.

The next morning at breakfast, Trevion is introduced to the rest of the clique along with a few other guys who always eat together. Darren 'Big Boats' Jones is a BM2 from Miami and James 'Suave' Patterson is in Supply Department, he's an E-3 Ship's Serviceman or SHSN. The guys all talk and joke around during breakfast while Trevion has a book

44

open and is quietly reading.

SKC walks up and gets in line. For each meal of the day an officer or chief petty officer must eat in the enlisted men's galley and fill out a report on how everything looks and tastes. As SKC gets his food and turns to the seating area, he sees Trevion and Monster sitting together. "Showing him the ropes, Parker?"

Monster looks up, "Yeah, making sure he's squared away, Chief."

SKC looks over at Trevion and asks what he's reading. Trevion shows him the manual of Returnable/Repairable procedures. "Whoa!" the chief exclaims, "that's pretty advanced, Carson. I'm not sure you'll understand that manual. And it doesn't even fully explain the job. Are you sure you're up to that assignment?" The SKs at the table, and the ones sitting within earshot, all stop eating and waits for Trevion's answer. His inner voice is telling him to accept the assignment if only to show up all of the SKs who resent him and don't even know him.

The manual is basically instructions on how to handle, order, store, and disburse parts that can be discounted if the old/damaged part is turned in. If the Engineering Department needs a large part for the salt water vaporizer, they can turn in the damaged part and order a new one, receiving a core discount which wouldn't hit their operational budget as hard. Trevion does a quick glance around at the SKs staring at him, "I can tell that it's a tough job, dealing with valuable parts, I have every confidence in myself so once you feel confident in me, I'd have no problem tackling that assignment, Chief."

SKC raises his glass of punch and says, "Finally, I have myself a go-getter! Once you finish your mess duty, the job is yours. That will give you time to get comfortable with how we run GSK."

SKC walks out of the galley and Monster looks at Trevion, "Lesson One; you pour water onto a fire, not propane."

45

The table laughs and returns to their conversations. Trevion asks, "What's mess duty?"

"Oh, you'll find out, Boot Camp." SK2 remarks as he's walking out. "By the time you're starting mess duty, you'll be begging for it."

Trevion watches as SK2 smirks then exits the galley, then turns to Monster "What the hell is that guy's deal?" Monster just shakes his head and says the word 'propane'.

2. No, I Really Hate the Navy

Trevion walks down several stairwells, down into the ship's engine area. Each floor is hotter than the previous and Trevion wonders how anyone works in such a hot, noisy environment. Finally, he gets to an office area within the engine room where four sailors are working. He walks in, and the men pause, staring at him. "So," Trevion says as he lifts the bucket that he'd carried down, "I'll give you guys three guesses what I've been sent here for." Which makes the four men erupt into laughter.

One of them says "So, you already know the routine?" Trevion says yes, that he worked for a vice admiral who tipped him in on all of the rituals. "Asking you guys for a bucket of steam, asking the Radio Room for a pack of fallopian tubing, asking the cooks for the part number to a bacon stretcher, yeah."

Again, they burst into laughter, "Bro, my advice is to act like they got you every time. Play really gullible, then when they send you somewhere you can just go to the berthing area or something."

Trevion begins the climb out of the engine area and reflects on his day so far; standing at Quarters just after breakfast and having the Supply Officer, or Suppo, embarrassingly read Trevion's school record to the group which consists of the Supply Department: Ship's

Servicemen or SHs, Disbursing Clerks or DKs, Mess Services or MSs, and of course Storekeepers or SKs. After Quarters, Trevion is sent with two others from Supply to clean the berthing area. The bottom bunk, as it turns out, is the most desirable of the options he had when choosing where to sleep.

The middle bunk was the best because it was easy to get in and out of and the coffin locker is at a manageable height. Those bunks went to the highest-ranking sailors in the berthing. The top bunk sucks because it's five feet from the deck so you have to climb in and out of it; plus, it has two stand-up lockers rather than one stand-up and a coffin locker. When you sleep on the bottom rack, you must lift the bunk at a tilt and secure it to the bunk just above it with thick strap and a large hook that's attached to it. The bunk is heavy, super heavy. So, when you're tasked with cleaning the berthing area and someone leaves their bunk down, it's beyond irritating.

Since Trevion is an E-1, he can't really complain about it and since he's new to the ship, he's the one who has to go around and lift all of the bottom bunks that have been left down. The berthing area includes the passageway leading to the door, from one end to the other must be swept, mopped, stripped of old wax, then re-waxed.

This is very difficult because this particular passageway, or p-way, doesn't have an alternate route, it leads to an area called Aft Moring where the large, hemp ropes used to tie the ship to the pier while docked are stowed. It's a very popular area and it's impossible to access it any other way than this p-way. The trio of E-1s and E-2s have a very hard time controlling the traffic enough to produce a finished floor.

After that, Trevion went down to GSK and was assigned Pick-Up. When supplies come aboard, they're separated and placed into large, wall-mounted slots so that the departments who ordered the supplies can come down, sign for them, then take them away. The SKs bring pallets of supplies, or stores, on-board to be separated right on the

Main Deck, then ask the Petty Officer of the Watch to announce a list of departments who have supplies for pick-up.

This reduces the number of boxes which will inevitably need to be hand carried down four flights of narrow, metal stairwells and three p-ways to get to GSK. Looking at the large amount of supplies sitting in the slots lets Trevion know just how hard the SKs had to work while he was asleep in Maui then hanging out with Dan the next morning.

Trevion had to stop whatever he was doing to go on 'messenger runs' for the imaginary items that Dan warned him about, further lengthening the amount of time it takes to complete an assignment. Then, like clockwork, at 1455 he hears "Hey, Boot Camp! Give me a full sweep before you go!" Last to leave GSK, last to the showers so there's no hot water, and last to get ready as the clique stand around mocking his fashion choices.

"Let's go, Boot! I want to eat before we hit the Cup!" Monster nags as he reaches into Trevion's locker and steals a splash of cologne.

"And bring a lot of cash," Moorish laughs. "The first two or three rounds are going to be on you, Boot."

The group of sailors leave the ship and head to a restaurant on the base, where Trevion has to leave the tip. Then they take a shuttle downtown, which Trevion has to pay for. They get to the Coconut Cup and the first two pitchers of beer are bought by Trevion, who isn't enjoying any of it. What's slightly amusing is all of the advice that the guys keep trying to give on picking up girls. Trevion just turned nineteen and he understands that he has a lot to learn about women, but these guys are flat out cheesy.

What's amusing is that they actually think that they're players and ladies men. Especially Suave, who seems to deploy the shotgun method, flirt with everything around him and he's bound to hit something. Trevion realizes that they're so confident because they're

48

servicemen in a bar that's known for having a bunch of sailors there, so the women who come there are looking for sailors anyway. He thinks about what the engineer told him and plays gullible, listening to their advice and acting as if they're teaching him something.

3. Anchors Aweigh

Trevion sits in at the table sipping his beer, he reaches into his pocket and counts his cash; eleven dollars and a bunch of change. "Hope they don't think I'm paying for the shuttle back," he says to himself as he stands to dance to a song that he likes. Moorish and Monster come stumbling up, bragging about the women chasing them around the bar.

"Whoa, hold the phone!" Suave yells as he sees two young women enter the bar. "Now, that's prime steak right there, Boot Camp. One day you'll evolve to this level, for now just watch and learn." The guys all begin primping themselves to speak to the two very beautiful native girls. Suave shakes his head, "I don't know what y'all are getting all spiffed up for, we all know who's getting that one."

"Bet money!" Fernandez yells out and the guys start pulling cash out of their pockets and arguing over odds. Trevion looks over at the young women that they're all drooling over, it's Lani and Gale. "What are my odds?" Trevion asks, to which they all pause, then laugh. SK2 leans in and offers 20-1 odds, to which Trevion pulls out five singles.

"What do you have left?" Suave asks, Trevion pulls out his last six dollars.

"I'll cover my young stallion," Monster says as he counts out money, "and when you lose this, you'll owe me double of what I put up, understand?"

Big Boats collects all bets and Suave slips away to make his move, and is shut down very quickly. Moorish is next and spends a few moments talking with Lani. "Looks like you won't even get a shot at it, Boot Camp." SK2 laughs as he asks Big Boats for his winnings. Moorish shakes Lani's hand and steps away, she makes her way over to where the guys are and Trevion grabs her hand and whispers in her ear. She giggles, then puts her arms around him, giving him a passionate kiss. She grabs his hand and begins to lead him away, pausing for a moment so that Trevion can collect the cash from Big Boats and see the faces of the guys. He shrugs his shoulders and leaves the bar with Lani.

"They're going to make me pay for that," he says as they stroll to the parking lot of the bar.

"Looks like they just paid for it," she jokes as they both laugh.

"The man is here!" Brenner yells from inside of a car. "Let's go set the island on fire before you leave forever!"

Trevion says to wait a moment as he runs back inside of the bar. He taps Monster on the shoulder and counts out triple of what he put up in the bet, "Thanks, big homie, I'll see you guys at Quarters."

Walking out, Trevion can hear Monster teasing Suave and SK2, "Do you see this? This is called respect; this is three times what I put up. You suckers better quit underestimating my protégé." Trevion smiles but still can't help feeling used by all of them. Walking to the car, he's feeling used by Lani and even used by Brenner who would never have had a shot at Gale, or anything close to her, if it weren't for him.

Lani runs up and jumps into his arms, kissing him wildly, "Tonight, I'm going to burn myself into your memory. You're never going to forget what I did to you!" Um, too late.

4. Sea Legs

Standing at Quarters, Trevion isn't feeling very good. His balance is suspect and his head is pounding due to the drunkover caused by how much he drank last night. He kept wanting to tell Lani how much he was hurting over their situation, but instead of talking he drank. It did make for a pretty wild night but the results are being felt now as he listens to Suppo read the orders for going underway, hoping that no one notices that he's still drunk from last night.

The ship must steam back to the Philippines to pick up ordinance then deliver it to their home base. There is a garbage detail happening right after Quarters where any and all trash is carried off of the ship before going out to sea and Trevion is assigned to it, along with every other sailor on the ship ranked E-3 and below.

The sailors work as a team, and the job is done in just under an hour, giving Trevion time to go to the berthing area and help with the floors. Everything is vibrating now because the engine room has come alive in preparation and traffic down the p-way is very heavy. "Don't worry about the floors today, guys." SK2 yells from the other p-way. "Wrap it up and get to work."

The ship's vibrations are not helping Trevion's headache, neither is the microfiche machine that he has to use to look up part numbers on each of the many incomplete order forms piled on his desk. Trevion knows full well what a request form is supposed to look like before it's signed and submitted, he learned it in A-School.

How an officer can look at this form and sign off on it, knowing that it's woefully incomplete is troubling to Trevion who, up to this point, thought everything in the military ran like clockwork and everyone followed the procedures set out by the Department of the Navy. The guys on this ship hand in incomplete paperwork and the guys down in GSK just accepts it. That's extra work for the SKs.

By lunch, Trevion has completed each of the forms and hands them over to Monster, who exclaims "Damn, Boot! Are you sure all of these numbers are correct?" Trevion looks at him with a confused face, but Monster's loud question catches the attention of SKC who asks to see the forms. After examining a few of them, SKC points out the areas where Trevion wouldn't need to fill out then passes the forms around to the other SKs.

"This is exactly how the form is supposed to look, tomorrow we will watch Carson's process and start doing it his way from now on." *Awesome, something else for them to hate me for,* Trevion thinks as he heads to lunch. The guys sit in their usual spots and have lunch; then, the ones that can, head topside to watch as the ship leaves, being taxied by tugboats out of the channel.

The vibrations from the ship have attracted millions of jellyfish, Trevion wishes he had brought his camera to take pictures of the beautiful sight as a countless amount of them can be seen through the clear, Hawaiian water. The tugboats turn back and the ship's engines roar to full steam, headed out across the Pacific Ocean.

The work day is very different when underway. Docked, the hours are close to regular work hours; 0830 to 1500 hours unless you had duty and couldn't leave the ship. Out to sea, the hours are 0700 to whenever they decide you've done enough. For Trevion, that means 0700 to around 2000 hours, which is what time he was finally released on his first day out to sea. Sleep wasn't had easily as the ship moves, tilts, and dips throughout the night, waking Trevion up.

By morning, Trevion's headache was gone but it was replaced by something else; seasickness. This condition causes its sufferers to have a distinct look on their faces, which Trevion figures must be on his because everyone who sees him asks if he's seasick. Yes, extremely! He makes it through breakfast and heads down to GSK, where the guys do everything they can to make him uncomfortable.

Three SKs would stand shoulder to shoulder by Trevion and sway in unison against the way the ship was moving. Even if Trevion tried not to look at them, seeing them out of his peripherals still made him nauseous. Finally, he couldn't hold it any longer and emptied his stomach into his waste basket, much to the delight of the crew who all stood and applauded.

Trevion had to walk around with plastic bags in his pocket for the next two days, everything he did was that much more difficult because of his out-of-control nausea, and that much more embarrassing because of the applause he drew every time he lost his stomach. "Two days and y'all still stand and cheer like it was the first time." Trevion complains as he watches four sailors play Spades on the berthing table.

"Oh, quit crying, titty-baby. Didn't that low-visibility watch you stood last night calm your tender little belly?" SK2 teases as he slaps a King down to win the book. "I heard that thick fog helps seasickness."

Monster looks at SK2, "What? Only thing that helps is time or a pussy-patch and it looks like my young son chose time, so give him his propers." Pussy-patch? That must be the circular little stickers that Trevion has seen some of the crew wearing just behind their ears. If he would have known what they were, Trevion would absolutely have been wearing one.

"The low-vis watch was pretty interesting," Trevion says. "I got to see glowing seaweed." SK2 chuckles and tells him to get used to standing that watch because he's the lowest ranking member of Supply Department, so he'll be getting all of the 'shit watches' for now.

Shit watches include, in no particular order; Low Visibility Watch where you sit next to the existing Look-Out Watch and be an extra set of eyes when fog or heavy rain makes it hard to see the horizon; Messenger of the Watch when the ship is in port and you're basically

53

a gopher for four hours, running all over the ship, carrying officers' bags, turning on or off lights depending on the time of day, all while keeping the Quarterdeck clean; and the dreaded Parking Lot Watch, self-explanatory.

Trevion is starring on all three of those watch bills, making multiple appearances on each. Trevion leaves the berthing area and goes back to his desk down in GSK. Working the long, underway hours isn't so bad for Trevion because at least he's away from the berthing area and constant hazing that exists there, but heading to the Philippines, or PI, then back to the ship's home port is a welcomed change as it seems to be making everyone a bit less grouchy. The ship will spend five days in PI then it will return to the US and dock at the Naval Logistics Base in Vallejo, CA for a week or so.

Then it will be steaming down to San Francisco for Dry Dock where the ship will be fully repaired and made ready. This won't be a traditional Dry Dock where the ship is lifted out of the water, but an abbreviated one where the ship will dock and stay for six months. The crew, those who don't have their own places out in town, sleeps on a barge tied to the next pier while civilian contractors repair anything and everything that needs fixing. Still, two more days of seeing nothing except water and sky outside then it's back on land.

5.   PI

The guys in Supply berthing take a look at the Watch Bill posted on the berthing message board. The ship will be in three duty sections beginning early in the morning when they pull in to PI. The first section will not be allowed to leave the ship on the first day, the second section will be on liberty as soon as the Quarterdeck is set up, and the third section will be allowed to leave at 1500. The next day, section one can leave at 1500, section two is on duty and cannot leave the ship, and section three is on liberty. This rotation allows for a day and a half of work followed by a day and a half of freedom in the port city of Olongapo. Most of the stories being told by the crew members who have been there before describes a man's paradise filled with fine clothes, cheap liquor, and legalized prostitution.

The latter doesn't interest Trevion at all, but the fine clothes has his antenna up. Before leaving Hawaii, and at the advice of SKC, Trevion went to the base commissary to buy packs of assorted thread. According to SKC, the clothes made in the Philippines are beautiful and made of excellent materials; except, for whatever reason, for the thread that they use. SKC tells him to bring his own thread when he goes into the shops to have clothes made. Knowing nothing at all about sewing or how much thread is used in tailoring cloths, Trevion spent $50 buying ten boxes of assorted threads.

Being in the second duty section meant Trevion was free to explore the city as soon as the ship pulls in. The ship is docked far from the actual base, over at the weapons magazine many miles away. There is a bus that will carry sailors from the ship, through the jungle, and to the actual base. It's not even noon yet but the sun is beaming and the air is very thick and humid.

Trevion climbs on the bus and tries to open a window, but cannot. Others on the bus also fail at opening their windows and their request to the driver for help go unanswered. As the bus gets underway, the air conditioning is on but is virtually ineffective as the inside of the bus gets hotter as they drive through the jungle on a winding road.

Everyone is complaining but the driver just looks in his rear-view mirror at everyone with indifference on his face. Trevion looks out and can see monkeys on the side of the road. They run alongside of the bus before vanishing into the jungle. Trevion watches this for a while until he notices something odd; there seem to me more and more monkeys with each wind that the road takes. '*They must be cutting through the jungle*' he thinks to himself as the bus begins picking up speed.

Bam! Something just hit the bus. Bam! Bam! "What the hell is that?" one of the sailors asks as they all begin to realize what's going on. The monkeys are throwing feces at the bus as it rolls through the jungle. Bam! Bam! Bam! Monkey crap splatters across the windows. The men can now understand why the windows do not come down as the revolting assault continues.

The whole bus smells like a dirty toilet as the sailors watch more and more monkeys line the road and throw feces at the passing bus. When they arrive, several of them are nauseous as they all try to get skinny as they exit the crap-splattered bus. Trevion is anxious to leave the base and doesn't even look around as he hustles to the main gate. He heads to the downtown area and walks around trying to find all of the places mentioned in the various stories being told on their way over. He goes into a clothing shop to have two outfits made, then presents a box of thread to the shop owner; who offers Trevion a huge discount if he's able to keep the thread once Trevion's order is done. This happens at each of the shops where Trevion places orders.

The clothes and shoes will all take time to be made so he arranges for them all to be paid for and picked up in two days since he had duty anyway. The women are very beautiful, some of them are clearly what's called 'War Babies' meaning they were sired by a serviceman so they're multi-cultural. The so-called legal prostitutes are the Bar Girls who stand outside bars luring men inside to either buy drinks or to pay their Bar Tab.

Once a man pays the Bar Tab, he can leave with the bar girl or, for a smaller fee, go to a room in the bar with her. "Handsome man, come buy a drink. I'll keep you company!" they say to the men walking by. Trevion is more concerned with getting all of his receipts back to the ship before he loses them than he is in messing around with one of the seductive bar girls. He heads back to the base so that he can take the bus back through the jungle and back to the ship.

6.   Island Girl, Vol. 2

The next day is duty for Trevion, and they somehow managed to give him three watches in one day. The SKs in the first duty section left a pile of work to be done and only Monster works hard to help reduce the load; that is until 1500 and he's free to leave the ship. Trevion is swamped with his duties down in GSK once everyone goes on liberty, SK2 is in his section and spends the entire time giving Trevion extra assignments. The day is capped off by a 4 to 8 Messenger-In-Training watch that robs Trevion of sleep.

Tired and frustrated, Trevion is very quiet during lunch as the guys plan the evening's festivities. This will be the only night that they'll all be able to go out together so they want to do an epic bar crawl. "We're going to break you in properly tonight, Boot. Show you what PI is all about." Trevion looks over at Monster, who is wearing civilian clothes because he's already on liberty, and mentions that he already went into town two days ago.

Monster says "Pfft, you got back to the ship before 9 o'clock. Trust me, you didn't see shit!"

By the time 1500 rolls around, Trevion only wants to go and pick his clothes up then check into one of the run-down motels lining the main strip so that he can sleep in peace. He rides with the guys through the monkey infested jungle and gets to the base where the men walk into town. Trevion wants to pick up his clothes, but the guys insist on first going to one of the bars which they claim has the 'prettiest, cleanest girls in town'. They're all in good spirits as the group heads to the bar, all except for Trevion who has walked past several of the shops where his clothes await payment and pickup.

They get to the bar and Trevion sits with Monster and Moorish in one of the booths where they're instantly descended upon by bar girls. One of them, an obvious War Baby, pays considerable attention to Trevion who tries his best to act uninterested. Every time she leaves the booth, she makes it a point to rub her butt across Trevion's lap.

Monster gestures towards her. "There you go, Boot. Half-Filipino and half-Black. You know what you get when you mix brown and black, don't you?" Trevion looks up at him, waiting for his answer. "You get a 'God Damn, you fine as fuck!' That's what you get." Everyone laughs, but Trevion isn't amused by the joke and really wants to get out of the bar.

The bar girl keeps whispering in his ear 'Pay my bar tab. Please, pay my bar tab so we can go.' As he looks at his half-finished bottle of beer, he realizes the best way to get out of there would be to actually pay for this girl. "How much?" he asks her. "Sixty dollars US and we can go." Trevion thinks about his budget, he wasn't planning on dropping sixty dollars on, basically, nothing since he had no intention of having sex with this girl.

Moorish mentions that after this, they're going to another spot where they have topless dancers. This helps Trevion make up his mind as he pulls three $20 bills from his pocket and hands it to the bar girl. As she hurries to the back, the guys begin to cheer and congratulate Trevion for buying his first bar girl. She comes back and says "Ok, let's go." Trevion says that he'd like to finish his beer, but the bar girl does not want to spend another moment in the bar and convinces Trevion to leave, not that he needed much convincing to begin with.

Finally standing outside, Trevion tells his newly rented companion that he needed to go and pick up all of the clothes that he ordered. They walk into the first shop and Trevion hands the cashier his receipt. The cashier brings Trevion's order from the back, then says "That will be $90." The bar girl begins arguing with the cashier in Tagalog and, after a brief exchange, the cashier says "$55." Trevion quickly pays then leaves with his order.

"That was incredible!" he says to her as they head to the next shop. "I'm sorry, I don't even know your name." The girl smiles and says that her name is Diwata. Each shop that they enter, Diwata negotiates a discount for Trevion, saving him much more than he had paid for her company. Trevion mentions that he hasn't gotten a hotel room yet because the guys brought him straight to the bar, Diwata mentions a hotel that she knows of, and the two travel by Jeepney to a hotel built into the side of a mountain.

The hotel is very quaint and reasonably priced with each room being like a 1-bedroom apartment. They walk a trail up to their room where they drop Trevion's bags off, then he takes her to eat in a small restaurant at the bottom of the hotel. By the time they're finished, Trevion is thoroughly impressed with Diwata's English and is moved by her story; having dropped out of college at seventeen and working at the bar where they met.

"I was safe as long as I was seventeen, you can't get a license to be a bar girl until you turn eighteen. I turned eighteen two weeks ago and Mamacita took me to get my license on my birthday. My certificate came in the mail today." She pulls out a card with her picture on it and shows it to Trevion, he notices that it has last week's date at the bottom. Trevion assures her that she won't have to do anything with him, "Tonight, you're just my date. We're going to go and party with my friends and have fun, no expectations; I'm just a guy taking you out for your birthday."

The two return to downtown and it doesn't take long before they locate the guys. "Where'd you go, Boot?" Franky asks. "You'd better go to the hotel and get a room before they sell out." Trevion tells them that he's already rented a room and begins describing the beautiful hotel made up of several separate structures and spread up the side of a mountain.

"How much did you pay?" Monster asks. When Trevion tells them how much the room costs per night, they all get upset because they paid more for a roach-infested, cigarette smelling motel room on the strip. The group tries to have a drink in each of the many bars and clubs along the main street. Trevion and Diwata dance the whole night. When they return to the room, Trevion gives her the bedroom and goes to lay down on the couch. He isn't asleep for long before Diwata wakes him up and pulls him into the bedroom with her.

The next morning, Diwata wakes up in a panic. The hotel is quite a distance from the bar where she lives and works and she's not going to make it back in time. Trevion looks at the beautiful young girl as she's almost in tears trying to get dressed to leave. "So," he asks, "how much would it cost you if you wanted to just leave and go back to school?"

Diwata looks over at Trevion, "Too much!"

Trevion grabs her and gives her a hug, "How much? Say you want to leave here later today and just go straight back to school. How much would that cost you?"

Diwata looks up into Trevion's eyes and can see that he's very serious. "It would cost me $600 in US money to get back home and then pay for school." Trevion looks at the lovely young girl and imagines her going back to the bar to slowly become one of the other girls who will spend their youth being sex objects; until they turn twenty-five and must go to the seedy brothels that line the side-streets.

Diwata saved him a bunch of money by arguing with the shop owners and now that he knows how much stuff should cost, he'll save even more in the future. So little money could save someone's future, the Boy Scout in him takes over and Trevion offers her the money. "Stay here," he tells her as he wipes tears from her face. "I'm going to bring all of these bags back to my ship. When I get back, I'll give you the money and you can get away from here."

7. Home Port

Trevion keeps a picture of him and Diwata taped to the bottom of the middle bunk so that he can stare at it while he lays in his rack. The guys all tease him, saying that he fell for the oldest trick in the book; the damsel in distress, and how Diwata probably took his money back to her Mamacita like she does to every sucker that she meets. Trevion tries not to listen to them but spending four days out to sea hearing all of them tell stories of servicemen being robbed, along with him just having been recently burned by a woman, twice, is making him think that perhaps he'd been conned.

The in-port watch bill is posted and Trevion is in Duty Section 4, which has a total of nine sailors who are E-3 or below. Watches are maintained 24 hours a day and are broken into 4-hour shifts. First Watch is from 0800 to 1200, this is the most desired watch as opposed to the Mid Watch which is from midnight to 0400. Trevion see his name on the Mid Watch for every watch bill underway and see him standing both the 1200 to 1600 or '12 to 16 Messenger Watch' and also the 0400 to 0800 or '4 to 8 Watch' in the parking lot once they pull in.

Surrounded by fellow crew members, Trevion has never felt so alone and isolated. He wonders if the sea will do to him what it has obviously done to all of these guys. SKC walks into the office and sees Trevion at the computer station and asks if he has a driver's license. The last time Trevion was asked that, he was given a dream assignment with Dan, so he says 'Yes, Chief.' SKC tells him that he'll be making a run to the ServMart before the ship leaves Vallejo and enters Dry Dock. "Whatever you need, Chief." Trevion responds, with his inner voice calling him a brown-nose. He has no idea what ServMart is but he's just enthusiastically volunteered for the assignment.

The ship finally makes it back to its home port of Vallejo, CA. The best thing about Vallejo, according to SK2, is that there are two freeways and a bus that can take you out of Vallejo. Trevion disagreed; the hangout spots reminded him of home. Most of the guys on the ship aren't really from a 'hood' so they don't relate to the inner-city style or their women, which is why they really don't like the city because the ladies there really don't like sailors. Trevion blends in seamlessly wherever he goes within the city and has to convince people around town that he's in the Navy due to his homeboy attitude and baby face.

Duty Section 4 finally rolls around and Trevion gets his first solo taste of Messenger of the Watch. His watch starts at 1600 so he stands on the Quarterdeck as those not on duty leave the ship, and rub that fact in. Trevion stays busy during the watch, running around doing things for the Petty Officer of the Watch, getting coffee for the Officer of the Deck, sweeping the area, etc.

Time flows by pretty quickly, and before he knows it, it's time to go. He heads down to GSK to finish up the work that he couldn't do because of the watch, but has to stop when he hears his name over the ship's intercom system, called the 1-MC, instructing him to call the Quarterdeck.

"Carson, I hear you have a driver's license. That's good because we need a duty driver, so get up here." Trevion receives keys to one of the ship's two vans and a map showing the van's route. There are six stops to be made before returning to the ship, the trip should take no more than an hour. The Petty Officer of the Watch makes an announcement that the van will be leaving in twenty minutes, giving Trevion time to go to GSK to wrap up what he was doing then to the berthing area to get ready.

"Hey, Boot. You're the new driver?" Fernandez asks as Trevion changes out of his coveralls and into his working dungarees. Fernandez mentions that one of his stops takes him next to a Chinese restaurant and offers to buy Trevion food if he picks up something for him, Trevion agrees.

By the time Trevion gets to the Quarterdeck, he has six separate orders from guys on duty and stuck on the ship. He can only eat once, so he gets to pocket all of the extra money. This is a good thing because getting all of those orders took time and effort, then a bit of speeding on the way back to make it in time. After eating, Trevion tries to get some rest before he needs to wake back up to stand the 4 to 8 Watch in the parking lot. And it feels as if he barely closed his eyes before the sound of his bunk's rack curtain jars him out of his sleep.

First week in February, 0700, almost zero visibility, so cold that the puddles of water left from a recent rainfall have frozen over. Trevion stands in a small guard shack with no glass in the windows so the wind whips right through it, as he watches the ship's crew slowly trickle in to work; and he's getting pretty tired of being asked if it's 'Cold enough for ya?' as they walk by.

Trevion thought that the sun coming up would mean higher temperatures, but it feels as if it's somehow getting colder by the minute. "Carson, what the hell are you doing out here?" Suppo yells as he walks past the guard shack.

"Freezing my balls off, sir," Trevion replies.

"No, I mean how is it that you're the last guy I saw when I left the ship yesterday and the first guy that I'm seeing as I'm arriving today?" Trevion shrugs his shoulders "R.H.I.P. I was told, and since I have no R, I gets no P."

Suppo laughs and says 'We'll see about that one' as he heads to the ship.

63

After his watch, Trevion hustles to the mess decks to try and scarf down some breakfast before Quarters. He enters just as the guys are leaving and must eat alone, with the kitchen staff looking at him and the two others who are keeping them from closing the galley. Then he rushes down to the berthing area to change out of his working blues and back into his dungarees to stand at Quarters.

"Glad you could join us, Boot!" SK2 exclaims as Trevion attempts to slip into the back of the ranks unnoticed. Suppo reads the announcements and assignments as usual, then makes a comment about tardiness directed to 'those who aren't aware' before he excuses everyone. SK2 looks at Trevion with a smirk before heading down to GSK.

8. Dry Dock – San Francisco, CA

"Alright, Boot Camp," SK2 barks at Trevion, "how about you go and handle Cleaning Gear before you go help clean the berthing." Cleaning Gear Distribution. It happens twice a week in-port and three times a week underway. Trevion goes to the small storage room just down the p-way from Supply berthing where various cleaning supplies are kept and distributed to each department on the ship. They all send someone to pick up supplies such as sponges, wire brushes, cleaning solvents and, most importantly, floor wax, which is requested by everyone.

Trevion opens the top half of the door and begins handing out cleaning gear, checking departments off of the wall-mounted chalkboard as he does. A sailor comes to the door that Trevion recognizes, it's the guy whose rack is directly across from his, MSSN Stafford. He asks if there are any gloves.

Those actually have to be ordered, they're not handed out with the cleaning gear. At least that's what Trevion tells him as he slips two pairs of gloves into his supplies. Stafford notices the gloves and gives a nod before walking off. When he's done, Trevion closes the door and takes a quick inventory of the supplies to see what needs to be replenished before the next time, then locks up and goes to help clean the berthing area.

Down in GSK, SKC is telling everyone what their assignments will be during Dry Dock since the entire ship will be under repair. Most of the SKs are being transferred over to the supply depot in Oakland, along with the Chief. SK2 and Monster will stay and run GSK since only emergency items will be authorized to get ordered. Trevion, since he's not an E-4 or higher, will be sent to a two-day Fire Watch school on Monday along with a group of other low-ranking sailors from throughout the ship.

They will all work with the civilian welders in LT Cruz's Fire Watch Team. Most of the Officers and Chief Petty Officers will get assigned to the cushy offices of the Pac Fleet Logistics Administration building, leaving the ship with a skeleton crew. The only thing that Trevion heard was '2-Day School starting Monday' which meant he was getting away from this bullshit for four days. Tomorrow is Friday and he has duty, Saturday morning he's planning on checking into a cheap motel, in a part of Vallejo that his shipmates are afraid to go to, and partying until he drops.

On Monday, the ship moves from Vallejo to San Francisco but Trevion will be heading to Oakland for the class. SKC hands everyone their orders then instructs them to square away their workspaces. For Trevion, that's not too difficult since he doesn't have an actual desk. Everyone else is forced to organize their belongings and box them up.

Monster is pumped about staying with the ship, but SK2 is highly upset. He wanted to go to the supply depot with the other SK Petty Officers because he has connections over there. He would have gotten a really soft assignment in a clean office instead of being on a dusty, loud, civilian-filled ship waiting for an 'emergency' to happen. Monster is happy because most of the clique will be staying with the ship, so they'll all be together living at the pier in downtown San Francisco.

Fire Watch will be led by LT Cruz from Operations and Senior Chief Roman from Engineering. LT Cruz is a Filipino who was born and raised in San Diego, CA. Both of his parents are Filipinos who were born and raised in San Diego, CA. LT Cruz was somewhat of an anomaly on the ship because the Philippine crew members all hung out together, except for LT Cruz, who doesn't speak Tagalog and, until just recently, had never even been to the Philippines.

Most of the Filipinos aboard the ship were born on the island and joined the Navy through a citizenship program at the Navy Base in Subic Bay. Once they retire, they're not only US citizens, but veterans receiving a pension. The circumstances of their entry into the Navy is a bond that they all share and keeps them together regardless of where in the Philippines they came from. SKC is one of their ranks, as is SK2. But LT Cruz is less a Filipino and more a California jock with his hair dyed a dirty blonde and his Southern California surfer accent.

Trevion never actually met him, just listened to him as he gave a lecture on the ship's Operations Department during orientation. Seemed like an alright guy. SK2 sounds like he's not too fond of the Lieutenant but Trevion isn't too fond of SK2 so, there you go.

Trevion stands in the hotel bathroom getting ready to go out, the guys all meet up at the base Enlisted Men's club to compare assignments. Moorish is going with Trevion to Fire Watch school while Fernandez got his orders to officially join Supply Department as a cook. Monster empties the pitcher into everyone's glasses, "Next time we all hang out, it will be at the world-famous Palladium in downtown Frisco!" The group all toast and chugs their beers.

Chapter Three

1.   Club Hopping

Fire Watch is a piece of cake. Trevion sits in a room with a fire extinguisher while a guy in the other room welds something on the wall. He's just there in case the welder goes through the wall and starts a fire. The hardest part of the job is carrying around the fire extinguisher from site to site. Senior Chief Roman makes his rounds to check on the guys, making sure no one is sleeping. Falling asleep is the second hardest thing about the job, and Senior Chief knows it, so he makes sure to do his walkthroughs a few times a day.

He has the shiniest shoes that Trevion has ever seen, so shiny that Trevion now sits with his brand-new shoe shine kit working on his boots while on watch. Senior Chief walks through and sees Trevion rubbing polish on the tip of his boot, "Looking good, Carson. You still have a ways to go but, keep it up." That was a challenge and Trevion accepts; all week he works on his boots until they're sparkling.

On Friday during Quarters, Senior Chief walks up to Trevion and puts the tip of his boot in front of the tip of Trevion's; equally shiny. After the assignments are made, Senior Chief makes an announcement, "Starting today and every Friday going forward, I will select one of you who was on time all week, didn't get caught sleeping, and maintained an outstanding uniform appearance. He will be given 72-hours of liberty starting right after Friday's Quarters. This week,

I've selected Seaman Recruit Carson. Regardless of duty section, you're off until Quarters on Monday morning. Anyone have any questions? Good, be alert. Carson, congrats now get out of here."

Trevion thanks the Senior Chief then almost runs over to the barge to change and pack. The bus station is only a few blocks away from the pier and Trevion can already taste his mother's cooking. In less than an hour, he's sitting on a bus headed to Los Angeles where he'll transfer to the city bus that'll take him to Beach City. Trevion hasn't been home in almost a year, so he's excited as he looks out the window and tries to forget what he's leaving.

That night, at the Palladium, the guys get to the club early to avoid the cover charge that begins at 9:30pm. Shooting pool and drinking beers, they ask what happened to Trevion. "Senior Chief gave him a Sweet 72 and he went home for the weekend." Moorish informs the guys, "And I ain't even mad at him. If I lived this close, I'd be headed home too."

They drink their beers then decide to hit up another club in the area until the Palladium comes to life. It's the only club in the bay area that stays open until 6am so, when the other clubs shut down at 2am but you still want to party, you head to the Palladium.

They end up at a club that's popular with college students and fall into their usual routine. Suave does two laps around the club to check out the ladies, Franky and Fernandez get beers then head to the smoking area, Big Boats and Monster stand against the wall looking like expensive bouncers and Moorish is on the dance floor, even if no one else is. Moorish is the party-starter wherever the clique goes, always the first-and last-person dancing.

Since he's a good dancer and a fancy dresser, he's never on the dance floor alone for too long, as is the case tonight, as two women dance their way over to him. Suave slides in and high fives Moorish then starts dancing with the other girl, but she moves to behind Moorish and keeps dancing which makes Big Boats and Monster laugh hysterically. Undaunted, Suave begins asking the girls that are standing around and just watching until one says yes.

In the smoking area, Fernandez is bragging to Franky about moving into Supply berthing. "Now I see why they don't let anybody hang out in their berthing area, it's always clean and it don't smell like shit."

Franky scoffs, "Because they don't do any real work! You're gonna be doing some real work in that galley, but Monster sits on his ass all day waiting for supplies to come to the ship and Suave is up in the barber shop cutting hair and shooting the shit. Me, Big Boats, Moorish, we do real work and real work don't smell too good all the time."

Fernandez reminds Franky that those other guys are Boatswain's Mates while Franky is a Gunner's Mate. "I do way more work than you do, and I go and help in the galley when I can. And what the fuck are you talking about? You sit your ass at a desk too. I can pick up one of the ship's phones and call you... at your desk!" Franky says not to compare the two and keeps reiterating that he's still a part of Deck department.

"Yo!" Big Boats yells into the smoking area. "Let's go girls, these punks think they can bowl so we're about to go find out." The guys head to a bowling alley where they make wagers on their games. Big Boats is the best bowler, at 10 his parents were in a bowling league so he grew up bowling. Now at 35, he's bowled for most of his life and can't wait to pluck money out of the guy's pockets. "Let's get it on, ladies. Don't be bashful, now. And I'll buy drinks later tonight if I end up taking all of your money in here."

The guys finish bowling and exit the alley, laughing and counting Big Boat's money, who ended up bowling the very worst of his life. They make their way back to the Palladium which, by this time is packed full of partiers and has a considerable line outside. The guys go to the front of the line and show the stamps that they got on their hands earlier then make their way through the crowd.

"The kings of the Get Laidium have arrived!" Suave yells as they head into the main area. They call the Palladium the Get *Laidium* because most of the people there have already been to other clubs or bars or house parties and have already consumed drinks, then they show up here where the drinks at the bar are mysteriously inexpensive. That multiplied by the fact that you can get into the club at eighteen years old means that millions of bad decisions have been made in this iconic club, and the guys plan on adding to that total tonight.

2.   Hello, Ladies

Monday morning and the guys are on the barge getting dressed for the day ahead. Monster and SK2 are putting on their work dungarees and Trevion is wearing a brand-new pair of coveralls. "Where did you get those from, Boot Camp?" SK2 questions as he walks up to Trevion to inspect the very nice uniform coveralls. "We don't carry these down in GSK, where did you get them?" Trevion explains how his trips to ServMart gained him a friend in the form of the manager at the surplus warehouse. ServMart is like K-Mart, only it's on a military base and you can't buy anything inside with money.

Everything is purchased via a special request form or SR-8, which must be filled out and signed before you enter. This means you must either find items in the catalog or make a dry-run trip just to find items and get part numbers, then fill out the form and get it signed. Hoop after hoop must be jumped through, but SKC knows that the catalog only has about 60% of what's actually inside of the store, so he sent Trevion to find his list of items and also scout things that GSK could use.

Being naturally curious, Trevion noticed the huge building next to ServMart and decided to take a look. There he met Pete, the civilian head shift manager in what turned out to be a building filled with surplus goods. Everything from office desks and file cabinets to engine parts to brand new computers. While talking to Pete, Trevion decides to write down the name of the facility so he could look up the forms when he got back to the ship.

His pen he bought on-board the ship, it had the ship's name and hull number on it and was able to write upside-down due to a pressurized ink system. Pete liked the pen so Trevion gave it to him, who returned the kind gesture by handing Trevion a blank form. "Look around, see anything you like just fill in the tag number on the form. Take it back and get it signed then come and pick up your stuff, but hurry because you ain't the only fellow shopping."

The coveralls, made for Navy pilots, were amongst the tag numbers that Trevion added to the form before bringing it back to SKC. "And all of this is free, even the office chairs?" Trevion says yes and that they'll even hold the chairs until after dry dock, then he can go and pick them up. After Trevion's story, SK2 asks, "So, where are my coveralls?"

Trevion looks over at Monster who tells SK2 that they're down in GSK. "He got a whole stack of them for us, I got two pairs of them and they fit like a champ!" The three head to the barge's galley to have breakfast and everyone there is buzzing over the news that their ship is about to start having female sailors.

"Um, I thought it was bad luck to have women on a ship," one of them jokes as they all discuss the prospect of having 'underway pussy' aboard.

During Quarters, LT Cruz reads an announcement from Pac Fleet naming the ships that will have females and detailing the integration process. All of the ships named are support-type ships such as submarine tenders, carrier tenders, and ammunition ships, none of which were designed for attack.

According to the memo, their ship will receive females in three waves; first will be three female officers followed by twenty women ranking from E-4 to E-8 a month later then a load of E-3 and below just a few weeks after that. Trevion now understands why the civilian contractors were doing so much work in the Ops berthing area, they're transforming that into the female berthing.

Over the next few weeks, Trevion and Moorish pay close attention to how they're changing the ship's layout. They notice that Deck berthing has been expanded and Engineering berthing is cut almost in half with all of the bunks having been removed. "That must be why they moved the cooks into Supply berthing last year," remarks Moorish as the two walk through the ship which now resembles a construction site. "This shit is going to be weird, don't you think, Boot?"

Trevion shakes his head, "There were girls where I went to boot camp, girls in my class at A-School, girls at the base in Hawaii; hell, being surrounded by a bunch of sausages for the past few months is what's weird to me."

The two exit the ship and walk over to the barge to have dinner. Monster and Franky are sitting with Big Boats discussing the training classes that the whole crew must take before the end of dry dock. "Hey there, Boot Camp," Big Boats says, "it's Friday and you're still here. I guess you didn't win the *Prettiest Sailor* contest this week, huh?" Everyone at the table laughs.

"Actually, I did, but I'm trying to save some money, so I decided to just stay here."

Moorish complains that Trevion keeps winning because of his spotless coveralls and shiny welder's boots. "The rest of us can't get those things, so I think the Senior Chief should make you wear the same uniform that the rest of us have to."

Trevion reminds Moorish that he could actually buy the boots himself, to which Moorish smacks his teeth, "What? You know how much them shits cost? Steel-toe, slip-on welder's chukka, in the military catalog... you know, the one that only we can order from and has all of the super-low prices? In there, those boots cost $269. Two sixty fucking nine!"

Trevion looks down at the boots, which cost him nothing because he put their tag number on an order form. "Is that too pricey for you?"

After dinner the guys decide to all go out since none of them had duty and Trevion was actually present for it. Typical night which saw them make their usual rounds before ending up back at the Palladium where Moorish is doing his usual King of the Dance Floor bit, until Trevion steps onto the floor with a young lady in tow and begins to take over the spotlight. The two try to outdo each other, which creates a dance circle around them and prompts the DJ to play more dance-friendly music.

By 4am, both are sweaty and tired as the clique walks out of the club. Suave is holding hands with a rather plump young lady and slips away with her. Monster sees him duck into a cab and laughs, "Looks like the Vulture has himself another carcass." Trevion looks over and sees the two get into the cab and leave.

"I thought you liked big girls, Monster?"

Monster turns to him and says that he does, but the one that Suave was with wasn't at all cute 'so she doesn't count.'

73

One of the girls that Trevion was dancing with walks by with her friends and thanks him for the good time. She's tall and fit with long, brown hair. "No, thank you!" Trevion replies, "I haven't had a good dance partner in a really long time."

As the ladies walk off, Big Boats slaps Trevion on the back of the head and scolds him about not continuing the conversation so that the guys could hit on her friends. "You need to get your Wingman License, youngster."

The guys all head to a 24-hour diner that's a couple of blocks away from the barge. They eat and flirt with the women, who are there fresh out of the club just like they are, when a young man walks up to their table, introducing himself to Trevion as Picasso. "I saw you out there, man. You got some dope moves! Come check me out, I tape a dance show every Wednesday night. Show them this card when you get there." Picasso hands Trevion a business card then walks away.

"Looks like Boot has a date," Moorish jokes from another table.

3. Picasso

Wednesday evening rolls around and most of the guys either have duty or are on their own little missions. Trevion sits in the common area of the barge watching TV when he remembers the conversation he had with Picasso. He pulls his wallet out of his pocket and looks at the business card, *Pure Picasso Entertainment*. He flips it over and sees the letters VIP along with a squiggle written on the back. Trevion looks up at the rerun of Happy Days that's on the wall-mounted TV and decides to go and check out what Picasso has going on. If it turns out to be some homo-erotic man-fest then he'll just leave and not tell anyone that he went.

He puts on an outfit that he bought during his last home visit and decided to walk the eight blocks to the address on the card, which led him through downtown and to a very tall office building. 'No, this can't be right' he thinks as he stands there looking at the building. He walks into the foyer and goes to ask the security guard for directions, but before he can speak the guard says 'Ninth Floor, sir.' Trevion gets into the elevator and hit's the '9' button.

When the door opens, he sees people lined up against the wall and can faintly hear music. He steps out of the elevator and can see that the line wraps around the corner, front and back. He walks towards the end of the line and sees that it goes halfway down the hall; then he walks to the front and sees that it goes all the way down, then continues around the corner. 'Damn' he thinks as he goes to see where the line originates. When he turns the corner, he sees that it goes halfway down and leads to an open door. Walking over to look inside, a man with a clipboard asks if Trevion is on the list. Trevion pulls out the business card and shows it to the man, who returns it and points to the entrance, "Go right ahead, they're about to start taping."

He walks in and sees a control room to the back and a very large, open area complete with a dance floor, a stage with a DJ set up on it, and three huge studio cameras set up between the dance floor and the control room. On the wall, just behind the DJ, there's a sign that reads *Oaktown Lounge*. "Trey! You made it!" Picasso yells from inside of the control room, "Hey, Betty, this is the guy I was telling you about. Dance with him tonight!"

Trevion follows Picasso's eyes to a young woman standing near one of the cameras. She walks over to him, "Hey there, handsome, looks like it's going to be me and you tonight."

4. Semi-Famous

With the six-month dry dock approaching its final month, the ship is beginning to look like itself again as fresh paint and new fixtures begin to return it to seaworthy status. With female sailors scheduled to arrive, the crew must all take a week-long training on sensitivity and sexual harassment. The training is held at the supply base in Oakland so Trevion has the opportunity to visit with his friend over at the surplus warehouse. On a Wednesday, during lunch, Trevion and Moorish head over to the warehouse to chat with Pete.

When Pete sees the guys coming, he signals for them to go around the side. They walk over to the side entrance and wait until Pete shows up carrying a large box. "So, this stuff came in with no paperwork and marked *Discard*. See if you can use any of it, I'll be back in a minute to get what you don't want." The box is filled with brand new blue flight suites and blue foul-weather jackets.

In boot camp, everyone is issued a black, wool petticoat and a green, denim foul-weather jacket with a padded, removable liner. The foul-weather jacket is very heavy and restrictive, but the ones in this box are dark blue, have a much thinner removable liner, and are actually fashionable. They're not as heavy as the boot camp issued ones but feel much warmer when the guys try them on. Trevion and Moorish both grab two jackets in their own sizes, Trevion grabs one for Monster and Moorish finds Big Boat's size.

The flight suits are smaller in size and only two of them fit Trevion and Moorish, who wear about the same size clothes. The rest of the box they return to Pete who looks in and sees what's left over, "Man, take as much as you can carry! I've already been through it."

They grab a few more jackets and coveralls, then hurry back to make it to the training in time. Big Boats puts on the jacket handed to him by Moorish, "Oh, this is quite nice. Where did you guys get these and what else do y'all got in those bags?"

Moorish looks at Trevion then says, "Don't even worry about that, just enjoy your new jacket, big dog."

They finish the class for the day then return to the barge. Trevion begins getting dressed to go to the dance show taping when Moorish walks up and asks where he's going on a Wednesday when nothing is going on. Trevion makes him promise not to say anything and tells him to get dressed because they're going to the show that Picasso mentioned when they all went out. After a bit of convincing, Moorish gets dressed and goes with Trevion to the filming.

After being on the show for a few weeks, the guy with the clipboard, who Trevion finds out is the Production Manager, knows Trevion and always just nods at him when he walks in. This time, Trevion isn't alone. "Hey, you in the yellow shirt!" he says to Moorish.

"He's with me," Trevion says as they walk into the filming area.

"Ok, everyone, please take your places. We have a local act performing tonight so I'm going to need you guys out of the shot during her show," Picasso yells through a tiny megaphone, "…we're using two cameras for this one so I need dancers on both sides and maybe three couples dancing in the middle; Betty and Trey, pick who you guys want in the middle with you and everyone else stay outside of my shot!"

Moorish, who is usually very confident and quick-witted, stands there in silence as he looks at the full scope of what's around him. Trevion pulls him to the middle of the dance floor and asks Betty to find someone for him to dance with. As they stand on their spots chatting and waiting for the taping to start, a young, Latina woman walks up to Trevion and taps him on his shoulder. "I remember you from the Palladium, right?" she asks.

It's the young woman that Trevion had danced with weeks ago when he went clubbing with the clique. "Hey, how are you?" he asks.

"I'm good, save me a dance, ok?" As she walks away, Betty asks how Trevion knows her, "That's Rissa Gold, she just signed with Sunshine Records! How do you know her?" As the show begins, Rissa is on stage performing when she gestures for Trevion to join her.

She stands in front of Trevion, facing the camera and holding the back of his neck, then wraps her right leg backwards around him as they dance while she's singing. The two move as if they'd choreographed the entire thing. After the show, Picasso thanks Trevion and invites him to a second show that he produces for the cable network which airs The Oaktown Lounge. "We film on Sundays so, if you're not busy or whatever, come by."

"That was bananas!" Moorish exclaims as the two walk through downtown and back to the barge. "I've never seen that many fine-ass women in one place in my whole life! How long have you been going on that show?"

Trevion tells him that it's been about two months then reminds him not to tell anyone about it. "I can't have a bunch of dudes trying to roll with me, one or two maybe but if you tell those guys about it, they'll all want to go and mess up what I got going over there." Moorish agrees and the two head to their bunks.

By Friday, the guys can't wait to go out and do the exact opposite of what a week's worth of sensitivity and sexual harassment training had just taught them. Same routine; Palladium at around 8pm to get stamped, bowling alley or pool hall, random bar, random club, then back to the Palladium. Only this time, at the bowling alley, a group of girls are there bowling next to the guys. Suave is busy trying to chat them all up when one of them keeps looking at Trevion.

"Do I know you?" she asks.

"Are you from Beach City?" he asks back.

She says no, but swears that she somehow knows Trevion. "Wait, are you on TV?" Trevion looks over at Moorish, who raises his eyebrows and gives an 'oh shit' look.

One of the other girls looks at Trevion, "That is him, the one that was on stage with Rissa Gold!" This makes the group of girls suddenly interested in the guys, which gives Suave an opening to invite them to the Palladium later in the evening.

One of the girls asks Trevion how he ended up on stage with Rissa Gold, Franky adds, "Yeah, Boot. Why don't you tell the pretty young lady how you ended up on TV with a famous singer?" Trevion spends the rest of the evening deflecting questions from the guys about how he's on TV, but enjoying all of the extra attention that the ladies are giving him in the bowling alley, on the street, and then later in the Palladium as Trevion keeps getting recognized for being on the dance show.

The next morning, Moorish, since the cat was already out of the bag, brags at breakfast about his experience at the show taping and how fine all the girls there were. By the following Wednesday, there are twenty or so guys trying to go to the taping with Trevion. Under massive protest from Moorish, Trevion decides not to go to the taping this week due to the large number of guys who are dressed, smelling like cologne and following him around the barge. "C'mon, Boot, stop being stingy!" Fernandez demands as he and the others try to convince Trevion to go, but he refuses to take off his sweats and then finally gets tired of being asked and goes to sleep.

5.   Wave After Wave

Thursday morning and there are only five weeks of dry dock remaining before the ship leaves San Francisco. The first wave of female sailors have already made their way to the crew and are with the Officers and Chiefs at Pac Fleet, so the guys haven't noticed it. But they can see the second wave coming because they wake up to find a second barge floating behind theirs.

"That's the ladies' barge," one of the crew members remarks. "It got pulled in early this morning and a cleaning crew has already been in and out of there." Trevion and Moorish glance at the new barge and comment on how it's a *new* barge compared to theirs which looks like it's been in constant use since WWII. They get to Quarters and notice that there are five females standing in the ranks. "Damn, that was fast!" Moorish whispers as they stand for Quarters. The fire watch team, after quarters, either receive assignments or sit in a room and wait for a civilian welder to show up and grab one of them.

Needless to say, all of the female sailors were selected first by the welders, leaving an all-male group waiting for assignments. "They ain't much to look at." Comments one of the sailors which makes the group laugh.

"Well," Moorish comments, "most of the guys who join the navy are ugly rejects so, what makes you think that most of the girls who join aren't ugly rejects? How many super-hot girls do you know that say, 'I think I'm going to join the military'."

"You'd be surprised," Trevion adds. "I went to A-School with some pretty dazzling ones."

At lunch, the females join the males on their barge to eat because the galley on the female barge isn't crewed. "Thanks a lot, Boot! We had a great time standing in the hallway last night like a bunch of jerky rejects." Franky says as he drops his tray down on the table.

"Who told you guys where it was?" Trevion asks as he looks over at Moorish, who is trying not to make eye contact.

"That ass hat with the clipboard wouldn't let us in. I saw your name on his list and told him that we were with you, but he still made us get in that line, the one that turned two fucking corners! Then, he walked back and forth grabbing people out of the line and didn't even look at us. I thought you had pull over there, why did we stand there with those losers?"

Trevion looks at him, "Did you just answer your own question?" Franky flicks him off and starts eating.

"Hey, I know you," says one of the female sailors from the table across from the guys.

Franky rolls his eyes, "Let me guess, you saw him dancing like a rabbit on TV, right?"

"No, I saw him in Meridian." Trevion looks over but doesn't recognize the female sailor. She tells him that when she saw him, he was at the airport with another guy and was about to fly to Hawaii.

"I had just flown in and was waiting for one of those expensive-ass taxis, I heard you guys talking about your orders. You're kinda the reason I'm on this ship, my number one on my dream sheet was Hawaii and my number two was San Francisco. I've been stationed at PacFleet waiting for the ship to be updated."

She introduces herself as SKSA Middleton. "Oh," SK2 says from another table, "you're one of mine. First rule, follow my example and steer clear of those two fuck-ups over there."

Monster looks up from his plate, "Fuck-ups? Fuck you, teacher's pet! You're just upset because your daddy has a new favorite son. And, while you're bullshitting, it looks like he just got a favorite daughter too if she's fresh out of A-School."

SK2 doesn't respond. Trevion looks at Middleton, who has a slightly concerned look on her face, "Welcome to the Mt. Wilson," he jokingly says. "My name is Carson."

SK2 quips, "No, his name is Boot Camp!"

Trevion hates being called Boot or Boot Camp. There are only a few sailors on the ship who are new to the Navy, the ship is called 'Top-Heavy' because the petty officers to seamen ratio was off balance. Trevion and Monster were the only SKs that weren't petty officers, the rest were either transfers or strikers from Deck department.

Monster came from Deck department; he and two other of the SKs were strikers and were allowed to take the advancement exam because of inevitable transfers and a retirement that left GSK understaffed. The others passed and made rank. Monster didn't make rank, but scored high enough to be given the rate of SK. In nearly two years following that, there have been no other strikers or new crew members until Trevion.

Each day saw new female crew members being added, unlike the earlier report which had them coming in three waves. By the time the ship was ready to return to the ocean, it had its full crew aboard and the guys were learning to get used to having women around them. Workspaces had to be cleaned up as calendars with nude models and magazine clippings with sexually suggestive pictures, jokes, or language could no longer be present.

The ship steams back to Vallejo where supplies have been piling up for months waiting for the ship's return. The SKs, with their new E-1 and E-6, have the advantage of a crane to bring up the pallets in the mornings, but after lunch the civilian crew is off to another site and the ship's crane, which had the most repair work done during dry dock, still hasn't been tested and cleared for use. So, the SKs must break open the plastic-wrapped pallets of supplies, carry the boxes up the gangplank to the quarterdeck, then down to the Main Deck where they separate it for pick-up by whichever department ordered it.

Anything that's been ordered for stock and whatever isn't picked up by the ordering departments must then be carried down to GSK. The guys worried that the two ladies wouldn't be holding their own, but both worked just as hard as their male contemporaries. Due to the two new SKs, and to one of them being an E-6 or First Class Petty Officer, the desk assignments are shifted. The new SK1 now sits in SK2's old desk right next the chief, SK2 now sits in the row against the wall.

Monster has to give up his desk and sits in the computer area with Middleton. SK2 assigns Trevion to a desk in the back of GSK, which hadn't been in use for years. That desk is just in front of the Returnables/Reparable storage area about three-quartes of the way to the back of the storeroom. It's pretty much set in stone that Trevion will be taking over that assignment after he finishes his impending mess duty, taking the job from SK2 who seems more than happy that he's about to be rid of the demanding and complex assignment. It takes a full week, including the weekend, to get all of the supplies on-board and down to GSK, but it's going to take much longer than that to finish processing and distributing it all as stacks of boxes crowd any available space in the storage area.

6.   Sea Legs

The ship is preparing to go on its Refresher Training or RefTra, which is when a group of naval inspectors come aboard the ship for three weeks of underway drills. The ship's captain schedules six days where the ship will go out to sea and get the crew ready for RefTra; especially since it now has female crew members and will be tested on their knowledge of the new procedures.

Much of the crew is upset because they'll be underway over the weekend and the playoffs are happening, which means they'll miss the games. But, the captain eases everyone's tensions by announcing that they'll be receiving the broadcast via an aircraft carrier that'll be in the area on that day.

Supply Department stands at Quarters and, despite the warnings from Monster, Trevion is wearing his new foul-weather jacket. SK2 tells him to take the jacket off because it's not approved uniform, but when Suppo walks up wearing an identical one, SK2 is forced to back down.

Monster whispers to Trevion, "How did Suppo get one?"

"Suppo and SKC," Trevion whispers back with a wink. "You can start wearing yours now."

SK1 stands in front with the brass, a place formerly occupied by SK2; which is why he's in such a foul mood. SK1 is pretty tall and has a strong, athletic build. She wears her hair very short and keeps a pair of gloves and a box cutter on her belt at all times.

Up to this point, Trevion has been impressed with the female sailors who pull their own weight and seem to work even harder than the guys on the ship; that is until they go out to sea as most of them are violently seasick. SK1 is fine, having previously served on a tugboat crew, so she already has her sea legs. But Middleton along with the majority of the other females are having a very hard time.

The watch bill is still very unkind to Trevion and with Middleton being so sick, he's forced to stand his watch and help cover her watch. Looking at the watch bill, he notices a different watch listed, Roving Security Patrol. This is the only watch that appears on both the underway and in-port watch bills. There are thirteen people listed as eligible to stand that watch, and only six possible watches to stand, meaning they never stand watch twice in one day.

Trevion speaks with SKC and asks if he could walk with the Rover during the 16 to 20 watch, the chief agrees and Trevion begins learning Rover watch instead of hanging out in Supply berthing or hiding at his desk. That is, when a drill isn't taking place of course. Battle station drills happen throughout day, as do emergency drills on fire fighting and watertight integrity in case the ship is hit by a torpedo.

With the endless drills on top of ordinary work, the crew is very relieved when the captain announces over the 1-MC that Sunday will be free of any drills so that the crew could enjoy the playoffs and so that the Gunner's Mates can conduct small arms qualifications on the ship's helicopter deck; since the ship's two helicopters nor their flight crew will be rejoining the ship until after RefTra.

The crew in Supply berthing all pitched in and bought snacks for the game before getting underway and everyone is wearing their team's hats or jerseys. The berthing area resembles a sports bar; minus the women and alcohol of course. The mess decks serve hamburgers, hot dogs, and chili and even turned on the never-used TVs hanging on opposite walls so that the crew can see the games being played throughout the day. It is a very welcomed break which ends dramatically when a drill begins at 0600 the next morning.

7.   Refresher Training

The week spent preparing for RefTra was nothing compared to the real thing. The crew may have been better off not preparing at all because the only thing the preparation did was lull everyone into a false sense proficiency. The reality was that none of them were battle ready, but the inspectors and trainers on-board would make sure that they were by the end of the three weeks. The crew had difficulty with one of the drills, so the next day the inspectors ran that drill over and over, all day. Tensions were high all over the ship and GSK was no different. The only one who had an outlet to release stress was SK2, who routinely would go to the back of the storage area to harass Trevion.

During a late evening drill, a hull breach was simulated taking place on the wall that ran along GSK. Most of the SKs were still there working when crew members followed by the inspectors came rushing in. The inspectors began testing everyone there, asking them what they would do in the event of a hull breach and personnel injury. Trevion is always first to answer their questions, especially the ones regarding first aid.

One of the inspectors tells Trevion, "Not bad, sailor. Are you on one of the ship's emergency response teams?" Trevion says no, that he was a Boy Scout and that he's trained hundreds of scouts on first aid. The inspector points at Trevion and calls out, "This guy is dying, transport to Medical!" Four sailors pick Trevion up and carry him up the flight of stairs leading out of GSK. When they get to the top, they put Trevion down and tell him to report to Medical until the end of the drill. When he gets there, the ship's Medical Officer points to an empty bed and Trevion lays down and falls asleep.

At 0200 the drill finally ends; Trevion isn't awakened until 0600 by one of the Corpsmen who notices that he's still there. A full night's sleep on a real mattress, in a dark, quiet room free of snoring and/or stinking sailors had Trevion feeling great when he woke up. He returned to Supply berthing and finds everyone just waking up, and they're all grumpy and tired. He dashes into the shower and is back before anyone is even fully out of their racks.

"Where the hell were you last night, Boot Camp?" SK2 demands as Trevion begins to get dressed.

"Dead." Trevion responds with a half-smile.

"You think that shit is funny?" SK2 asks as he walks up on Trevion. Monster has to get between the two arguing sailors. "We'll see, Boot Camp! This ain't over." SK2 yells as he walks past Trevion and heads to the showers.

"Fuck is wrong with that guy?" Trevion asks, but Monster looks at Trevion.

"Fuck is wrong with you, Boot? Stop trying to outdo everybody and stay in your damn place!"

8.   Propane

RefTra ends and the inspectors begin to debrief the command team on what needs improvement and what they actually excelled at. As the ship slowly steams towards Vallejo after doing circles in the ocean for what felt like forever, Big Boats walks into Supply berthing carrying the watch bill. "Y'all ain't gonna like this." He posts the watch bill on the tag-board and removes the old one.

As the guys look at the new watch bill, Monster yells out, "What the hell is this? Why isn't Boot on the Low-Vis watch? I outrank Boot but I'm on this bitch like... eleven times!"

Fernandez asks how Trevion is on the Rover Watch. "I qualified."

He responds, "Qualified?"

Monster asks, "We've been out to sea for less than three weeks, I know dudes that's been trying to get Rover qualified for damn near a year! How can you possibly be qualified?"

Trevion explains how when he would follow RN2 Baker around on his watch that Baker would give him the gun belt and say, 'I'll follow you', and let Trevion walk the route around the ship.

Moorish demands, "How can he do that? Baker wasn't supposed to give you his sidearm! You're not..."

"Gun qualified?" Trevion interrupts. "I am now, remember that Sunday when you guys watched that blowout that they kept rebroadcasting all day? I got my gun quals. LT Cruz is the guy that gives the test for Rover, he was with the Gunner's Mates helping to run the gun range on the fantail and Baker mentioned to him that he followed me on watch. LT Cruz gave me the test on the spot, I passed, now I'm off the Lookout watch."

Moorish pauses for a moment then says, "That means, when we get back to port you'll be off of the Messenger watch too, right?" Big Boats laughs very loudly and says that he feels sorry for the guys in Trevion's duty section.

SK2 slaps Trevion on the back and says, "You know what, Boot Camp? I guess you're not so bad after all. I'm all for one more rover on the watch bill, means I won't be standing that Mid Watch anymore."

Moorish isn't as pleased, "Damn, man! Our duty section is full of Petty Officers, we got just enough E-3 and below to cover Messenger when we're pulled in. If this punk is off the rotation, somebody will always be on the watch twice!"

Big Boats gives out another laugh, "Told you that you weren't going to be happy, Boot is fucking up the grading curb."

"Curve..." Trevion begins to correct Big Boats when Monster again complains about Trevion not being on the Low-Visibility watch bill.

Big Boats asks Trevion if LT Cruz put him on the Security Squad. "Yeah," Trevion answers, "aren't all Rovers assigned to the Security Squad?"

Big Boats looks over at SK2 and says no, but that's why Trevion is off of the Low-Vis watch bill. "He's on the Squad now so they're going to change his General Quarters station since he'll be one of the assholes running around the ship when we lose power or whatever…"

"Bullshit!" Monster shouts again as he punches the watch bill and walks away.

"I guess you gotta kiss a lot of ass, eh Boot?" Fernandez jokes.

Trevion looks at the group of disgruntled sailors and says, "If by kissing ass you mean standing three watches a day this entire trip, working extra hours to make sure all of the orders are processed, and missing my team destroy yours and move on to the championship round, just to get qualified? Then, yeah, I kissed a whole crowd of ass!

"Y'all can't get mad at me because I decided to get qualified while all of you sat on your asses and played cards or watched sports instead of getting it in."

SK2 slaps Trevion on the back again, "I take it back, you're not alright. You're an overachieving little show-off, and I can't wait to see you crash and burn." Trevion looks around at the men who were supposed to be his friends and can see that they're not happy with his achievements.

A culture exists on the ship that Trevion has noticed but, until now, figured that it wouldn't affect him. Everyone seems to do just the bare minimum, the base requirements for everything. That way, if they want to prove a point, they can step it up and make themselves look good by doing just over what's required. Trevion lives in the over what's required zone, and took offense when SK2 called him an overachiever.

Trevion's father always taught him to aim for no less than just past his mark, to always go above and beyond and to not worry about what slackers would say because 'You're making them look bad by just being yourself. If any of your friends aren't happy when your hard work pays off, they're not your friends. They're your rivals.' These words, coupled with his mother's favorite phrase 'Play a fool to catch a fool' keep ringing in his head whenever the harassment and bullying begins to make him overemotional.

Perhaps he should take Monster's advice and just slow down, be average and pay the sweat equity that seems to be the preferred currency on the ship. But his inner voice, which suspiciously sounds like his father, won't let him slack off. At least, Trevion thinks, he should keep what he's doing as quiet as possible. They know that Trevion is on the Security Squad, but it seems as if no one knows what the Squad does, only that they're comprised of E-4 and above, and that they guard the special weapons on-board the ship.

Trevion crawls into his rack and looks up at the picture of Diwata. "You know why he's so pissed off, right?" a low voice comes from Stafford's rack.

Trevion opens his rack curtain and whispers back, "No, why?" Stafford explains that SK2 has been trying to get on the Security Squad for over two years. "Damn," Trevion whispers back, "I can't win for losing, can I?"

By the time the ship returns to port, the crew is very tired from the constant training and drills, and the SKs are especially exhausted because they also had to deal with the giant pile of supplies that they brought aboard just prior. The rest of the female sailors are waiting on the pier as the ship pulls in, along with more pallets of supplies. "We got stores on the pier," SKC informs his team, "I know everybody is tired and you want to go home, I do too, so the sooner we get supplies to the main deck, the sooner we can leave."

Trevion thinks to himself how that pep talk had to have been aimed at the SKs who live off-ship, which would be all of them with the exception of Monster, Middleton, and himself. SK1 was stationed in Oakland with the tugboat team so she was already living there for years. The rest of the guys are either married and living out in town or in military housing, or have apartments somewhere in the Bay Area. SK2 isn't happy about having to deal with the supplies before he goes home and is taking it out on Trevion, making him carry up all of the heavier boxes and speaking to him like a child.

"How hard is it, Boot Camp? Pick up the box, bring it to the Main Deck! You don't need to go to A-School to figure that out!" Once all of the supplies are either on the Main Deck or inside of GSK, most of the SKs go home. Trevion has duty so he'll be bringing down the remaining boxes from the Main Deck to GSK since its only him and SKC in the duty section. Middleton and SK1 haven't been assigned duty stations yet, so SK1 goes home while Middleton decides to stay and help Trevion get the boxes downstairs.

"What did you do to SK2 to make him not like you?" she asks as they stack the last of the supplies.

"I was born, I guess," Trevion responds.

9. More Propane

SK2 takes great delight in informing Trevion that his six-month mess duty is about to begin. So much delight that as soon as he finds out about it, he searches the ship for Trevion so that he can personally deliver the news. SK2 checks the normal areas then finally finds Trevion in the head sitting on the toilet.

"Boot Camp, are you in here?"

Trevion debates answering, "Yeah, what's up?"

SK2 give out a, "Whew! First thing is, stop eating whatever it was that you ate last night. But, good news, you start mess duty next week on Monday. So, congratulations, have fun and I'll see you in six months!"

SK2 laughs as he exits the head, but Trevion sits with a confused look on his face, "Its only Tuesday so, he'll see me today after lunch."

Trevion returns to the berthing area where the guys are getting ready to play basketball in the Fleet League, which is a league of teams from each of the sixteen ships in the area. "What's up, Boot, can you ball?" Monster asks, to which Trevion says that he's played ball in the street since he was very young and was on the high school team before he left for the Navy.

Monster hands him a jersey and they all leave to play in the preliminary tournament. Coincidentally, MS2 McKay, a cook famous for his fried chicken recipe, is making a soul food menu for dinner on the ship. The guys know that there will be no chicken left when they return from the game because even the officers come down when he cooks the southern-style chicken.

The anger from missing out on a once in a blue moon event along with Trevion's surprising production off the bench drives the team to victory in the tournament. They return and head straight to the galley but, as expected, all of the chicken is gone. The ribs and steak strips are very good, but nothing compared to the chicken.

As the guys stand in line grumbling, Stafford motions for Trevion to step out of line. He walks around to the kitchen crew door and the young cook takes Trevion's tray. A few moments later, he brings it back with three pieces of chicken atop the rest of the food. "Oh, shit! Thanks!" Trevion says as he heads to the table to sit down.

"Precisely where in the fuck did you get that?" Franky asks when he sees the chicken on Trevion's tray, which makes everyone else take notice. A few minutes ago, the guys were praising Trevion for coming off the bench and scoring eighteen points in the final game of their tournament, now they're all upset with him because he has the coveted chicken on his tray and they don't.

Their grumbles and insults do nothing to Trevion, who is lost in how delicious the chicken actually was. The breading was amazing and the meat tasted as if it had been marinated overnight. He looks over at Monster's tray and sees that he's almost finished with his food. Trevion points at his tray. "Grab that thigh right there, big homie."

In one motion, Monster grabs the chicken from Trevion's tray and takes a big bite; which brings more grumblings from the guys. With a mouth full of chicken, Monster mumbles, "Shit, fuck y'all."

The rest of the week is spent handing off assignments and hearing SK2 make jokes and casual threats, "I'm going to make sure that my friends up there take good care of you, Boot Camp!" On Thursday, SKC tells Trevion to keep studying those manuals and gives him the afternoon off. Friday morning, Trevion stands at Quarters for the last time because he'll be reporting to the mess decks immediately after for an orientation, then he'll have his last weekend off for the next six months because there are only two duty sections for mess duty; on duty and off duty, so there'll be no two consecutive days off.

Suppo reads the announcements as usual, then calls everyone's attention to the Yeoman standing next to him who begins to read a paper; "Pacific Fleet – Naval Operations is proud to announce the following servicemen have been promoted... um, the relevant name on this list is Trevion Carson, who is, as of January 1, 1990, hereby promoted to the rank of E-3 with all rights therein. Blah-blah-blah-blah, Seaman Carson will be eligible for the E-4 exam at the next offering and will receive E-3 pay in retro. Congratulation to Storekeeper Seaman Trevion Carson from Pac-Fleet Naval Ops."

The Yeoman and Suppo begin clapping, followed by SKC and the heads of the other Supply divisions with only a spattering of applause given by the crew. "Thank you, Petty Officer Warren, and congrats to our stellar team member. Make sure you adjust your rank on your uniforms, Carson. Alright, if there's nothing else, everyone turn-to and commence ship's work."

"How in the hell did Boot jump to E-3 like that?" SK2 asks as the SKs head down to work. SKC informs him of his three letters of recommendation; one from Trevion's CC in Boot Camp, one from his Chief Instructor in A-School and one from Vice Admiral Dan Unger. Trevion tries to sit quietly at his desk in the rear of the storeroom, but the SKs are all abuzz with what just happened and are standing around his desk. "As of January 1st, that's six months of retroactive pay!" SK2 comments as he looks at Trevion, "Drinks on you then, right Boot Camp?"

As the group discusses the rare promotion, Suppo comes down to GSK and makes a bee line for Trevion's desk, "Carson, Pac Fleet is watching you now. From what I've just heard, Vice Admiral Unger rarely signs a letter of recommendation, let alone hand-write one and fax it to Admiral Cobb's office. Brass tax; you do good, I look good. You do bad, I look bad, then you'll feel bad! Are we clear?"

Trevion says 'Yes sir' and Suppo storms out.

Monster looks over at Trevion, "This guy hasn't done a damn thing yet and he already has Pac-Fleet watching him. You just can't fly under the radar, can you?" Trevion begins to wish that he could.

10. Mess Crank

For six months, each crew member ranking E-3 and below must serve the mess decks. The duties are familiar to Trevion, having been through Service Week in boot camp. With the sudden promotion that Trevion received, Stafford convinces the MS1 to allow him to pull Trevion down to the storage area with him. Stafford is in charge of the dry foods, cold storage, and freezer areas on the lower decks of the ship. MS1 LeRoy "Bubba" Thomas runs the galley with an iron fist so, at first, he is reluctant to let Trevion escape his legendary wrath. But the fact that Trevion is an SK, which means both he's familiar with keeping a storage area and he's a fellow member of Supply Department, Bubba agrees to assign Trevion to Stafford.

"The only bad thing is," Stafford warns, "when we're underway, we have to work Mid-Rats. Even on the weekends." Trevion remembers his first time eating Mid-Rats, which is short for Midnight Rations; he was standing the Mid Watch so he got up early to wash his face to wake up. A shipmate told him to get coffee from the mess decks but when he got there, he found that they were serving re-heated leftovers from dinner. This meal was designed for those crew members whose schedules are irregular while the ship is at sea.

"Thanks for pulling me down here, man. I really appreciate it." Trevion says as Stafford gives him the tour.

"Don't trip, even if you are a crab." Trevion looks at Stafford, who makes a 'b' with his fingers.

"How did you know I was a Crip?" Trevion asks. "You're from Beach City, you ain't Asian and you ain't Mexican. Everybody knows that there ain't but three hoods in Beach City, and Bloods ain't one of them."

The two laugh and joke about each other's neighborhoods, Stafford being from Compton. In the mornings, Trevion and Stafford must help out with opening the galley and prepping the more difficult dishes. Trevion isn't a cook so he's not allowed to do any food prep, so instead he assists the other cranks in their duties. After the whole kitchen crew has breakfast, he and Stafford head down to the lower decks to get to work.

The cold storage locker and the big freezer are nothing compared to the very hectic GSK, so Trevion has lots of ideas to help Stafford reorganize the refrigerated areas as well as the dry storage room. For the first two weeks of his mess duty, Trevion and Stafford complete the inventory and draw up their reorganization plan to present to Bubba.

"So, this is what you two have been doing for the past weeks?" Bubba asks with a frown on his face, "You both think this is a good idea? You think that it's a proper use of the Navy's time and manpower?" Trevion begins to second-guess what he and Stafford have been doing, but Stafford says that it's a great idea, and when they're done, that it'll save valuable time in the future.

Bubba hands the papers back to Stafford and says, "Yup, I think so too. And since we're leaving for West-Pac in a few weeks, it's perfect timing. Damn good job, both of you get to work on this and make sure you give me all of the credit for it!" Trevion is beginning to figure out that Bubba is always mean, he's always yelling; even when he's being nice or giving a compliment.

The two return to the lower storage area and begin setting up their plan. The work that Trevion is doing with Stafford is not at all typical of what a mess crank does. Aside from the mornings when Trevion helps out for an hour or so, he spends his time hanging out with Stafford. The other mess cranks are working very hard in the galley, under the eagle eye of Bubba, all day with very few breaks.

Bubba walks into the food prep area and asks where one of the cranks went, the others play dumb even though they knew he had slipped down to the Deck berthing area to hang out with the guys who were doing morning cleaning. When the crank returns, Bubba asks "Where did you go?" to which the crank says that he got his pants dirty and went to change them.

Bubba looks at the sailor and says, "You just gave me the wrong answer. I need you to take all of the pots and pans from under the kitchen island and wash them all, dry them all, then put them back under the island; and they'd better be organized. You have one hour to get it done, failure results in penalty." Penalty means extra duty and Bubba hands out penalties in 3-day increments. All of the cranks are afraid of Bubba, and are growing jealous of Trevion and his very favorable assignment.

Most of the cranks are from Deck department so Trevion isn't present in their berthing area when they complain about how he's getting the Supply treatment while they bust their asses all day. He can only feel the resentment and hear the passive aggressive comments in the mornings as he helps them set up. It's only been three weeks and somehow Trevion already has the workplace against him, just like the workplace down in GSK. It causes him to self-reflect as he lays in his bunk at night, staring at a photo of a girl who most likely scammed him out of hundreds of dollars.

The photo was taken by a wandering photographer at the mountainside hotel. Trevion paid to have two pictures taken; one with them sitting next to each other and smiling, the other with Diwata wrapping her arms around him. She kept the first and Trevion now stares at his picture wondering if she kept the other one because she's just sitting and smiling and not hugging him like in his picture; easy to cut someone out of a photo if you're not all over them.

One night, Trevion is awakened by a conversation in the berthing. Everyone begins exiting their bunks to hear what's going on. The ships scheduled WestPac has been pushed back, they're on stand-by until further notice. "What's going on?" Monster asks as he rolls out of his rack. Big Boats walks in and tells everyone that there's tension in the Middle East so the entire Pacific Fleet has orders to tool up and be ready.

Trevion returns to his bottom bunk, he and Stafford talk briefly about the possibility of seeing actual combat. "I hope not," Stafford says as he pulls his blanket up past his shoulders, "if we get attacked, this ship is designed to either go straight up, exploding into a million pieces, or go straight down and sink super-fast so that the enemy can't get to our cargo."

He pulls his rack curtain closed and Trevion does the same, but even when the berthing slowly returns back to quiet, he can't return back to sleep. He was looking forward to WestPac, when the ship does a six-month deployment and visits multiple countries along the way. PI is a country that was scheduled to be visited twice, since they have a naval weapons magazine and can accommodate a ship carrying powerful ordinance. Trevion needs to walk into that bar and find out if he's been tricked or not, but that will have to wait until whenever Pac Fleet decides to let them go.

11. Wait, We're Really Going?

The ship spends the rest of June and the entire month of July preparing for the worst-case scenario, completing Underway Replenishments, or UnReps, with several warships and stocking up on everything. The SKs are being hit hard as they are being tasked with making sure that the ship's inventory is at near-max while dealing with the increased requests from the ship's other departments as they too prepare for what could come.

The reorganization of the cooks' storage areas drastically improves their efficiency, prompting Suppo to comment on how great the area looks during Quarters. Trevion isn't there to hear the praise, he stands Quarters with the mess cranks. But his fellow SKs aren't happy about Trevion not being there to help them as they're slammed with incoming supplies almost daily, so the news of him excelling elsewhere only really makes SKC proud.

Trevion has tried to go home every other weekend. Mostly to see his family, but mainly to be counseled by his father. Trevion's dad wasn't happy about his choice to join the military, but is very proud of him and happy to listen to the new set of life obstacles that his son is wrestling with; giving him encouragement and advice.

Trevion hasn't told his father much about Diwata, calling her a 'potential' when his dad asked about the picture that appeared in a frame on Trevion's last visit home. With the picture off of the ship and sitting in his bedroom back in Beach City, Trevion hopes that he won't think about her as much.

The first few days with the picture missing from his rack, he thought about her twice as much. Which is why he had mixed emotions when it was announced that the ship's battle group was heading to the Persian Gulf. Finally, his ship would go to the Philippines, and he'd be able to confront Diwata but, at the same time, he's heading into an actual war.

The coming conflict brings out the best in some of the crew, and the worst in the rest. It has been quite a while since America has been at war, so the vast majority of the crew have never seen conflict. Trevion is not alone in his anxiety over the whole thing as past tensions begin to fade away in light of what's to come.

"That's it," Big Boats announces as he enters Supply berthing, "Iraq just invaded Kuwait! They're threatening Saudi Arabia now so we'll be heading out day after tomorrow." The words ring in Trevion's ear as he listens to Big Boats' report. Iraq has the fourth largest army in the world and their leader uses chemical weapons, even on his own people. This isn't going to be a walk in the park.

The next day was surreal as everyone prepared to leave for war. Trevion gets an unexpected visitor at Supply berthing; Middleton shows up while Trevion and Stafford take their turn cleaning. "Hey, I just want to know," she asks, "how were you able to process so many requests every day? I looked at the files and you got so many requests done every day, more than anyone else on file, how did you do them so fast?"

Trevion fills Middleton in on his method of searching part numbers, Middleton comments that she remembers that from A-School. "That's exactly where I got it from, they showed us the shortcut right in the text book. I remembered it because I taught it to my dad over the phone so that he could use it in his store. It works like a dream. But do me one favor, don't share that secret. Just use it and kick ass."

Middleton agrees and returns to GSK. "That was pretty cool, man." Stafford tells Trevion as the two prepare to wax the p-way floors.

"Thanks, but I told her to keep her distance so they won't start fucking with her just because she's cool with me." Stafford agrees with the decision and they continue their cleaning duties.

In the officers' lounge, Suppo is sitting in an impromptu meeting between LT Cruz, the ship's Executive Officer or XO, and himself regarding Trevion. The ship's Security Squad needs to complete a training series on the leg from Hawaii to PI to be ready for the special weapons transfers that will be happening, and LT Cruz needs to have

Trevion present at each of the sessions.

This is the first time of Suppo hearing about Trevion being on the Security Squad, but pretends that he put Trevion on mess duty so that he can be more available just in case. The XO grants LT Cruz permission to pull Trevion from wherever he is to attend any trainings or meetings with the Squad, and Suppo gives his support for the decision.

After the quick discussion, Suppo hurries to his cabin and calls a Personnelman at Pac-Fleet to relay a report on how well Trevion is doing, under his personal leadership of course. He ends the call with only a few moments to spare as all phone lines are disconnected from the pier in preparation of the ship's departure.

Chapter Four

1.   Slimy Pollywog

The crew of the USS Mt. Wilson, along with two other ships, steam south to meet up with three others who are in their battle group. They will all steam further south so that the USS Mt. Wilson and one other ammo ship can receive ordinance from a NATO fleet in the South Pacific, then meet the remaining ships from their battle group in Hawaii. The once lively Supply berthing area is now mostly quiet and solemn as they watch the wall-mounted TV which plays news and updates from the Armed Forces Network.

Suave shakes his head at the reports of what the Iraqi leader is doing to the Kuwaitis and what he's done to his own people. "This guy is a damned medieval overlord! How has this gone on for so long without someone doing something about it?"

Moorish reminds Suave not to believe everything on the screen, "My brother, this is the AFN we're watching so, of course they're going to paint whomever the enemy is as a bad guy. They can't have us doubting if we should be fighting…"

"How about you shut the fuck up?" Monster interrupts with a staredown, "I ain't tryna hear none of that silly-ass panther shit out of you right now so either shut your hole or beat feet out of here!" Moorish nods and looks up at the TV, but Monster is still staring at him. The tension is broken when Big Boats walks in to inform the guys that after the UnRep, the ship is going to dip beneath the equator.

A few of the sailors begin cheering and clapping while most of the others look around, confused by the statement. SK2 slaps Trevion on the back then very firmly grabs his shoulder, "Boot Camp, I'm going to be looking out for you. We're going to have lots of fun!" The statement is hilarious to Big Boats and the three or four others who understand what SK2 is saying.

"We have a boat full of slimy, disgusting pollywogs," Big Boats announces on his way out, "and you will all feel my sheleighly!"

Pollywogs? Trevion looks over at Stafford who raises his eyebrows and mouths 'Oh, shit'. Bubba addresses all of the cooks, informing them that although the initiation is voluntary, he fully expects his crew to participate. "Participate in what, Bubba?" Stafford asks. Suave laughs at the question "Ha! These guys don't even know what they're in for. When the ship crosses the equator, we have a ceremony turning all of your filthy wogs into true and trusty Shellbacks."

Trevion remembers Dan telling him about this back when he was driving him around Hawaii; how when a ship crosses the equator there is a ceremony involving garbage and swats with a sheleighly. Dan also filled him in on a few items that he should buy before deploying on WestPac.

The news actually has a positive effect on the whole crew as everyone talks about what's going to happen and how so many pollywogs can be initiated by so few Shellbacks. After cleaning up following midrats, Trevion and Stafford begin to make their way back to the berthing area, but Stafford takes a detour to the freezer.

Trevion keeps going and is in his rack dozing off when Stafford finally arrives, "I fucking knew it," he whispers to Trevion, "they're freezing garbage from the galley. They have five of those 4' paper bags all taped up and tucked in the back." Stafford crawls into his bottom bunk and tells Trevion that they're going to be dumping frozen garbage for the next few days, "Right after midrats." The two chuckle and then drift off to sleep.

The next day, Trevion begins training with the Security Squad and learning his responsibilities. Whenever the ship transports what are termed Special Weapons, the Security Squad sets up a perimeter around the entire route from the munitions storage area below decks all the way to when it leaves the ship, and vice versa. Trevion will use twine to string off an area, then defend that line against any and every one. No one can cross his line once it's established; to gain access they must go to the designated entry/exit point.

The unrep will take thirteen hours from beginning to end and Trevion must be present for all of it so Suppo instructs him to skip going to midrats so that he can be well rested. "You need to shine tomorrow; I'm putting my neck on the block for you with this. Failure is not an option!" he says to Trevion in front of the other mess cranks.

"In fact, how about you get your ass out of here right now and get some rack? Unless you have to take a piss, I don't want your head off of that pillow until 0430 when you have to report." Trevion looks around and can see the disdain on everyone's faces, but is snapped out of it when Suppo asks, "Which part of what I just said has you confused enough to still be standing here? Go! Now! That's an order!"

While lying in his rack, Trevion wishes he hadn't taken his picture of Diwata home and left it in his room. He tries to understand how he keeps finding himself in such stressful situations with his peers all disliking him for trying to advance. His father warned him about people like that but, until now Trevion's never seen so many of them in a single concentration; not even in high school. Trevion wonders if he'll be able to sleep with all that's swirling around in his head, but is startled when he's awakened by the Rover at 0400.

The unrep went very smoothly and the ship brought on-board several pallets of bombs and missiles, all with a yellow or white tip. Trevion nervously stands his position as double-bladed helicopters dropped off pallets to be taken by fork truck to the freight elevator where Trevion's line extends. He's relieved from his post twice, as are all other Security Squad members, to use the restroom or grab a quick coffee but he hurried back both times. After the transfer was complete, there was a debriefing where the XO praised all involved for their hard work; then informed the meeting that the ship will be crossing the equator in the morning.

"As of right now, there are only two ranks; Shellback and pollywog. If you chose not to participate, you may be assigned a watch post so that others can attend this sacred event." LT Cruz says a few words then introduces the two newest members of the Security Squad to the PRP.

Everyone involved with the movement of special weapons are part of the Personal Reliability Program, or PRP, and are given conditional secret-level clearance. Trevion stands when he's introduced and is given praise for being the only person in the room that isn't at least a Petty Officer.

The group is dismissed and Trevion heads to the galley with some of the Security Squad members. He sits with them and learns all about the Shellback Initiation that's about to happen. With females aboard the ship, the event had to be toned down quite a bit, and they discuss what's no longer acceptable.

Flush with new information, Trevion heads down to the berthing area to share with his shipmates, but is greeted with questions on why he chose to sit away from the usual tables. SK2 is especially critical, "He's over there with the Ops guys talking shit about us."

After everyone gets their jabs in, Trevion yells out, "I didn't sit with you jackasses because I was learning about what's going to happen to us tomorrow! Tonight is supposed to be Wog Uprising, where we terrorize all of the Shellbacks. It got cut short because of the unrep but, they know that none of us have a clue about what's going on; and they're not about to tell us that, for the rest of the night, we're allowed to mess with them. All of them! SK2, tell me I'm lying!" SK2 just waves Trevion off and walks back towards his rack.

"See? Right now, we need to be tying him to a chair and having him face the wall or something. Tomorrow, they're going to kick our asses. Tonight, we're supposed to be earning those ass-kickings!"

Bubba interrupts and warns Trevion that he still has to work for him up in the mess decks, but Monster replies, "Shit, I don't. How about you guys?"

All of the pollywogs in the berthing area begin surrounding the Shellbacks. Suave tries to slowly close his rack curtains but gets pulled out of his bunk. For the rest of the night, the pollywogs throughout the ship, who outnumber the Shellbacks by a 15:1 ratio, launch a barrage of college-level pranks. Trevion and Stafford slip down into the freezer and begin carrying the 4' paper bags of frozen trash out and dumping them overboard. By midnight, they've gotten rid of all of the trash hidden in the freezer.

2.   Sheleighlys and Shenanigans

0300 and most of the crew are asleep. Trevion, Stafford and the other pollywogs are awakened and ordered out of the berthing areas. "On your knees, you filthy wogs! You don't deserve to walk like a Trusty Shellback!"

Stafford looks over at Trevion. "I'll be damned, you were right," he whispers.

Trevion looks down at Stafford's pants and asks, "Are you wearing them?" Stafford knocks on his knee and the sound of hard plastic is heard. Trevion gives a quick smile as the two are forced down and made to crawl from their berthing area all the way up to the main deck where they join the other pollywogs being herded around.

Trevion recalls what Dan told him in Hawaii about the initiation and warning him 'If you know what's good for you, you'll invest in some really good knee pads. I'd go with the kind that skateboarders use, I'm sure you know the ones I'm talking about, being from Beach City' which is why both he and Stafford are wearing the heavy-duty knee pads which they purchased just days before deploying. A conversation in the dry storage area turned into a trip to the sports store and a bet. If they returned from war having never used the knee pads, Trevion would have to pay Stafford back for the purchase, and vice versa.

"Best thirty-nine bucks I ever spent!" Stafford yells out as he makes it to the non-skid covered main deck. Non-skid is a military-grade epoxy deck paint containing countless tiny metallic ball bearings, it is ridiculously hard. The ship had just received a fresh coat during dry dock so it is particularly abrasive. "There's my prize wog! You can crawl out of line, Boot Camp, bite this." SK2 lowers his sheleighly down to Trevion's mouth, but Trevion just looks up at him which brings a frown to SK2's face. "I said, bite this! Or do we need to soften you up first?"

There is absolutely no way Trevion is about to put that dirty thing in his mouth. He looks over at Stafford, but notices that several Shellbacks are walking towards him. "What's going on, SK2? Is this one a wild buck that needs to be broken?"

"What do we got over here? A deaf wog?"

"Move it, wog! Do as you're told!"

Trevion has his final defiant thought, which must have shown on his face because one of the sailors walks over and swats Trevion with the sheleighly, signaling that his initiation has officially begun.

Up until this point, Trevion didn't have very much respect for the cut sections of an old fire hose with one end wrapped with twine to make a handle. "How bad can it really be?" he asked last night during the uprising. Bad. So, so bad. The swat made Trevion shout out 'Oh, shit!' as he struggled to comprehend how much pain the sheleighly caused.

"Put this in your fucking mouth, you slimy pollywog!"

Trevion bites down on the end of the sheleighly and is lead out of the line and over to the side where he's forced to do a variety of embarrassing, degrading things while receiving the random swat from whomever felt like delivering one. He's put back into line, which is now crawling in a gigantic circle around the Main Deck. Random wogs are pulled out of the circle to sing or perform dog tricks for the Shellbacks.

After two hours of what basically amounts to an ass whooping, the wogs are allowed to lay on the deck and rest. Trevion and Stafford look at each other and can't even muster a joke to lighten the mood. Monster is on the other side of the Main Deck fuming over the fact that he's getting hit and can't do anything about it, which is why he took so many swats in the beginning.

"Carson, how you holding up?" Trevion looks up and sees the XO wearing a headband that says 'Death to Wogs' and holding what looks like a custom made sheleighly.

"Piece of cake, sir." Trevion answers in a hurt, quivery voice which brings a chuckle to everyone in earshot.

"Well, I advise you to close your eyes and rest, all of you; we're just getting warmed up." Those words make the Shellbacks in the area laugh diabolically, which brings a sinking feeling to Trevion as he closes his eyes and tries to rest up for what's to come.

Aft, or to the rear of the ship, there is a helicopter deck where the finale of the ceremony took place, but it's been cleaned off and turned into what's called a 'Steel Beach' as barbeque pits are pulled out and the crew is treated to a bit of R&R. The ship's Captain has authorized all Shellbacks to receive two cans of beer with their meals.

Trevion doesn't like beer very much, but after the thirteen-hour long stomping that he's just received, those beers are wonderful. "Here you go, buddy!" a sailor says as he hands Trevion another beer. "You deserve this after what you just went through." Trevion laughs along with the sailor and thanks him for the extra brew, but inside he curses him and everyone else involved in what had just happened.

Aside from the thirty-minute nap that was offered to the wogs, which Trevion took full advantage of, and another forty-five minute break that he only got to sleep through half of, there was no rest. He and Stafford were among the first ones led to the Main Deck, but there were only three sailors behind Trevion when it was over.

Trevion knows that he's going to have the very best night's sleep of his entire life, until Bubba walks up and says "Don't go too far, Carson, you're going to help break all of this down and stow it away. Then you're going to head up to the galley and help get everything clean, then you and Stafford can take care of midrats."

Trevion looks at Bubba with a stunned face, asking why he's piling all of that work on him. "I told you, I warned you not to fuck with me, didn't I? Hope you had fun during your stupid little uprising, enough fun to make up for the next two months that I have in store for you." Bubba stares hard at Trevion before walking away. "You just be looking for shit to step in, don't you?" Monster's words and the guys' laughter echo in Trevion's head as he opens then chugs his final beer.

Knees rubbed raw from the inside of the knee pads, palms looking like he'd been attacked by a cheese grater courtesy of the non-skid, butt cheeks bruised from the countless sheleighly swats, spirit all but shattered by Bubba and the delighted laughter of everyone who overheard the exchange; Trevion puts his plate in the garbage bag and his cans in the recycle bucket next to it.

Judging by the line that each of the grilling stations still has, it'll be a while before Trevion will be needed. But he can't take a nap because there's no way he'd be able to wake back up and be functional. Sitting down is painful and standing is exhausting.

But the ship is now steaming towards Hawaii, then a two-day stop in the Philippines. Trevion tries to think about seeing Diwata again, whether to see that she's on track or to know if he'd been played like the guys keep telling him. "Hey Carson, want another one?" a sailor asks while holding up a beer.

"Fuck it!" Trevion replies.

3. Headed In

The eight days that it has taken for the ship to get to Hawaii, then to the Philippines, has been among the longest that Trevion has experienced in his young life. Bubba's wrath is unyielding. Trevion used to look forward to being called up to attend a training or meeting with the Security Squad, now that time must be repaid to Bubba before Trevion is dismissed for the day.

Trevion stands inside of the dish-washing station, receiving trays from the crew then spraying them down with high-pressure water before loading them onto the dishwasher conveyor belt. The trays are stacked up because there are supposed to be two or three people in this area of the station, but Bubba insists that Trevion can handle it solo. Whenever there isn't traffic at the window, Trevion is able to tackle the stacks of dirty trays that have piled up or to inspect then stow the ones coming out of the dishwasher.

"Carson? What the hell are you doing in here?" Trevion looks and sees LT Cruz standing at the window holding a tray.

"Mess duty, sir." Trevion replies as he takes LT Cruz's tray.

LT Cruz looks around inside of the dish-washing station, "And, how long have you been doing this job? Do you guys rotate or what?"

Trevion laughs at the question, "We do whatever Bubba tells us to do down here, sir." LT Cruz gives out a 'Hmph' then walks away. Trevion continues to play catch-up with the stacks of trays until another rush of sailors shows up, and he's forced to man the window.

After about an hour, the rush dwindles and Trevion is able to get all of the dirty trays, cups, and silverware onto the conveyor. "Can I get a trash dump over here?" he calls out, bringing one of the mess cranks from inside of the galley into the small area of the dish-washing station. Trevion pulls out the bag of food trash that he'd dumped from the trays and hands it to the other crank, who gives Trevion a replacement bag. "Carson, get your ass out of there!" Bubba's voice booms from inside of the mess deck.

Trevion uses the sprayer to wash off his hands and forearms then walks into the galley, "Yes?" he asks. Bubba doesn't say anything, he just stares at Trevion. "Um, did you call me?" Still nothing. Trevion stands around six-three and Bubba is about six inches shorter than him; but Trevion feels like a grade school kid looking up at the principal.

"I just wanted to see your face so I could know the truth." Trevion thinks really hard, but can't figure out what Bubba is talking about. "You just got requested up to the Officers' Wardroom so, go and wash your stinking ass and put on a clean uniform then report upstairs."

Trevion had only been up there once, when he had to deliver a huge bag of ice when their machine broke. Most of the female mess cranks worked either there or in the CPO galley for the Chiefs. Only a couple of females work down in the crew's galley. Trevion showers and puts on a clean uniform then heads up to the Wardroom. There is a much smaller, infinitely cleaner galley with a large wall opening which looks into the Officers' Lounge area.

Chief Petty Officer Kale, or Chief Cooks as he's called, greets Trevion and gives him a quick tour before telling him to return in the morning for breakfast, "We start up here at 0400, the second crew starts 1600 and we overlap for an hour so you'll be on duty from 0400 to 1700. Get some rest and we'll see you in the morning." In the morning? The ship pulls into port in the morning. Trevion will be on duty until 5:00PM, then he'll be free to go! His excitement is exploding from his face as he walks into Supply berthing.

"The hell you so zip-a-dee-do-da for, Boot?" Suave asks when he sees Trevion's smiling face.

"Sleep," Trevion replies. "Me and sleep haven't been on the best of terms lately, but tonight…" Trevion pretends to hug a woman, making gyrating movements with his hips. Suave bursts into laughter and gives Trevion a high-five.

As Trevion gets to his rack, he realizes that he didn't tell Suave about his good fortune; he didn't tell him about how he had just been pulled from the hot and sweaty dish-washing station and gently placed up in the 'penthouse', he didn't mention how he'll be able to go on liberty both nights that the ship is in the PI while the rest of the crew will be operating on fifty-fifty duty.

He kept all of that to himself and claimed that his good mood was because he was about to finally get good sleep. This, he thought, should be his tactic going forward. Maybe then he'll quit 'stepping in it' all of the time. Where he comes from, you tout your accomplishments and your peers congratulate you. Everybody on the block wanted to see you do good, but here it seems like the exact opposite.

After changing into the sweat suit that he sleeps in, Trevion crawls into his rack and pulls his curtains. As he's dozing off, he overhears a conversation between two of the SKs discussing the massive amount of supplies that awaits them once the ship pulls in to PI. Their gripes make Trevion want to help them out once he's done in the Wardroom, he considers it as he drifts off to sleep.

In the morning, Trevion is actually having fun with the very laid-back cooks in the penthouse. He's what's called a *runner*, bringing trays of food to the waiting officers. While the rest of the crew receives free meals, the officers must pay for their food monthly. But the financial hit is the only downside of the whole thing because their menu is filled with dishes that the crew could only get in a restaurant.

Trevion brings a tray of food to one of the 4-person tables and delivers it to LT Cruz, "See, that's more like it. I should see one of my guys in a clean, white apron and with a smile on his face; not sweating his ass off in a filthy hole in the wall." Trevion realizes how he suddenly got transferred to the penthouse and thanks the Lieutenant. Trevion works until the transition hour where the cooks actually tell most of the mess cranks to leave and get out of the way. Trevion is one of the lucky dismissed ones and heads to Supply berthing to get ready.

"What's up, Boot? Are you rolling with us tonight or do you have duty?" Monster asks as Trevion enters the berthing area.

Moorish adds, "Hey, don't start acting all stupid when your little bar girl is still in the bar." Everyone laughs but Trevion isn't sure what he'd do if she were there. Right now, she's an awesome fantasy that he uses to take his mind off of everything. He hurries to get ready so that he can leave with the guys.

The downtown area is packed with sailors heading out to the Persian Gulf. The last time Trevion was at the bar where he met Diwata, he and the guys were the only customers. Tonight's quite different as the place is filled with tipsy Americans. Trevion looks around, scanning the girls in the bar, when he gets slapped on the arm. "You are not allowed here! You go, now! No more girls for you!" Mamacita begins shoving Trevion towards the door.

"What did I do?" he asks, but she's not answering any questions.

The guys follow Trevion out of the club, "You know they staged that, right?" Suave says as he begins walking towards another bar, but Moorish is upset and yells at Trevion for still getting them kicked out of the bar. Trevion isn't sure what to feel; it sounded as if Mamacita was upset that Trevion gave Diwata money to escape the life of prostitution that she had set up, but what if it really was just an act to get him out of the bar so that Diwata can return to entertaining the servicemen. Either way, she's gone and Trevion decides to accept that fact.

As the guys try to enter another bar, they notice everyone else exiting it. In fact, all of the clubs and bars are emptying. "What's going on?" Monster asks one of the guys leaving the club.

"War has been officially declared and everybody needs to return to their unit." Fernandez tries to dash into the bar and grab one more drink, but Shore Patrol officers are standing at the bar making sure that no serviceman buys another round.

Big Boats looks around then yells, "Dammit! I'm about to go to war, and I didn't even get my dick wet, what kind of bullshit is that?"

4.   The I.O.

The battle group that Trevion's ship is in has two nuclear submarines that shadow the fleet and that most of the crew are unaware of. Trevion is aware of them; they're referenced frequently during the Security Squad meetings that he once again looks forward to attending. Outwardly, especially when he's in the berthing areas, Trevion presents the look of defeat. He laughs along when made fun of rather than defending himself. He joins in when the sailors around him grumble and complain about things rather than offer alternate viewpoints like he did before. He doesn't talk about working in the penthouse at all, because there is nothing to complain about.

The officers are grateful and polite, quite the contrast from when they're interacting with the crew on a day-to-day basis. Listening to their conversations has given Trevion both insight on several levels and a deeper respect for the officers on his ship. Plus, they tip so, that's always good. But three weeks of the easy life came to an abrupt end once the battle group entered the Indian Ocean.

Trevion's time as a mess crank was cut short due to his new General Quarters station in the Small Arms Magazine, all Security Squad team members are to report there when an emergency or combat situation occurs and the ship goes into General Quarters. In a Squad meeting, the XO decides to pull Trevion from mess duty and will make sure that his duty sections when docked will first consider the amount of Squad members in each.

Trevion returns to GSK and to his desk, which is located on the opposite end of everyone else's and completely buried in unprocessed paperwork and stacks of supplies that required processing and stowage. As he looks at the pile, Trevion recalls SK2's remark when he walked into GSK after being relieved from the Wardroom, 'Make sure you clean off your desk before you get comfortable.'

Trevion can't even see his desk; it's surrounded by boxes stacked high and secured with plastic twine. He can hear that the office is suddenly quiet as if they're waiting to hear his response to what he's looking at. Rather than give them a show, he opens the file cabinet against the bulkhead and pulls out his little boom box, pops in a hip-hop mix-tape, and gets to work.

Each box has a plastic pocket on the side containing the paperwork for whatever is inside. This shows whether the contents were ordered by one of the ship's departments or if it is to replenish the supplies in GSK. The latter must be processed by computer, the paper receipt filed, and the part placed into supplies according to its location number. Some boxes are combo packs, meaning they have many different parts for the same requester.

Trevion notices that most of these boxes are combo packs filled with small parts, which are the most time consuming and frustrating to process and store. Trevion is used to these due to his dad's gun shop and the 'God-illion' little parts and pieces that his father made him work on. Trevion's dad showed him a process that he uses here to make stowing the parts much quicker, he stacks the boxes in a way that blocks the view of his desk and begins working on the mess.

"Hey, Boot!" Monster calls out, "Let's get some sweepers going before dinner." Dinner? Trevion didn't even go to lunch. The music and his dad's method of processing small parts had Trevion in such a zone that he missed lunch completely. He grabs the large stacks of processed receipts and brings them into the main office area.

"Where is the filing box?"

SKC looks up and sees the two handfuls of invoices that Trevion is holding and asks where it all came from. Monster throws SK2 under the bus and explains what Trevion's desk looked like this morning. "I don't even think my man went to lunch, Chief. When we went, his music was playing in the back and when we got back, his music was still bumping in the back."

SKC stands then walks back to where Trevion's desk is located, which really isn't what Trevion wanted because then SKC could tell that he'd stacked the empty boxes in front of his desk to block the view. SKC comes back and asks to look at the invoices, scanning them quickly, he asks if Trevion had already stored everything.

"Almost, there's some cleaning gear that I'd rather take to the aft storeroom and some repairable/returnables that I'm not authorized to process but…" SKC asks how many of the returnable items were back there, Trevion tells him three boxes. SK2 runs to the back followed by a few more SKs, Monster tells Trevion to follow him to the mess decks for dinner.

While they stand in line, Monster explains to Trevion that those parts had been requested by the battle group's aircraft carrier and that no other ships in the battle group had them. "All three of those showed up on our inventory, but we couldn't find them anywhere. SKC made us pull everything out of the R/R cage and we couldn't find them. SK2 fucked up, big time."

Every ounce of restraint was needed for Trevion not to say aloud that SK2 is getting what he deserves or something about universal karma coming back to slap him. Instead, he asks if it's too late to send over the parts. "No, that's why they started scrambling just now, Suppo is going to be on fire."

Returning to the clique side of the mess decks for the first time in months, Trevion is greeted with the usual playful insults that comes with being there. Fernandez is missing from the area because he's now one of the cooks and is working in the galley.

Trevion tries to keep quiet and only give short responses when questioned about his time upstairs and with the Squad, in an effort to downplay how great both were. Suddenly, the 1MC announces *SKSN Carson, report to the flight deck. SKSN Carson, report to the flight deck ASAP.* Trevion looks down at his less-than-half-eaten dinner then up at Monster who asks him why he's still sitting there. "Move your ass, Boot!"

Trevion tries to scarf as much food as he can on his way to the dish-washing station then heads to the flight deck where Suppo is standing there talking with the Aviation's Officer. "Carson!" yells Suppo as he waves for Trevion to come over. "Well, I see you're already wearing a flight suit," Suppo remarks as he looks at Trevion's coveralls, "that's good because you're about to fly over to the carrier with these parts and complete the process." Suppo hands Trevion the three invoices for the returnables, "Sir, I'm not authorized to…"

Suppo grabs Trevion's shoulder and says, "You went to the cooks' storerooms and now they have a new storage and inventory process; you came up to the Wardroom and service improved dramatically; you've been back down in GSK for one day and found missing parts that our carrier needs to be able to keep going. How about you shut the fuck up with all of that modest, humble bullshit and go kick some ass for me? Do you know how to process this?" Trevion says yes, but again tries to explain that the repairable/returnable storage belongs to SK2 and that only he is authorized to process these items.

Suppo again asks if Trevion knows how to process the order, but in a very threatening and frightening way. "Yes sir, with your authority, this is a piece of cake." It isn't a piece of cake. Trevion knows how to process a returnable item, in theory that is. But, actually doing it, not so much. A female Airman begins to strap safety gear onto Trevion and echoes Suppo's comment about already being in a flight suit. "Where did you get this one? It's the Special Forces jumpsuit, pretty pricey."

Trevion is too nervous to explain how he got the coveralls from his friend at the surplus warehouse, he can only ask about safety procedures and 'what if' scenarios. The Airman reassures Trevion that it's going to be a smooth ride and gets him strapped into the large, twin-engine Chinook helicopter.

5.   Smoove Criminal

The urge to look outside at the beautiful sunset is too great for Trevion to resist as he sits on the Chinook that's flying across the ocean. The aircraft carrier is several miles away so the fastest way to get these parts over to it is by flying them there via helicopter. Trevion's ship, the USS Mt. Wilson, has two on-board helicopters; a Chinook and a smaller Seahawk helicopter used by the Explosive Ordinance Disposal or EOD team. Once the parts were discovered in GSK, word was sent, and the Mt. Wilson's air team began preparing for flight. Trevion only had time to get his food and begin eating before the parts were loaded onto the Chinook and ready to go.

From this height, Trevion can see a few of the other ships in his battle group along with land on the horizon. Land is a welcome sight, even if he won't be walking on it. The Chinook lands on the carrier and a team removes the very heavy boxes. The airman tells Trevion that they have another delivery request and that they'll return afterward to pick him up. Trevion is greeted by an SK1 named Noel Aikens who brings him down to one of the processing areas.

When the paperwork is complete and Trevion has the three used parts all boxed up and ready to go, Aikens compliments Trevion on his knowledge of the process. "I've never seen paperwork so thoroughly completed before, you filled in information that I even forgot how to pull up. Usually, the whole form never gets completed, only the red boxes need to be filled out, but you not only filled it all in, but you knew where in the book to find the data. How long have you been working on R/R?"

Trevion looks at his watch. "To be honest, for about an hour and forty-five minutes. It took us an hour and a half to fly here and we've been working on the paperwork for fifteen minutes so..." Aikens is impressed with Trevion and brings him down into the Logistics Office or LogOff to introduce him to the processing team and their Suppo, and then gives him a quick tour of the supply work areas.

Their ship's stores are huge and stocked with far better items than the small one on Trevion's ship. The snack options and uniform items are much broader than on his much smaller ship. They even sell the basic uniform coveralls that can only be ordered by departments on his ship. He looks behind the counter and notices that they carry Newport cigarettes, the Mt. Wilson had been out of that very popular brand for a long while and although Trevion only smokes when he drinks, he was well aware of the shortage.

"My ship is out of those right now; I know some guys who would have a fit if they saw those cartons sitting there."

Aikens pauses for a moment, then looks back at the SH3 standing behind the register and says, "Isn't this kid just the most adorable thing?" and the two burst into laughter. Trevion stands there with raised eyebrows at the awkward statement, then Aikens explains how Trevion should buy as many cartons of Newports as he can afford, then sell them back on his ship for double or triple of what he pays for them. Again, they burst into laughter when Trevion's face shows the light going off in his mind.

Earlier that morning, Trevion was working up in the Wardroom for the last time. The officers all gave him huge tips to say thanks for his excellent service while he worked for them, so he had a pocket full of cash. He unzips his coveralls and reaches into the pocket of his dungarees "Let me get, how much would five cartons cost?" Aikens shakes his head and asks how much Trevion has, suggesting that he spend whatever he has on him.

Trevion ends up buying an entire case of Newports, which Aikens plastic-wraps along with the returnable parts. Trevion tries to buy a bag of chips, explaining how he didn't get to finish eating, but Aikens takes him up to one of the smaller mess decks that serves only burgers, hot dogs, and fries.

On Trevion's return flight, he didn't have the nagging urge to look out of the window anymore, the slight cloud coverage is enough to block out the light from the moon so outside looks like something out of a horror movie or a nightmare. He closes his eyes and tries to remember what Aikens told him; hide the case of Newports in the storage area and only pull out two cartons at a time, don't start selling cartons until half of the case is gone, give away the first pack one cigarette at a time, never give discounts to anyone who doesn't directly affect him.

The Chinook touches down and Trevion gets the supplies down to GSK where Suppo is there waiting with the crew. "You did it again, Carson! Made me look like I'm kicking some major ass over here, you just earned yourself a 72-hour liberty pass, pre-approved and available upon demand." SKC informs Trevion, and everyone else, that Trevion's now in charge of the R/R supplies. This job takes him out of most of the day-to-day functions down in GSK and puts his focus more on the control, distribution, and processing of the R/R items.

"Attention on deck!" Monster yells out as he stands at attention. Everyone in GSK pops to attention as the ship's Captain walks in and asks for Trevion. "This is our guy, sir." Suppo says as he pats Trevion on the back.

"Well done, son; very well done. I've received word that you made quite the impression over there, made our ship and its crew look very good. And it's your first day back from mess duty, first day handling R/R items, and first time performing an emergency transfer, is that accurate?" Suppo steps in and confirms all of that, adding that Trevion is also a member of the Security Squad.

The Captain shakes Trevion's hand and says, "I expect you to maintain this level of excellence, are we clear?"

Trevion gives an enthusiastic 'Yes, sir' then the Captain and Suppo exit GSK.

Monster laughs, "Alright, I need to quit blaming you for this shit, I can see now that you're not doing a damn thing to bring all this extra light on you; shit just keeps happening to you, don't it?"

Trevion shrugs his shoulders. "I think I'm part shit-magnet or something!"

The next morning, Trevion wakes up and does his normal morning routine, except this time he heads up to the ship's smoking area with a pack of Newports. He stands in the middle of the area and begins packing the Newport Box until he hears a few people mention what he's got. Opening the box, Trevion lights one up.

"Yo, Boot, where did you get that?" a sailor asks.

"Last night from the carrier, I did a supply run and grabbed some from their ship's store. Want one?" Trevion offers the sailor a Newport and ends up giving out half the pack to the sailors who normally smoke them but have been forced to smoke the less popular Kools.

Following Aikens' instructions, Trevion turns down offers to buy packs from him by saying, "No telling when we're going to get more Newports, I don't want to sell my stash and then be assed out." By lunchtime, word has spread amongst the menthol smokers that Trevion had a stash of Newports. Stafford agreed to let Trevion store his case in the refrigerated area to keep them fresh and the sales began. By the time the ship reached its first liberty port, Dubai, Trevion had sold half of his case and had already made nearly double his investment. Stafford received a share for the use of refrigerated storage and the two began planning their liberty in the city famous for inexpensive gold jewelry.

One of the sailors that Trevion served mess duty with asked him for a loan until payday, but when payday came the sailor was a no-show. Monster overhears Trevion telling Stafford about the delinquent sailor as they talk in the berthing area. "How much does he owe you?" Monster asks. Trevion explains that he borrowed $50 and promised to pay back $100. "I'll go and get it right now, but you gotta give me $20 out of that hundred." Trevion agrees, and Monster rushes out of the berthing area.

"Do you get liberty tomorrow?" Stafford asks. Trevion says no, that he has duty and won't be able to leave the ship until the following afternoon. As they discuss plans to go sightseeing, Monster returns and counts out $100 to Trevion, who gives him twenty of it back.

"Pleasure doing business with you, Boot. Let me or Big Boats know if you need any other collection services."

Stafford looks at Trevion and says, "This kind of feels like the start of a cartel, blood. We slanging Newports and slushing money, might be time to invest in this shit for real." Trevion laughs it off, but is intrigued by the idea.

6.   The Invisible Box

When the battle group first entered the Persian Gulf, the conflict was called Operation Desert Shield and had several nations involved. A massive buildup of troops, artillery, tanks, and aircraft had taken place as the nations prepared to face the world's fourth largest armed force. The USS Mt. Wilson was very active since it was the only ship in the Gulf with Special Weapons storage magazines and a trained Security Squad.

Trevion had been called up to stand his line on an almost daily basis. This often interfered with his reorganization of the R/R supply cage, which had been an ongoing project ever since it was assigned to him. Another barrier had been the frequency of R/R parts that had been requested since Desert Shield began, which pleases SK2 who was, up to that point, very bitter over losing the assignment to Trevion but now laughs at him and the amount of extra work that he has to do.

Word around the scuttlebutt was that this would all be over before Halloween, but as Thanksgiving approaches, the crew begins to feel the effects of the almost constant UnReps, the extra-long work hours, and being away from home as tensions begin to run high. Adding to this stress is where the ship rests for most of its time in the Persian Gulf.

The Mt. Wilson is assigned specific coordinates in the Persian Gulf, an invisible box that they are to remain in until called upon. The box happens to be in a very popular fishing area, so there are always several fishing vessels scattered about. The crew hates being there because of what are known as Iraqi Gunboats, which are fishing vessels with 50 caliber machine guns mounted to its deck.

They float alongside a Navy ship, looking quite harmless, then a tarp is pulled back and the bullets begin to fly. To the crew, every fishing vessel within sight is an Iraqi Gunboat so they watch each one attentively. Trevion is so busy that he doesn't have time to stress out over being in the box, his plate is completely full. Any free time he has away from his duties is spent on managing his budding empire.

With his connection on the aircraft carrier, Trevion had begun not only buying cigarettes, but also chewing tobacco and a few other items which were in high demand around the ship. But, by far, the most lucrative part of his business was slushing, or loaning money at interest. The normal interest rate for a loan was 100%; that's the hard standard. In desperate times, some would pay up to 200% for a loan. Trevion set his interest rate at 80% which was very attractive to borrowers. Whenever the ship would finally go to a port, the loan requests would begin to pour in.

Trevion's team consisted of Stafford, who stored their supplies and provided cash to loan out; Monster and Big Boats, who handled collections and helped with sales; a Radioman named Justin Martin, who is on the Security Squad with Trevion and also provides cash to be loaned out along with helping to communicate with Aikens over on the carrier; and Middleton who loans cash to the females.

In the three months that the team, who call themselves Smoove Criminal, has been operating, there have been six pay periods. As the ship steams towards Dubai the loan requests are at an all-time high as everyone wants to shop and enjoy themselves in the growing city.

On the night before making port, Smoove Criminal had run out of cash to loan out, shocking them all since they had built up quite a large pot of money. Trevion, Stafford, and Middleton gave up the last of their personal money in order to cover the final loans. Trevion counts out the eighteen dollars that he has left and wonders if it was worth giving up this opportunity to go shopping on the famous Gold Street, where the purest and least expensive gold jewelry can be found. He knows that they'll be back in three weeks because the last Security Squad briefing gave the port schedule for the month.

As they all get dressed to leave the ship, Trevion tells Monster, "I can miss this one, do a bit of window shopping then come back and get draped in gold!"

Monster replies, "You're a bigger man than I am, Boot. No way I was gonna give up my shopping money to the cash pot, fuck that." The guys plan on going to a local restaurant to sample the cuisine then heading down to Gold Street and the many other businesses surrounding it. Shoppers from all over the world flock to Dubai to get jewelry and designer clothes at inexplicably cheap prices.

As Trevion is spraying cologne in the air above him, the 1-MC announces, "All Security Squad members are to report to the small arms magazine immediately."

SK2 laughs very loudly, "Looks like you're not going anywhere just yet, Boot Camp!" Trevion hurries down to the magazine where Squad members are gathering, LT Cruz informs them that half of the Squad would be spending the next twenty-four hours as part of a security detail for American and Canadian military heads who are meeting in town.

Being the most junior member of the Squad, Trevion's name was called first on the detail list. "You guys change into your Working White uniforms and meet up on the Quarterdeck in thirty minutes, the rest of you will have the detail in three weeks when we come back. Dismissed."

7. Shinehead

Trevion stands on the Quarterdeck in his white uniform and carrying a small duffle bag. A Chief Petty Officer from Deck Department is standing the Officer of the Deck watch, "Hey there, Carson. I know you've got a carton of Newports in that bag. Sell me a pack." A pack of smokes in the ship's store costs $1.75, Trevion sells his packs for $3.00 since the ship frequently runs out of Newports.

"I'll give you a discount, Chief. Two for five." The chief pulls a five out of his pocket and Trevion hands him two packs of cigarettes, then the Petty Officer of the Watch asks for the same deal. Trevion refuses "That's a khaki deal, bro, you gotta be E7 and above to get that price."

Before long, the two cartons that Trevion had brought with him had been sold and he had two packs for himself along with a bit of money in his pocket. LT Cruz arrives and leads the detail to a waiting van where they drive to the large hotel hosting the meetings. They are all issued special uniform items to wear while they're there, a gold and white shoulder cord, white gloves, leggings, a side-arm, and a shiny, silver combat helmet. They are broken up into two-man teams and are assigned to various posts throughout the luxurious hotel.

Trevion and Martin are assigned to a Canadian general, whom they follow around as he attends meetings. Since the Security Squad had a clearance level of Secret, they are the obvious choice for such assignments as they'd be able to hear what's being discussed. What the two Squad members overhear is that things are getting worse and a full-scale war is coming.

LT Cruz sends two Squad members to relieve Trevion and Martin for fifteen minutes. They take this chance to use the restroom before meeting with LT Cruz who informs them that the general has requested them for the rest of the assignment so they won't be going back to the ship until tomorrow afternoon.

"You guys made a really good impression on the General, so the UN guys got you both a room here in the hotel. Here is a stipend so you can buy underwear or whatever." He hands them envelopes containing Durhams, the local currency. They return to their post and proceeds to guard the General and his staff for the rest of the day. At around 1600, the General dismisses his staff and tells Trevion and Martin that they're required to accompany him to dinner at 1800, after which they'll be off duty until 0800 tomorrow.

The sailors find their room keycards in the stipend envelopes and discover that they each have their own room. Walking in, Trevion is taken aback at how stunning his room is. He goes into the bedroom and lies back on the very soft bed. "Well," he says out loud, "this wasn't such a bad assignment after all, was it?"

He closes his eyes and enjoys how great the bed feels, but is interrupted by a knock at the door. Thinking it's Martin to harp on how sweet the room is, he opens the door saying, "Yeah, yeah, yeah, I know..." but is embarrassed because it's not Martin but rather one of the Canadian officers from the general's staff, Second Lieutenant Betty Highland.

"You know? Then we can just get right to it then, eh?" she asks as she pushes Trevion back into the room. As soon as the door closes behind Second Lieutenant Highland, she grabs Trevion and begins kissing him. Trevion is half frozen in shock, not knowing whether or not to touch her since she is an officer.

"Don't be shy, lover, we may not get another chance at this so let's do as much of everything as we possibly can."

Trevion thinks really hard for something clever or witty to say. "Permission to come aboard, ma'am."

Second Lieutenant Highland makes a pleased moaning sound and says, "Permission granted, sailor!"

The encounter is equal parts awkward and awesome. Thirty minutes of aggressive passion and Second Lieutenant Highland gets dressed and rushes out, leaving Trevion breathing heavily in the king-sized bed. After a shower, he realizes what the money in the envelope was for as he's forced to put on the same underwear that he'd just taken off.

He puts his uniform back on then calls Martin's room so see if he's still there, Martin answers and agrees to go shopping before they're back on duty. The hotel has a nicely stocked convenience store and the two are able to find decent clothing to wear once they're off duty later that evening.

"Hey, Carson," Martin says as the two ride the elevator back to their floor. "That Canadian officer was really checking you out today, wasn't she?"

Trevion looks over at Martin, "Yeah? How come I didn't notice it?"

Martin laughs, "Because you were too busy checking out all of the Arab girls that work here at the hotel. But that Second Lieutenant couldn't stop looking at you, I think she's the one who convinced the General to keep us tonight. If that's the case, then I need to thank you, man. Now, take one for the team tonight so she can get us into the mixer that's happening after dinner." Trevion smiles and looks down at his highly polished welder's boots, thinking to himself that he may have already sealed that deal.

The dinner was elegant, Trevion and Martin sat at a very long table directly behind a table full of dignitaries and high-ranking military personnel. Martin keeps looking at Trevion and nodding towards Second Lieutenant Highland, urging him to ask her for passes to the evening's event. The USO hired a popular American band to perform for the guests and Martin wants very badly to go. But, before he can ask her, the Second Lieutenant gives him two passes and insists that he show up. When the dinner is over and the General excuses the guys for the evening, Trevion hands Martin one of the VIP passes that Second Lieutenant Highland gave him.

Martin squeals, "VIP? What? Are you serious right now? We get to be on the floor right in front of the stage with these! How did you pull this off, Carson?" Trevion shrugs his shoulders and tries to play it off like it was nothing, but Martin is beside himself with excitement and doesn't even go inside of his room, instead he runs back to the elevator to go and buy different clothes for the mixer.

Trevion doesn't get into his room either because Second Lieutenant Highland peeks her head out of her room and calls him over. "So, obviously we can't be together at the mixer," she whispers to him, "but afterward, I expect you to be tapping on this door. Are we clear, sailor?"

Trevion smiles. "Aye-aye ma'am," he says, which produces another moaning sound from the Second Lieutenant, who quickly kisses him then ducks back into her room.

8.   Who Ordered the Propane?

The USS Mt. Wilson returns to the invisible box after being in Dubai for three days. The crew got a chance to blow off a bit of steam, as much as could be blown off in a very religiously strict country, and buy a few things. Many of the sailors buy Persian rugs and send them home, Trevion is one of those sailors as he's unable to resist using the very generous stipend to purchase a large Persian rug and send it home to his mother. But the next day, the crew wakes up to payday and everyone is issued their paychecks.

Immediately following dinner, the mess decks are set up with check cashing stations so that the crew can cash their checks. Money comes flowing in from all of the loans that were given out, and the cash pot is replenished and reset to a higher amount. The members of Smoove Criminal pocket unusually high profits and Trevion does his usual routine of heading to the ship's Post Office and turning half of his profits into a money order and then mailing it back home to himself.

His father collects the letters and locks them in the family safe. But even after Trevion drops the envelope into the mail slot, he's left with quite a bit of cash. He's considering buying more than his usual supplies from the aircraft carrier when he goes to complete a scheduled supply swap tomorrow.

Being on the ship with lots of disposable income is like torture to the crew, and as a result, the ship's store runs out of stock very frequently. The only thing to do with your money is to either save it or gamble it. Trevion isn't at all a gambler so that doesn't appeal to him; nor to Stafford for that matter as they both have jokes and comments for the guys who become extremely emotional over a high-stakes game of cards.

One such game is taking place in Supply berthing as sailors with recently-cashed checks gamble away their salaries. SK2 can't stop ribbing Trevion about missing out on liberty due to the special detail that he was on. Trevion tries to stay quiet and not brag about the amazing time that he just had at the hotel, but SK2 is relentless and refuses to drop the subject. "See, that's what you get for trying to be Super Sailor! We had liberty all day and you were all uniformed up and standing watch." The rest of the guys in the berthing begin piling on, telling stories about where they ate and what they had bought.

In his mind, Trevion walks over to his locker, opens it and pulls out the paper key card from the hotel and a flier from the USO mixer then puts them on the table. "While you Cinderellas had to be back on the ship by midnight, I was staying in this hotel. At midnight, when you were all here in this stinky berthing surrounded by each other, I was in bed with a hot Canadian officer; after we watched the Red Hot Chili

Peppers perform, that is." But, instead of rubbing it in, he just absorbs the verbal abuse and agrees that he has bitten off more than he could chew.

The next morning during Quarters, Suppo keeps looking over at Trevion with a smirk on his face. Trevion notices and begins to get uneasy, thinking that perhaps his little romp with the Canadian officer was discovered, and he was about to be in deep shit. After the daily report is read, Suppo begins reading a message from the Canadian High Command thanking the US Navy for providing honor guards during the Joint Task Force meetings.

The Suppo pauses then clears his throat before reading "...*and a special thanks to the USS Mt. Wilson for providing guards RM2 Justin Martin and SKSN Trevion Carson, who displayed the highest level of professionalism and performed their duties in an exemplary manner.* Carson, you just got the ship mentioned in a global communiqué. The Skipper is beside himself upstairs trying to spin this gold into platinum so, stay on your toes and keep up the good work. Does anyone else have anything? Then turn-to."

Trevion swims through all of the sarcastic 'Golden Boy' and 'Super Star' comments given by his peers as he makes his way down to Supply berthing to change into his coveralls. Everyone has jokes about Trevion being mentioned in the communiqué and they make sure to walk over to him and share those jokes.

Monster can tell that Trevion is close to exploding so he walks over and shoos away all of the hecklers. "Stay calm, my son. We don't want to do anything to draw attention to the business, good or bad, so maybe you should step back and be a silent investor for a while."

Stafford asks where they'll be getting their supplies of cigarettes and chewing tobacco if Trevion steps back, to which Monster has no answer. Stafford and Monster go back and forth about how things should proceed with Monster trying to make changes and Stafford demanding that nothing needs to change.

The debate between the two gives Trevion a bit of insight on how his little crew works and how important he is to the crew's success. Finally, Trevion says that nothing is going to change and if anyone would rather break off and do their own thing then that's fine.

The comment is directed at Monster who has been acting very obnoxiously since their big payday. "We just made more than we ever had," Trevion whispers. "Payday is the day before we pull back into Dubai so we'll have bread but we won't be getting a bunch of loan requests. Don't spend too much in Dubai because you know that everyone else will. Then, when we get to Bahrain, they'll all be broke and begging for loans."

Monster and Stafford look confused, but Trevion explains that the ship will spend three days in Bahrain right after they leave Dubai, but not to tell anyone. Monster and Trevion head down to GSK, and Trevion heads to the back and his desk. He's not there long before SK2 sends him to pick up the mail which had been delivered from the carrier last night.

Trevion brings the mail down to GSK and begins handing it out when he notices that a large, official-looking packet is addressed to him. He brings his mail back to his desk and opens the letters from home first, but his mind is on the packet until he sees that one of the letters is from the Philippines. He rips it open and a picture of Diwata falls out.

The letter is written on stationary from De La Salle University in Manila. Trevion smiles from ear to ear as he reads how Diwata was able to enter college with the money that he gave her, then reads that she qualifies to transfer to an American college if she has a sponsor. Trevion opens the packet and sees that it contains applications for him to fill out in order to sponsor Diwata, but there is a fee of $2500 that must be paid upon submission.

"What you got there, Boot Camp?" SK2 says, startling Trevion out of his thoughts. "What, are you applying to the Naval Academy or something?" Trevion quickly gathers everything and puts it into the packet, but the picture of Diwata is still on his desk. SK2 picks it up and looks at it, mentioning that his niece goes to that school. "Who is this?" SK2 asks.

"It's your niece, asshole!" Trevion snaps as he pulls the picture out of SK2's hand.

"Why are you back here, don't you have work to do or something? Some other high-level assignment that you can slowly neglect to the point of complete disaster so that I can step in and fix your fuck-up?"

SK2 pauses then bursts into laughter. "Finally! It's about time you grew some balls, Boot Camp. Now you're ready for the next level, let's see how you handle that."

Trevion spends the next week focusing on the R/R cage in the back of the storeroom, bringing forward all of the parts that have been requested in the past five years and pushing to the back the items that haven't. The items are mostly very heavy engine parts and moving them around takes quite a bit of effort, which is why the area was in such disarray before Trevion took it over. But the constant unreps and Squad details couldn't keep him from finishing the area and redesigning it so that he's able to walk all the way to the back of the cage and see every box's invoice sticker.

He stands in front of the cage, admiring his work, when SKC comes walking up. He whistles when he sees the cage then calls everyone back to the area. "Do you see this? I've never seen an R/R area this organized and efficient before." As SKC begins to mount praise upon Trevion, SK2 asks about the paperwork and the log book. But SKC gives a 'one step at a time' speech, saying that the cage is proof of progress then sends everyone back to work.

Trevion locks the cage and sits at his desk. The paperwork and the log book are, of course, both in order since he would need to organize both of them before he could arrange the boxes inside of the cage. Perhaps SKC knows this and is giving Trevion a bit of a break; doubtful, so Trevion thinks it would be best if he didn't report that everything is in order just yet. Trevion looks over at the cage, still in disbelief that all of his very hard work has finally paid off. Maybe now he'll have a bit of time to focus on other things.

9. Storm Watch

As weeks became months in the Indian Ocean, the crew of the USS Mt. Wilson have grown used to the isolation and long work hours. The few port visits that they get are not as exciting as they should be due to the fact that in Muslim countries, alcohol is extremely expensive and the women are all covered from head to toe. You are not allowed to even look at them or you may be arrested, causing an international incident during a conflict, so the females on the ship began looking more and more attractive.

The same applied to the females who wouldn't give the time of day to any of the obnoxious men on-board the ship, but months away from any better options does wonders for a man's looks so, several not-so secret romances have developed.

Not even the members of Smoove Criminal are immune to the love bug as Stafford and Middleton have begun fooling around. Having spent Thanksgiving, Christmas, and the New Year together, the crew have moved from being testy and short-fused to acting more like a family. The ship began allowing sailors to go fishing out of the Aft Moring area after work hours while they're anchored in the invisible box, which further bonds crew member who would normally never coexist.

Supply berthing is abuzz with rumors that the conflict is about to end without any serious warfare, but Trevion knows that's not true. The last briefing given to the Security Squad is that Iraq is not only refusing to withdraw from Kuwait, but is threatening to attack Israel if any coalition forces intervene. This conflict is far from over.

One of the very few upsides to being in the Middle-East is the shopping. Thanks to the additional income that Trevion and the rest of Smoove Criminal have been making, they've been mailing home a steady stream of gifts to their loved ones.

Everything from Persian rugs and silk fabrics to gold jewelry and tailor-made suits have been shipped from military members in the Gulf and back home to their countries, and Trevion is no exception. He has sent three beautiful Persian rugs home, along with purses and scarves for his mother, and shoes, watches, and leather hats for his father; along with his usual money order for his father to put into the family safe.

His father owns two pieces of jewelry; his wedding band and his class ring, he wears both every day. Trevion is hoping that the gold watches will inspire him to buy more bling, but understands that the chances are very slim. Shopping in the Arab countries using the profits from his side-hustle has become his emotional escape as time in the invisible box weighs heavily on Trevion and the rest of the crew.

The new picture of Diwata is taped above his rack where the old one was, but it is now accompanied by a picture of Second Lieutenant Highland and a picture of a Stinger from another supply-type ship deployed in the Gulf.

Stingers are military reserve personnel who have been activated and trained in using the Surface to Air Missile launcher, they're called

Stingers because that's the name to the particular type of SAM launcher that they use. The Mt. Wilson has several Stingers aboard who joined the ship in Hawaii, they're assigned to whichever department their particular rate happens to be.

Most military reserves don't really think too much about their rate since they're only part-time, a few try to specialize in whichever field they work in back in the civilian world. Those are the lucky ones. Only one of the Mt. Wilson's Stingers got assigned anywhere but Deck Department, where those unfortunate Stingers are given the hardest, dirtiest assignments and are treated as second-hand crew members since they'll all be going back home after the war.

Trevion met Daisy out in town while in Bahrain, she is another lucky one who made rank while in the Reserves so was assigned to the mess cooks on her ship. Every night, Trevion looks up at the three photos as he lays in his rack and tries to imagine a future with any of them.

Stafford and Middleton have broken up and gotten back together so many times that Trevion is convinced that being with a military member is out of the question, or at least one who lives on the ship with you. Love letters and occasionally being in port at the same time keeps things with Daisy fun, but Stafford and Middleton have the advantage of having each other when the ship is away from port.

They're able to comfort one another during the stressful times, but will also cause each other stress at times. There are a couple of female sailors on the ship who flirt with Trevion; Middleton has even tried to hook him up with one of them. But he sticks to his guns and resists saying, "No offense to you and Staff but, I don't want to piss where I drink, if you know what I mean."

Each port visit is filled with discovery as Trevion explores each city's shopping areas. The buying frenzy has died down by this time and Trevion is much more of a particular shopper, looking for rare and wonderful items to send home. When their schedules match, First Lieutenant Highland accompanies Trevion on his shopping expeditions and offers her personal insight on the local cultures and cuisine.

The First Lieutenant had been stationed with the UN Ambassadors in the Middle East for over a year before the conflict began so she had quite a bit of knowledge about the area. As time passes, along with the expectation of hard work, long hours, and occasional shopping sprees, the crew of the Mt. Wilson begins to settle into a routine that helps keep their spirits up as they spend time in the invisible box.

10. All Hands On Deck

The energy on the ship drastically changes when Operation Desert Shield becomes Operation Desert Storm. Suddenly, the endless drills and training are taken very seriously by the crew, and the lessons learned from the weekly General Quarters drills have greater value. A wave of confidence sweeps across the ship as the crew feels as if they've mastered their individual duties and that their skill along with their proficiency will be more than enough for anything that could come up. Liberty while in port has been greatly restricted, Cinderella liberty is the new norm and a list of off-limits areas circulates.

The crew are all issued their own gas mask and are given refresher trainings on how to properly use them in case of a chemical attack, which the enemy is more than willing to do. They watch the AFN nightly to get reports of the battle in Kuwait which is the US Military's first real war battle that isn't currently being discussed in high school history class.

The Mt. Wilson is very active, supplying munitions and supplies to the fleet almost daily and mostly in the evening hours. Standing his line during nighttime Special Weapons transfers is very unnerving to Trevion due partially to the many fishing vessels in the Gulf but mostly because of a Lieutenant Junior Grade or LTJG named Charles Brown who harasses Trevion during every move.

LTJG Brown is an officer who works in Operations Department, but Trevion isn't sure exactly what he does; other than give him a hard time whenever his line goes up. LTJG Brown will do things like attempt to exit the restricted area through Trevion's line, question Trevion on his duties, or try to strike up a conversation to distract Trevion from his line.

"*Carson!*" he would yell from inside of the restricted area, *"what would you do if I tried to break your line?"*

Trevion would respond, "I'd remind you that you must enter and exit from the access point, Mr. Brown."

"And what if I tried to exit through your line anyway?"

"I'd warn you until you reached five feet of my line, then I would stop talking and wait for you to touch my line, sir." Trevion had to be mindful of rank while trying to tell Mr. Brown that if he took his test too far and actually touched Trevion's line that he'd get the butt of Trevion's rifle, at the very least.

Trevion takes his post very seriously and Mr. Brown knows it, so he uses that fact to pick on Trevion whenever he can. Tonight, the UnRep was with the carrier that Aikens is on so Trevion is expecting his order to be fulfilled. When the transfer is over, Trevion heads to GSK to get his supplies and finds double of his normal order along with a note saying that since the war has started that there'll be no more stock. Aikens doubled his order as a parting gift to Trevion.

Monster and Big Boats are most affected by this because they're the ones who do most of the selling of the products and make the most from their sale. Other than Trevion, that is, who makes the most on all fronts; but makes sure that it's not by too much in order to keep everyone happy. All extra activities are suspended so there's no more fishing or basketball, not that there's time for any of that as the Mt. Wilson is now outside of its invisible box more than its in.

A port visit is coming up and the Security Squad has again been requested as guards, much to the delight of Suppo who has been spending much more time down in GSK than ever before. Trevion always makes sure to give both Suppo and SKC credit for being flexible and allowing him to pursue Security Squad activities whenever he's in Squad meetings with the XO; so Suppo tries to visit GSK often to appear to be mentoring Trevion.

Both know that it's a sham, but it's a mutually beneficial one. Trevion can't wait for the guard duty because in the three days leading up to it, the Mt. Wilson will be highly active in the Persian Gulf and Trevion will be busy with incoming supplies as well as outgoing special weapons, so he's looking forward to the rest.

The reports given by the Armed Forces Network are the most reliable, the aircraft carrier in the area also broadcasts news from home which give inaccurate to downright false reports about the war. Each time Trevion visits a port and is able to call home, he has to calm his mother down and remind her not to believe everything that she sees on the news. He's looking forward to hearing her voice and finding out which of his shipped items has made it home.

The Mt. Wilson had just finished its final UnRep and was steaming towards the invisible box as Trevion heads up to the mess decks to catch midrats. Stafford tells him to bring his tray into the office on the other side of the galley and the two eat and joke about the reports that some of the Iraqi soldiers are surrendering to civilian news crews because they were hungry and out of ammo.

As they laugh about the 'World's 4th Largest Army' an alarm goes off and a voice is heard over the 1-MC, *"General Quarters, General Quarters! All hands man your battle stations!"*

Trevion and Stafford look at each other. "Is this a real GQ?" Stafford asks. When the announcement repeats, Trevion leaps from his chair and runs down to the Small Arms magazine then begins to suit up with the other Squad members; who are also confused as to what's going on.

The ship will go into GQ if it loses power or if the Rover doesn't check in on time. "Probably the Rover," Martin says with an angry expression. "I had just gotten to sleep; he'd better have a good explanation for why he was late checking in!"

The detail begins making its way through the ship in its usual route when they're ordered to the main deck. There, they are instructed to assist the Gunner's Mates on the port side. Trevion is the doorman and moves to the large hatch, pulling the long handle and releasing the door's watertight seal. He swings the door open and holds it as the other members of the detail rush through the door, just as they had done countless times during training.

Only this time, they are immediately met with gunfire. A small vessel had pulled alongside of the ship and has opened fire. The detail gets low to the deck and makes their way to a covered position as bullets ricochet all around them. Trevion looks over at the Gunner's Mate who is supposed to be manning the 50-caliber machine-gun which is mounted to the side of the ship; but he's crouched down and holding his head. "Man down! Carson, go and man that gun! Martin, Baker, pull that guy out of there! Get a medic up here!"

There were only two seconds between Trevion hearing those words and him dashing to the 50cal, but in that time he had considered all of his options and determined that the only way he'd make it back home in one piece was to man that gun and take out those attackers. But other options such as turning around and running back through the door preceded that decision and were preferable by far. Trevion says to himself 'There is no fucking way I'm not going home' as he grabs the mounted machine gun and pulls the trigger, nothing.

He checks the ammo feed and sees that the dummy rounds which start the chain were not properly inserted so he pulls them out and rethreads it. As soon as he's ready to fire, one of the ship's Signalmen turns a bright spotlight onto the vessel. There are roughly a dozen men and one of them has a rocket launcher pointing at the spotlight. 'You first' Trevion says as he begins firing at the vessel. The sudden return gunfire is enough to make the men on the vessel take cover and allows the Squad to also return fire. Trevion targets the mounted machine gun then the vessel's bridge.

After only a short while, there is no one firing from the vessel; but the assault coming from the Mt. Wilson is undying. They continue to fire upon the vessel until it catches fire and begins to sink. The smoke coming from the vessel isn't black or white but has a greenish color when the spotlight hits it. "All hands don your gas masks!' screams the voice over the 1-MC, which is the only thing able to make the defenders stop firing on the vessel.

Trevion secures his mask and screws on the canister, then closes his eyes in an attempt to calm his nerves, but he can't because one of the crew is running around screaming hysterically that he can't find his mask and that he's going to die. The Mt. Wilson pulls anchor, cranks its engines up to full then steams away from the area as attack helicopters from the carrier arrive to finish off the vessel and sweep the area.

Chapter Five

1. Glass Slipper

With reports of repeated, decisive victories on all fronts, the number of UnReps have begun to decrease and port visits are more frequent. Mina Jebel Ali is the port that the Mt. Wilson is pulling into and Trevion is relieved to learn that no supplies or munitions will be coming aboard, which means it's a liberty port. The guys are all excited about finally leaving the ship and hanging out. A hotel in the middle of the desert is the destination and most of the guys leave at first call but Trevion has to attend a brief meeting with the Squad before he can leave the ship, so he gets dressed in his civilian cloths then slips into coveralls to go to the meeting. Once he's done, he goes to the berthing area and finds that everyone has already left. He'll have to catch a cab to the hotel to meet up with the guys.

The walk from the portal door to the Quarterdeck is only around twenty to twenty-five yards, but by the time Trevion gets there, he's dripping with sweat as the hot, desert sun pushes down on everything. The walk across the pier to the cab was brutal, but not as brutal as the armpit odor that the cab driver had.

As they drove to the hotel, Trevion considered opening the window to let some fresh air into the cab, but the cab was air conditioned and he didn't want to let in the unforgiving heat. So, he had to just suffer through the smell. The cab driver was actually quite nice, offering

used

143

information about the town and its history as well as areas where the best shopping can be found.

Trevion tips him well once they get to the hotel then dashes inside to get back to the A/C. The large hotel had a bar area where the guys were sitting. "Thanks for waiting for me," Trevion sarcastically says as he walks up.

"Man, we have to be back by midnight! I'm not trying to waste one minute," Monster says as he sips on his drink. The guys are all upset over the steep prices for drinks in the hotel.

Suave complains, "Drinks everywhere else cost an arm and a leg. Here they cost an arm, a leg, and a dick! Glad ole boy showed up."

Trevion asks who *ole boy* was and is told that Big Boats knew a guy who was selling the little miniature bottles of alcohol, like the ones you get on airplanes, and the guys were all just buying soda from the bar then spiking it with the little bottles. Trevion asks if any are left, but no one wants to share their stash. 'Fine' he says as he heads over to the bar. He stands for a while waiting for the bartender to notice him, but the bartender seems to be purposely ignoring him.

Already upset at his buddies and the fact that he's about to pay an absurd price for a drink, Trevion is further annoyed by the three Arab fellows sitting at the bar looking at him. Trevion tries not to look over at them, but can see out of the corner of his eye that they're smiling at him. The bartender again walks past Trevion without glancing in his direction. Finally, Trevion decides to look over at the Arab guys staring at him.

One of them says, "Hello, are you American soldier?"
Trevion says yes, "American sailor."

The very well-dressed man explains that he's Kuwaiti, and that he and his family were displaced due to the war. "Thank you for fighting for us, thank George Bush for helping us. We are very grateful."

Trevion watches the bartender speed past again then says, "I'd be very grateful if this damn bartender would stop acting like I'm invisible!"

The Arab man says something to the bartender who quickly comes over to where they're sitting. "What is it that you want, my friend. Please allow us to buy you a drink." Trevion isn't too big on letting some random dude in a bar buy him a drink but, with these prices… "Well, I wouldn't mind a shot of that Hennessey but if a mixed drink costs…"

The man says something in Arabic to the bartender, who hurries off then quickly returns with a bottle. The man pulls out a wad of cash and pays for the bottle of cognac, which is unopened and still in the box. "For you, my friend. Please enjoy."

Trevion looks at the box then back over at the men. "Wow, this is actually too generous. I don't think I can accept this."

One of the men begins laughing and says, "There is no such thing as too generous, my brother. Please, enjoy!"

Stafford and Middleton had gotten a room at the hotel, so Trevion slips out of the bar and up to their room. He knocks on the door and after a few moments Stafford, half dressed, opens it and asks, "Dude, really?"

Trevion holds up the box of cognac and says, "Yeah, really!" When Stafford sees what Trevion is holding, he pauses for a moment then yells for Middleton to put her clothes on and lets Trevion in.

"Damn, blood!" Stafford exclaims as Trevion pulls the beautiful bottle out of the box. "How much did that cost you?"

Trevion explains how the Arab businessmen at the bar bought it for him. "Monster and the guys had some connection that sold them a bunch of shot bottles, and they were being all funny-style with them. I went to the bar to buy myself a drink and came up on a bottle. So, fuck those dudes! We're about to get bombed up in here."

After a few shots, Trevion lets Middleton talk him into letting her go down to the bar area and bring back one of the female sailors from the ship, YN3 Brooks, so that they can have a fourth to play cards. Middleton has been trying to hook Trevion up with Brooks for the past few weeks, so he knows that Middleton isn't interested in having another person in the room to play cards, she's trying to play Cupid. But a few drinks made Trevion open to having Brooks join them for drinks and cards, and a few more drinks made him open to the private conversation on the balcony. Before he knows it, he's in the bathroom with Brooks making out.

Trevion has never drank so much that he's blacked out before, so when the phone in the hotel room wakes him up, it shocks him out of his sleep. He frantically looks around the dark room but can't move because someone is laying on top of him. "Hey!" he calls out. Brooks moves a bit and Trevion is able to see her face. The memory of what had happened slowly tries to return to him as the ringing phone suddenly fills him with dread.

He pulls his arm from under Brooks and looks at his watch. "Oh my Sweet Jesus!!" he screams. "Staff! Staff, wake up! It's 2330!" The four sailors desperately try to get dressed and out of the hotel, bribing the cab driver to break laws in order to get them back to the ship before midnight. It does not help as they reach the Quarterdeck fifteen minutes late and must surrender their ID cards as they board the ship.

2.   Fall from Grace

Trevion stands at Quarters still feeling intoxicated from the night before. He looks up at Suppo and can tell that he knows Trevion has missed the midnight curfew because he's standing there with his arms crossed and a frown on his face. Trevion can only imagine how this is going to affect his life; the Security Squad is held to a much higher standard than the rest of the crew, so he's sure that he'll be either suspended or kicked from the Squad.

That means, no more color guard details and romps with First Lieutenant Highland; no more time away from his desk to hang out with the Squad in one of their 'Trainings' where they spend two hours relaxing in the Secured Library; perhaps even disciplinary actions such as extra duty or restriction. Not to mention the situation that will undoubtedly occur when he sees YN3 Brooks who probably thinks that the two are now a couple since they fooled around last night.

SK2 usually has something to say to Trevion during quarters, but he's suspiciously quiet this morning which makes Trevion even more anxious. The daily report is read and Suppo begins to speak, mentioning the high number of crew members who didn't make it back by midnight. "As you know, unless there are unusual circumstances involved, I always come down hard on missing curfew. Very hard! To those of you who missed curfew, there is an unusual circumstance which occurred last night. I have your ID cards, you can come to my office to get them but, if you were just late, then expect my usual punishment. Anyone have anything to add?"

Trevion wants to publicly apologize for being late last night but can imagine how slurred his speech would be if he did. His inner voice is arguing with Monster's voice in his head about speaking up and owning his mistake. Monster's voice is telling Trevion to keep quiet and don't make it worse, while his own inner voice is demanding that he take responsibility for his own actions. Monster's voice wins as

Suppo tells his crew to 'Turn to' and ends Quarters.

After a few tender moments with the toilet followed by a thorough tooth brushing, Trevion makes his way up to Suppo's office and knocks on the door. "Enter!" Suppo yells as Trevion opens the door and walks in on what seems to be a meeting. When Suppo sees Trevion, he reaches into his pocket and pulls out a small stack of ID cards. "Who was with you last night, Carson?"

Trevion feels suddenly cold as he tries to quickly decide whether or not to name any names. This meeting was all khaki, consisting of Chiefs and Officers; one of which was the OOD last night who took Trevion's ID. "Stafford, Middleton, and Brooks, sir." Suppo shuffles through the ID cards and pulls out three of them "Brooks isn't one of mine so, I'll let her Divo know that she was with you. Take these to Middleton and Stafford for me."

He hands the ID cards to Trevion who says 'Yes sir' then turns to leave, waiting for Suppo to stop him and inform him of their punishment. The tension in his head isn't relieved until he closes the office door behind him and walks away.

"God damn, Golden Boy! I'm glad we're homies!" Stafford exclaims when Trevion hands him his ID card.

"Don't celebrate just yet, cuzz. This is going to cost us something, I just don't know what yet."

Trevion's warning is brushed off by Stafford who thanks him for such a wild night. Trevion mentions that it's too bad they had to leave that bottle of Hennessy behind, but Stafford says, "Well, maybe it's not so bad after all." Revealing that he had smuggled the bottle aboard the ship and hid it in the walk-in freezer.

Then Trevion remembers the word 'wild' being used to describe last night. "What do you mean by wild?"

Stafford looks at Trevion. "You don't remember what happened last night?"

Trevion thinks back, remembering making out with Brooks in the bathroom then whispers... "Oh! Oh, wow! Wait a minute, bro, did we... wait, did we like... switch girls last night?" Stafford bursts into laughter at Trevion's spotty memory and fills him in on what the four of them did once they were all drunk.

As Trevion walks into GSK and hands Middleton her ID card, he tries not to look her in the eye. When she gets her ID from him, she jumps up and gives him a big hug. "Oh my God, I thought we were toast. Thank you." Trevion tells her its nothing then heads back towards his desk, but not without hearing a comment from SK2 about how much browner his nose is than the rest of his face.

For the next few days, Trevion tries to focus on his duties and avoids the questions from his shipmates, but he can't help but wonder what's going on behind the scenes. Suppo is notorious for handing out extra duty and written reprimands for missing ship's movement and being late back from liberty. Once an ID is taken from a sailor, he or she is basically stuck on the ship until they get it back.

Therein lies the rub as Suppo makes his sailors pay in sweat to get their ID cards back. But, Trevion not only got his back, but he also got Stafford's and Middleton's back with zero effort; which should be cause for celebration. Instead, Trevion is thinking of the possible dues that he'll have to pay not only to Suppo, but to the guys in the berthing who will be trying to find out how he got off so easily.

Trevion didn't go back on liberty the two more days that the ship was in port, opting to stay and organize his desk and also mail off anything that he hadn't had a chance to. Being back out to sea is a relief and being on the Rover watch every day helps to kill time and avoid the questions.

Sitting at his desk, Trevion organizes the invoices that he'd just processed so that he can file them when he hears, "Carson, you back there?" It's Suppo yelling from the office area.

Trevion stands up and can see that he's with the XO. "Yes, sir!" Trevion responds.

Here it comes, Suppo is making his way back to Trevion's desk followed by the Executive Officer. When they get there, the XO orders Trevion to tell him where he was from the moment he left the ship until he walked back across the Quarterdeck fifteen minutes late. The question makes Trevion suddenly weak, and he can feel sweat beginning to cover his skin.

"I left the ship and took a cab to the Hilton to meet up with the guys. I went to the bar to buy myself a drink and these three Kuwaiti businessmen bought me a bottle. I took the bottle up to Stafford's room and we got drunk; we meaning Stafford, Middleton, Brooks, and myself. We all passed out and woke up at around 2330 hours and made a mad scramble to get back in time. We failed, sir."

The XO looks at Suppo who gives him a proud smile. The XO thanks Trevion for being courteous to the three men then the two officers leave GSK, and also leave Trevion more confused than before. Who were those men anyway? Only one way to find out, get in contact with Martin up in the Radio Room. He'll know what's going on. Trevion knows that he can't just call and ask him, he'll need to get a message to Martin via the Hush Network utilized by the Squad.

Trevion goes up to the Secured Library and hangs out for a few minutes until another Squad member shows up. He tells that guy that he's trying to talk to Martin after lunch, which means in the last few minutes of the lunch hour. The word will get to Martin who will show up at the Secured Library before lunch is over. This time, Trevion doesn't need to wait because this Squad member is also an RM and works with Martin. "I know what you want to ask him, it's about those dignitaries from Kuwait, right?"

Dignitaries? Not businessmen? Trevion listens as the RM explains how those dignitaries mentioned him when they met with the UN officials, saying that the American servicemen were kind and respectful and how Trevion made them feel comfortable when they were in the hotel. "That's why anyone who was late coming back to the ship, but were at the hotel that night, got a pass for missing curfew. I wasn't there but, I told them I was, so if anyone asks make sure you look out for me and say that you saw me there."

3. Steaming Home

Operation Desert Storm was a quick and decisive victory for the coalition forces and Trevion's battle group, which had been there from Shield to Storm, is finally steaming out of the Persian Gulf. Minus a bit of shrapnel to the head, a heart attack, and one heat stroke victim, the crew of the USS Mt. Wilson leaves the war unscathed and is in a magnificent mood as the ship heads out for the last time. Everyone down in GSK is talking and laughing and sharing stories; even SK2 is laughing and sharing stories with the rest of the SKs.

The Port List is published throughout the ship and everyone clamors around their respective bulletin boards to see where they'll dock on the way home. Two port visits, then Hawaii, then home. One of the ports is familiar to most of the crew; the Philippines, but the other is new to much of the crew; Thailand. The Mt. Wilson will anchor out and run ferries to and from the ship, which means Thailand is a liberty port; which also means that loan requests will start pouring in.

The pot is unusually large this time because Monster and Big Boats are contributing to offset the losses from no longer selling cigarettes and chewing tobacco. Smoove Criminal is prepared to cover all loans, until Martin contacts Trevion via the Hush Network and tells him that the fleet is looking to make an example of anyone caught loan sharking.

During the war, several incidences occurred over non-payment of 100% interest loans between servicemen. There was even a casualty as an Army Corporal beat a Private so severely over a loan that the Private ended up dying. There are more than a few sailors on the Mt. Wilson who slush money and all of them are on Pac Fleet's radar.

Smoove Criminal meets on the mess decks and Martin suggests breaking up the team at least until they get back home, a suggestion that does not go over well with Big Boats, who was counting on the extra cash to spend in PI. "What if it's just me?" he asks. "What if I just handle the pot and if I get caught then it's on me. But, when everything goes as smoothly as I know it's going to, then we all get breaded. Then, after all of this dies down; like I know that it will, it's back to business as usual."

Trevion thinks that Big Boat's idea sounds really good and wouldn't mind having extra money to spend either, but Martin insists that they just split the pot and cut ties for now. "I don't know about the rest of you, but I kind of like my rank. I'm pretty fond of going on liberty. They're going to hammer anyone that they catch and they're planning on catching every slusher on the ship. I'm out, I'll take my cut of the pot and will be waiting in the wings for all of this to blow over."

Martin pulls out a small duffel bag with a lock on it and hands it to Middleton who pulls out a key and unlocks the bag. She pulls out a canvas money bag and hands it to Trevion who enters the combination and dumps the bills out onto the table. As the cash is being divided, Big Boats continues to protest, trying to convince everyone that nothing is going to happen.

Trevion shakes his head. "Boats, have you ever seen Martin lose his cool? This is the most level cat that I've ever seen, and he's shook right now. That means we need to kick back and watch this one from the rafters. Like you just said, this will all blow over, and it'll be back to business as usual."

Though still quite upset, Big Boats thanks Trevion and leaves the galley followed by Monster. Trevion leaves too, headed towards the ship's Post Office to buy money orders. Martin sits for a while with Stafford and Middleton until finally heading over to Ops berthing. Middleton asks Stafford if he agrees with Martin, that they should all break up until they get back home, Stafford takes the question to have a hidden meaning; that he and Middleton should break up. This sparks an argument between the two which ends with Middleton storming off to Female berthing. Leaving Stafford sitting alone in the galley.

"Damn, what the hell just happened?" he says aloud as he stands up then walks down to Supply berthing. He lays down in his rack and listens to the guys talk about going home and wonders if he's going home single or if he's bringing Middleton to meet his mother. Trevion walks in and asks him what's wrong. "Blood, I should have listened to you and not fucked with a broad on the ship, she flipped out on me in the galley just now. I don't even know if it's worth it to try to fix it."

Trevion smiles and reminds Stafford of all the times that he and Middleton messed around on the ship while the rest of the guys had to take matters into their own hands, but Stafford brings up the three women that Trevion managed to sleep with during their time in the Persian Gulf, "You even bagged a Canadian Officer, man! Her bikini picture is taped above your rack right now."

When Trevion says the words "More than that now", Stafford rolls out of his bottom bunk and pushes Trevion aside, then crawls into Trevion's rack to look at the new pictures that he has taped up.

"What? They let you take butt-nakeds of them? Damn, she got some perky titties!" Stafford rolls out of Trevion's rack then gives him another shove, "I guess you weren't corny for buying that instant camera after all. I see you even managed to get a bra and pantie shot of ole Brooks."

That sentence got the attention of Suave. "A bra and pantie shot of who?" Trevion frowns at Stafford who quickly tries to clean up his statement, but Suave persists until Trevion confesses to going out with her a few times.

Suave gives a look of disappointment and walks away. Stafford asks what that was all about, Trevion tells him, "Maybe he's been trying to hook up with Brooks, dude looked at me like I just stole his sweetheart or something. Hell, he can have her, I heard Thailand was crawling with single women who love American sailors. Last thing I need is a bucket of sand on my way to the beach. Oh, sorry bro."

4.   Three Stops from Home

Channel Fever has spread throughout the ship and the sailors aboard the USS Mt. Wilson find it quite difficult to sleep the night before arriving in Thailand. Midrats is unusually crowded and actually runs out of food with much of the anxious crew finding their way to the mess decks in the middle of the night. With the Watch Bill already posted and duty sections assigned, the clique begins planning their days ashore.

It's rare that they're all in the same duty section, but with the Stingers aboard and Fernandez now on the cooks' rotation, they'll have three of the five days of liberty together. None of them can sleep as the ship steams very slowly towards port, timing their arrival at 0700 the next morning. Big Boats, Franky, and Moorish sit on the mess decks with Monster and Suave planning the second day of liberty since they'll all be on duty when the ship arrives to port.

Franky is extremely excited. "Man, I just can't wait to get some pussy! Months with nothing to look at except fleet chicks, completely covered Arab chicks, and you swinging dicks; pussy is very high on my to-do list. So, I don't care what we do afterwards, but we need to hit some kind of hoe house or brothel or something as soon as we get there."

They all laugh, but whenever they start planning their liberty, Franky brings the whole thing back to having sex first, everything else afterward. Two sailors who aren't especially hard up for sex are Trevion and Stafford, who sit in the cook's office with Fernandez and Middleton discussing the liberty port. Fernandez and Stafford are on the cook's rotation so they will be able to leave the ship at 1900 if they're on duty, 1500 on work days, and they have two days of unrestricted liberty.

Stafford and Middleton already have plans together for the first day so Fernandez is taunting Trevion who has duty on the first and last days at port. "I'll try to save some fun for you, Boot. I won't turn the whole country out before you're finally allowed to touch land."

Trevion sits and absorbs his ribbing with a smile because he's not going to be stuck on the ship in the morning, the XO has scheduled an off-ship team building exercise for the Security Squad. They're supposed to be gone from 0900 to 1400 hours, but Trevion doesn't see his nor Martin's names on the Rover watch bill, and they're the lowest ranking Rovers so it's not unusual to see one of their names on the watch bill twice in a day. But, having neither of their names listed makes Trevion think that they'll be gone much longer than 2pm.

Morning comes and the ship is met by two tug boats and a ferry, then anchors out at around 0630. By 0800, the 1-MC announces *'Liberty call, liberty call! Liberty call for all non-duty personnel!'* Trevion and the other members of the Security Squad are instructed to wear their Dress Whites and to bring a set of civilian clothes with them, including skivvies, and meet on the Quarterdeck at 0845.

"Looking good, Boot Camp!" SK2 yells from across Supply berthing, drawing the attention and lots of whistles from the guys getting dressed. SK2 walks over and inspects Trevion's uniform, making fun of the marksmanship ribbons that he earned on the helo deck. "I told you that overachiever shit was going to catch up to you, now you have to go stand in a room full of officers being their little errand boy while they sit around getting drunk."

"Shit," Monster says, "I'll take leaving with the XO over staying here on the ship any day." Trevion zips his small duffel bag containing his civvies and skivvies then makes his way through the guys and up to the Quarterdeck.

The first ferry that leaves is called the Khaki Cruiser because it's reserved for officers and chiefs, the XO and the Squad board that ferry with the high-ranking crew members and begin the twenty-five minute trip to shore. "Congratulations, guys, you all performed admirably." Mr. Brown says to the Squad, followed by several officers concurring with the statement. "Especially you two, Carson and Martin, great job back in Dubai with the UN guys. You both deserve this." The members of the Squad look around at each other to see if anyone knew what *this* was.

The XO, along with the Captain and a few other officers from the battle group, has blocked off a floor at a resort in Thailand and the XO has arranged for the Squad, along with a few privileged other non-commissioned personnel, to be treated to a night at the resort.

Martin leans over and whispers to Trevion, "If I had known, I would have brought more cash with me."

Trevion whispers back, "I got you covered, bro." Just before pulling to the pier, the XO announces to the Squad that they'll be off duty once they reach the resort and can stay for two nights, but cannot tell anyone else about it.

"As far as the rest of the crew knows, you guys pulled color detail for a bunch of officers; gopher duty, getting drinks, and providing armed escorts. Your duty section heads all know that you're not coming back tonight, so if there was something back on the ship that you really needed to get done tonight then I guess it should have gotten done before we left. What happens from the time we step off of this boat until you go back to the ship is strictly Need-to-Know."

The private resort is beyond breathtaking. Each room that the Squad will stay in has two bedrooms, one with double beds, and will house three Squad members. The XO arranges for Trevion and Martin to share a deluxe room on the 'Commanders End' of the floor. By lunchtime, the two young sailors have already gotten a massage, had a swim, and shared a pitcher of Margaritas with a group of pilots from the aircraft carrier.

Just down the road from the resort is a small village which makes its living catering to the travelers at the resort. The Squad walk around all day shopping and eating authentic Thai cuisine with the group of officers. The XO recommends a tailor in the village who makes the most unique silk suits so Martin persuades Trevion to go with him to buy a suit. Trevion isn't very big on suits, having only worn them for the funerals of his classmates back home who were caught up in the violence of his neighborhood.

Therefore, suits reminded him of death, but the tailor had a very unique style. His suits were fun and colorful with unique touches. Trevion began to soften on the whole idea of buying then wearing a suit as he watched Martin being sized for his suit. "Last chance, Tray. They won't be ready until Sunday and we have duty on Monday; and then we're gone forever. Trust me, these suits will more than pay for themselves in the long run."

The tailor looks over at Trevion with raised eyebrows "Size you next? Young man need at least two suit, one for business, one for social. I make you both deal, three suit, only pay for two." Martin looks over at Trevion and asks if he has that much cash on him, Trevion says that he does, and the Margaritas that he's been downing says that he should buy the suits and stop thinking about it so much.

After spending a considerable amount of money in the nearby village, the sailors and officers travel to the populated downtown Bangkok area to spend the rest of the evening dancing and drinking. At a crowded club which plays mostly hip-hop and popular R&B music, Trevion is very popular due to him being an excellent dancer. He's not able to stay off of the dance floor for too long before a young woman walks over to their table and pulls him back to dance with her.

Months at war, miserable hours spent in the Persian Gulf stuck in an invisible box, paranoid as every fishing vessel around him could potentially open fire; Trevion dances all of that stress away and leaves the club covered in sweat.

A trolley takes him back to the resort where Martin is already in bed asleep. Trevion takes a quick shower then climbs into bed, but doesn't get the chance to doze off before he hears a banging on the door "Carson! Martin! Open this door, ASAP!"

Trevion jumps out of bed and makes a beeline to the front door, passing a groggy Martin along the way. "You have five seconds to open this door!" the voice insists as he continues to beat on the door. Trevion recognizes the voice, its LTJG Brown. He scrambles to open the door and finds Mr. Brown standing with a group of young women. "That's him, girls, the other one is in there somewhere. Take them both down!" The giggling young ladies, wearing blouses and bikini tops but no pants or panties, rush inside and push Trevion back into his room.

Three of them push him onto his bed while the other three attend to Martin. Mr. Brown closes their room door and walks away as the ladies tie both Trevion and Martin to their respective headboards with scarves that they had in their hair. Trevion wonders why the ladies were bottomless rather than topless, but the thought was fleeting as they dance around the bed then begin to have their way with him. When it's over, they untie Trevion then quickly rush out of the room, leaving Trevion and Martin dazed by the sudden and very passionate event.

As Trevion looks up at the ceiling fan, he can hear Martin ask, "Damn bro, what just happened?" Trevion revisits the shower and tries again to fall asleep but the sound of the officers partying outside has him curious to find out what they're doing down in the common area. To satisfy his curiosity, he gets dressed and heads down to take a peek and is surprised at how many people were there. The girls who rushed into his room were there, but they were accompanied by many more beautiful young women.

"Carson, get your ass over here!" the XO yells from a corner booth. Sitting with him are LT Cruz, LTJG Brown, and a few of the Squad members. Trevion sits as the group continues their conversation, which he can tell contains some confidential information. LTJG Brown motions towards Trevion and the XO knocks on the table three times, then once.

Everyone at the table takes turns doing the same. Trevion is not sure if he should also do this or not so he just sits there. "First test passed, Carson!" says the XO with a confident smile. "We all knocked on the table, but you didn't blindly copy us, well done. A man needs to know when to lead, when to follow, and most importantly, when to just stand fast. Are there any objections?" The men around the table all shake their heads 'no'.

The XO looks over at LT Cruz, who explains to Trevion that they belong to a secret group on the ship, and that the group is part of a larger organization which exists throughout the entire fleet. "None of us asked to become one of Davy's Boys, we were all selected. You were selected before you even came aboard our ship, back in Hawaii." Trevion tries not to show the shock on his face as he realizes that Vice Admiral Unger did more than just recommend him for early advancement, Dan seems to have been pulling strings from afar on Trevion's behalf.

The XO begins to speak, but Trevion is now recalling some of the things that's happened since he's been on the ship; how he was encouraged by Baker to follow him on his Rover rout and learn how to stand the watch, that being qualified for Rover is necessary to be selected for Security Squad, which is ran by the XO and LT Cruz; how LT Cruz qualified him for Rover on his first attempt immediately after Trevion passed his gun qualifications; how he seemed to be the only Squad member that Mr. Brown would pick on and test during Special Weapons transports; and why Suppo, who is absent from the table, keeps trying to connect himself to Trevion's accomplishments.

Slowly, The XO's words return to Trevion's attention. "You still need to have a steady anchor in order to qualify to serve Davy Jones, but that's the only qualification that you haven't already met. So, keep up the good work and enjoy yourself. You and Martin are welcome to stay here tonight and tomorrow night. But after that, only you are allowed to return. Your room will remain available to you until we sail, you come highly recommended so don't let us down, Carson."

5.   With the Clique

Trevion is good at hiding his emotions, a skill that he's mastering every day in Supply berthing. He talks to Martin in the morning and swaps stories about the three girls that were in their beds, even though he'd rather talk about the meeting with the XO after Martin had went to sleep. He'd rather discuss the secret club on the ship that has been watching him since he arrived. He wants to ask how Martin knew about the sweep that's happening on the ship with all slushing and gambling is being halted and anyone participating is being sent to Captain's Mast where they are tried and sentenced by the Commanding Officer of the ship.

The guys from the ship went on liberty at 0900 so they should be downtown by noon, giving Trevion about ninety minutes to make his way there. The patio of the resort has a stunning view of the common area with a lush backdrop of colorful, tropical landscape. Trevion considers not going to hang out with the clique and just staying at the resort filled with wealthy travelers, military officers, and beautiful women.

But Martin is excited to go and hang out with those guys. The clique really doesn't hang out with too many people from the ship, especially not guys from the Ops Department. Martin loves being the only Ops guy allowed to kick it, and Trevion is his ticket in with them so he's keeping Trevion from deciding to just stay.

"Hey, shipmate!" a voice calls out from behind the privacy wall of the balcony.

"Ahoy!" Martin responds. "Anyone have a menthol?" Martin looks at Trevion's pack of Newports sitting on the table. Trevion yells that he has six left in the pack and that the sailor can have them. He walks to the door and opens it, waiting for the guy to open his door. When he doesn't, Trevion walks over and knocks, and Betty opens it.

"Oh my God, what are you doing here?" she whispers frantically. Trevion can't think of anything to say, so he holds up the pack of cigarettes. A voice from inside calls out, "Many thanks, shipmate!" Trevion smiles but can feel that it's a very pathetic attempt at one, then walks back to his balcony, telling Martin to get ready so they can go and meet up with the clique.

Trevion was quiet on the trip from the resort to Bangkok. He was very deep in thought, pondering everything that had happened up to that point. The bus ride in was close to an hour, but it didn't seem as long to Trevion who was lost in his own mind, nor to Martin who was asleep with his mouth wide open. As the bus pulls into the station, Trevion sticks Martin's fingertip into his own mouth and then into his ear "Self-Wet Willy!" he says, which wakes Martin up and starts a shoving match.

The two walk around for a while until they see a McDonald's. "If they ain't in there, they will be." Trevion says as they make their way to the restaurant. Sure enough, the guys are occupying three tables in the back. Monster looks up, "And, there's my young apprentice! Big Boats, pay up!" Big Boats looks over at Trevion in disbelief, then hands Monster three dollars.

"I told y'all, didn't I? We can be miles apart in a foreign country, the clique will find the clique." The guys all greet Trevion and Martin and ask if they're going to order food, they say no. Suave laughs, "Good thing because I have no idea what this bullshit is, but I know for sure that it ain't Micky Dee's."

They all hang out until everyone is finished eating and then head out to experience the town. As the afternoon begins to become the evening, the clique heads back to the ship to drop off everything that they've purchased and to shower up and dress for the legendary Bangkok nightlife.

Everyone in Supply berthing is comparing scouting reports about where to party, where are the best places to eat, and where they can buy a good time if they strike out all night. As usual, Trevion is mostly quiet, listening to everyone else talk. But today he's thinking about the secret club that's been on-board the ship this whole time, and he didn't know about them; until he became one of them.

He thinks back to the faces around the table and realizes that the only ones who were not officers where Squad members. And not all of the Squad members were there. He wonders if SK2 is aware of Davy's Boys, it would explain why he wants so badly to be on the Security Squad. What about SKC? Trevion has seen him with the XO several times, but he was also absent from the resort.

Moorish snaps him out of his thoughts by asking about the dance clubs in town. "Yeah, I heard of a really good one," Trevion replies. "Two sides; one side plays Hip-Hop and the other plays Pop and R&B. It's a couple of blocks away from the river."

"Is that right?" Suave interrupts. "Think you know how to get there, Boot?" Trevion says yes and the guys all agree to go there first to see if their technique of getting stamped at the club and then returning later will work in Bangkok.

As the ferry brings the group of sailors to shore, everyone is their normal selves again. The shadow of war is gone and spirits are very high as they head towards the awaiting arms of the club scene. Trevion looks over and sees Baker sitting on the other side of the ferry. Baker asks if Trevion is 'headed back'. "Not just yet, how about you?" Baker nods an enthusiastic yes which brings Trevion to laughter.

6.   Different Country, Same Clique

It seems as if there is no such thing as early with the nightclubs, they're all packed at 7pm. A few of the guys want to check out a popular club that's on the way to riverfront club, but the enormous line outside of the club dissuades them, and they keep going to their original destination; only to find an even longer line at that club.

The guys all exit the two taxis that they were traveling in and stand in awe of the club and the amount of people outside of the club trying to get in. Suave doesn't mind the line, saying, "Will you look at all the prime-choice pussy in that line. I may not even need to go in!"

One of the security guards recognizes Trevion from the night before and stares at him until they make eye contact, then motions for him to walk over. Trevion points at the group of sailors who are with him and the guard gives a thumbs-up. By this time, the clique is split between those who want to get in to the club and those who want to flirt with the young women in the line. Trevion says, "Hey, if you guys are ready to go in, I can get us in right now. Just follow me."

Big Boats laughs at Trevion saying the words 'follow me' and reminds Trevion that he's had more time aboard the USS Mt. Wilson than Trevion has had in the Navy. He suggests that they get in line and flirt with the women until they get in. Moorish has been in a situation before when Trevion says that he can get them into a place with a huge line, so he follows as Trevion shrugs his shoulders and walks towards the entrance.

Martin also follows, along with Stafford and Middleton. As they reach the security guard, Trevion pulls out a brand-new pack of Newports along with ten dollars and shakes the guard's hand with them. The guard stamps each of their hands but gives Trevion a wristband with Thai letters on it.

They walk into the crowded, smoky club and find a table for the group to occupy. Moorish looks at Trevion and says "Downtown San Francisco, I can sort of buy that. Picasso actually invited you there, I remember. But this is Thailand! How can you possibly have pull here?" Martin laughs and is about to explain how they were just at this club last night, but Trevion clears his throat and tells Moorish that it's all in the way you approach people. Martin turns white at the realization that he had almost spilled the beans on last night and sits quietly while

Stafford flags down the waitress to order drinks.

A very beautiful young Thai waitress comes and takes their order, she's dressed like the rest of the girls working in the club; black shoes with pink thigh-high stockings, an almost-not-there white skirt and a pink, studded bustier with her hair in two pigtails. She's not gone long before returning with their drinks.

Everyone pulls out money to pay, but she tells Trevion that his is free, pointing at his wristband. Trevion looks down at the wristband, which he can't read, then gives the waitress a big tip. Moorish waits until she walks away then asks Trevion, "So, the way you approached the bouncer made him give you a free drink wristband?"

Trevion shrugged his shoulders, "That or the cash that I slipped him when I shook his hand."

It took the rest of the guys two hours to finally make their way into the club. Big Boats is forced to concede that he should have listened to Trevion as the girls in the line didn't seem to like American sailors, so the two hours were long and boring. "Except for one funny thing that happened," he says, which brings the guys to an instant laughter.

He tells a story of how, when they were standing in line, one of the guys from the ship came running out of the hotel across the street screaming with his pants half-way down. "I looked and recognized him, he's one of my Third-Class BMs, so me and Monster ran over there thinking that he just got robbed or something. This fool was super drunk and babbling about something, I couldn't understand him.

Come to find out, this idiot bought some pussy and brought it up to his room, only it wasn't pussy that he bought. It was dingaling! He picked up a ladyboy! He said that he was upstairs in his room and had her, or him, or whatever bent over and he was hitting it from the back when he tried to do a reach-around and felt a dick and balls! He said he just ran out of the room."

Trevion and the others burst into laughter as Big Boats explains how he made the sailor go back into the room and kick the ladyboy out. Everyone stops laughing when two Thai girls walk up to Trevion and ask him to dance with them. As he leaves with the two attractive young ladies, he's looking at both of their throats to see if either has an Adam's Apple. As he dances with them, he looks around the club and notices that there are more than a few questionable women there, ones who could actually be men.

He now realizes why the girls at the resort were running around bottomless; to show that they were actually girls rather than boys. This jogs his memory, flashing him back to the time he was driving Dan to a lunch date in Hawaii. Dan said, "In some countries, like Thailand for example, if a family has five boys, the fifth one is treated like a girl to help the mother. If the family is rich enough, they'll actually turn him into a her with surgery." Throw-away comments like that one didn't have very much merit to Trevion back then, now he's trying to remember some of the other things that Dan would ramble on about.

The guys spend the rest of the evening enjoying the benefits of Trevion's popularity in the club and Trevion enjoyed the free drinks that the waitress kept bringing to him every time his glass was empty. They all stumble out of the club, some with girls that they've picked up inside, and start looking for taxis.

Trevion is still inside talking to the waitress who spent most of the night coming on to him. She's tall and athletic, so Trevion is scrutinizing her heavily, and clumsily, due to all of the drinks that he's had.

"I don't close." She tells him, "I can leave in ten minutes if you want to hang out?" Trevion looks very closely at her neck, which makes her smile because she can tell that he's afraid of her turning out to be a male. She hugs him then grabs his hand and slips it under her skirt then whispers "Born a girl."

Outside, some of the girls have decided against leaving with the clique because they were all going to the same hotel room. This sparks a heated debate over allowing the guys with females to use the room while the others either waited somewhere else or just went back to the ship.

Trevion walks out with the waitress and they listen to the debate for a while. Stafford asks Trevion where he's going, saying that he and Middleton have a room and that he's welcome to come with them. "No thanks, bro. I have somewhere to go." Trevion quietly walks away from his arguing shipmates and jumps into a cab around the corner.

The cab lets them out where the resort shuttle stops and the two wait there. Just before the shuttle arrives, Martin pulls up in a cab to catch the shuttle as well. "Yo, Trey! The guys started fighting outside of the club, then the cops showed up. I'm not sure if anyone went to jail or not, I just walked away and grabbed a taxi."

As they sit on the shuttle, Martin tells the story of how the heated debate escalated into a fistfight between Big Boats and Monster, and how the other guys were actually placing bets on the outcome. As the shuttle reaches the resort, the waitress gasps, "You have a room here? This very exclusive resort, how can sailor get a room here?" Trevion's ego swells as the waitress clings to his elbow as he shows her around the resort. They get to the common area to party and have another drink before going back to his room.

7. Trevion vs SK2 – Round 1

The next morning, Trevion walks the waitress to the shuttle stop and kisses her before she leaves. Martin, along with most of the Squad members, need to be out of the resort by noon so Trevion plays the role as if he has to leave as well. He and Martin head back to the ship where they learn that four of the guys were arrested then released to the ship's Master at Arms, who placed them on restriction until further notice. Somehow, Big Boats and Monster, who were the ones actually fighting, were never arrested.

"Man, fuck Thailand!" Suave shouts. "You can't tell if the girls are actually girls and the cops are just as racist as the ones back home!" Trevion laughs, but Suave tells him to shut up. "Where the hell did you go, Boot? I saw you with that waitress, where did y'all go? All the hotels were either sold out or too expensive, where did you take her?"

Trevion tells Suave that it's none of his business, which starts an argument between the two that Monster had to break up before it turned physical. Trevion storms out of Supply berthing and heads down to his desk in GSK to cool off. He notices that someone has been going through his R/R files because the book is not where it's supposed to be, which increases his anger.

"Fuck this, I'm out of here!" he screams aloud as he leaves GSK and returns to Supply berthing to pack for another two days at the resort. Suave is still there, and still talking trash to Trevion who tries to ignore him. Finally, Trevion says, "You know what, you're right. My bad. Come on, let me buy you lunch downtown. Oh, wait... you can't leave the ship, can you, jailbird? Oh well, maybe we can go next time we're in Thailand." Monster has to physically restrain Suave as Trevion walks out of Supply berthing and leaves for the resort.

Trevion spends the next two days hanging out with the Naval officers and pilots who serve Davy Jones, learning about the network and what's expected of him as a new recruit. They insist that he not call them sir, but rather put the title of Sir in front of their first names; Sir Chuck, Sir Keith, Sir Jason, etc. By the second night, Trevion has become close with many of the Davy's Boys who are staying at the resort.

Since he knows that he has duty the next day, Trevion decides to sleep on the ship so that he's not late getting back due to the very unpredictable transportation methods in Thailand. He packs up his belongings and makes a pass through the common area to say good-bye, then walks down to the village to pick up his and Martin's suits before taking the trolley back. When Trevion walks into Supply berthing, the guys from the clique are all there, talking and gossiping as usual. Trevion looks over at Suave and asks if they're cool.

"Man, fuck you!" Suave replies with a smirk. "I'm the only one in here that's cool, you're just like the rest of these assholes." He gives a fist-bump as Trevion walks by. "But don't let that shit happen again, Boot." Trevion puts away his things then brings his new suits down to GSK to hang them near his desk. Before he can get to his desk, Trevion notices SK2 sitting there going through his very well-organized record book.

Quietly, Trevion leaves GSK and goes to Supply berthing to get his instant camera. He comes back and sneaks as close to SK2 as he can, then snaps the picture. The flash startles SK2. He looks over and sees Trevion hurrying away and waving a photo to develop it faster. SK2 yells out as he chases Trevion out of GSK. But when SK2 gets to the top of the stairwell, Trevion is nowhere to be found. He runs to Supply berthing but Trevion isn't in there. "The hell wrong with you, SK2?" Monster asks.

"Don't worry about it," he replies as he walks out of the berthing.

The next morning, there is duty section Quarters where the oncoming and off-going duty sections receive their orders and are relieved of duty respectively. SK2 stands with the sailors coming off of duty, looking over to the oncoming duty section to see if he can find Trevion. As Quarters is called to order, SK2 finally sees Trevion standing over to the side and talking to LT Cruz. He waits for their conversation to be over, but they instead walk further away from everyone else and continue to speak.

"So, you need to study really hard, Carson. Once you get to E-4 then we can submit your name for the program, but only if you make first or second increment. That means you need to know your shit and know it well, understand?" Trevion gives a 'Yes, sir' and the two begin walking back to Quarters, just in time to hear the Duty Chief send the outgoing section on liberty.

Trevion walks away with SK2 right behind him, until he sees that Trevion is walking to the Quarterdeck to relieve the 8 to 12 Rover watch. Once he has assumed watch duties, Trevion walks over to SK2. "Look, I really don't care about why you have such a beef with me. I honestly don't. Whatever your reasons are, I'm sure that they're valid and good. But what you're doing is sabotage, you're trying to hurt my good name, you're trying to mess up my good work. That I do care about, a lot. I know that you have your connections, but I have a few connections too; and a picture of you in my shit. With all due respect to you and your rank, back off or I'll be forced to defend myself."

SK2 looks hard at Trevion, but Trevion maintains eye contact. "Ok, I'll leave you alone as long as you keep doing your job." SK2 says as he backs down and walks away. Trevion keeps the hard, confident expression on his face until he gets inside of the ship and away from everyone's eyes, then has a baby panic attack.

Trevion has had these little episodes throughout his life, his father taught him to do breathing exercises to calm himself. He closes his eyes and begins breathing deeply, thinking about what he'd just done. SK2 could possibly put a bad mark on Trevion's record, which has been unblemished and impressive up to this point despite all of the obstacles.

He thinks back to the restroom stall inside of the courthouse where he had to calm himself after avoiding jail; in Lani's bathroom in Hawaii after narrowly avoiding a beat-down by her brother and his gigantic friends; in the aft storeroom after fighting the Iraqi gunboat, and now in a passageway after confronting SK2. Like he did in the past, he thinks to himself *You did it, it's over, move on!* He composes himself and continues his rounds, at least he'll be on watch until noon and out of SK2's path, hopefully until he eventually leaves on liberty.

8.   A Taste of Home

The trip from Thailand to the Philippines felt like a luxury cruise to Trevion with the tasks of selling tobacco and slushing money no longer on his plate; and SK2 no longer on his back. Trevion focuses on inventorying his supply locker, to make sure that SK2 hadn't messed anything up, and learning from Davy's Boys what's expected of him. The evening before reaching PI, the mail arrives from the carrier and Trevion brings down a bag full of letters and packages from the ship's Post Office.

As he begins distributing it down in GSK, he notices that he has two letters with no return address; those are most likely from Daisy. There's a letter from Thailand that has to be from 2nd LT Highland, since the waitress doesn't know Trevion's full name or rank, a bunch of mail from home, and a care package from his grandmother. That's the one that Trevion wants to see first.

He opens the thick, waxy box and finds a bunch of cold, moist towels wrapped around a large food container. Whatever is in the container is still frozen solid, which surprises Trevion since it's postdated to over a week ago. "No way!" he says in a voice loud enough for the SKs up front to hear him.

Monster is the first to come back to Trevion's desk to investigate. "What you got there, my young apprentice?"

Trevion opens the container. "Authentic Louisiana gumbo! My granny must have packed it in dry ice or something because it's still frozen. It's a gang of it in here, and I can't eat it all…"

Monster makes a face. "Naw, I really don't like seafood. That shit got shrimps and crab legs… ugh! Thanks though."

Trevion brings the container to Stafford, who almost has a heart attack when he sees what's inside. "This is a whole pot's worth! I'll make some rice upstairs and we can get down tonight for dinner." Trevion tells Stafford to warm up half of the container. When asked why so much, he says that he wants to give some to the XO, who is from New Orleans and would appreciate real gumbo.

That evening for dinner, the mess decks served goulash and rice so Stafford didn't need to make any. Goulash has a very powerful aroma, but the half-pot of gumbo simmering on the stove overpowered its smell and Trevion gets a whiff of it once he gets to the mess decks. He walks past the line and over to the Cook's Office where Stafford and Bubba sit talking.

Bubba looks over at Trevion and asks, "So, you think that a bowl of that delicious gumbo is going to just magically put you in my good graces, huh? Is that what you think?" Trevion looks over at Stafford who is nodding his head yes.

"I'm pretty sure that it'll put me on the right track," Trevion replies. Bubba smiles at Trevion and tells him that he just gave the correct answer and walks out.

Stafford asks if he's going to bring the XO a bowl before he starts eating, but before Trevion can answer, the XO storms into the office holding a bowl and a soup spoon. "Carson, I can smell it, where the hell is it? Stop fucking with me!" Stafford grabs the XO's bowl and walks into the galley; the XO looks at Trevion and says that if it tastes as good as it smells then he'll owe Trevion 'a huge solid'.

Stafford returns with the bowl and the XO immediately takes a spoonful. His face goes blank, he stops chewing and closes his eyes for a moment, then finishes the mouthful. "Ok, maybe two huge solids. Thanks, Carson." The XO leaves and Trevion, Stafford, Bubba, and MS2 Santos sit in the Cook's office quietly eating the gumbo.

MS2 Santos has never tasted gumbo before, but is a huge fan of seafood, so when he asked what was cooking, Trevion offered him a bowl. Santos, one of the senior members of the Filipino crew, loves the rich seafood stew and says that it reminds him of a dish that his mother makes back in the Philippines.

Full and satisfied, Trevion returns to GKS and remembers that he has a bunch of mail that he completely disregarded once he had seen the gumbo. The two letters from Daisy had pictures inside of them; three nice and one naughty. The letter with the Thai post mark is from Highland who apologizes to Trevion and explains that she was there with her husband when he saw her. He opens the first letter from home and is confused about the 'paperwork' that his parents mentioned completing and how thrilled his mother is. Thrilled about what? Trevion has no idea but as long as she's no longer worried about him being at war then he's fine waiting until they speak to find out.

9.   One Down, Two to Go...

As the USS Mt. Wilson pulls into port, the usual call for all personnel E-3 and below to report for garbage duty goes over the 1-MC. Trevion and Middleton are excluded from that call because there are a large amount of supplies waiting for them on the pier. Luckily for the SKs, the crane is working and the pallets are hoisted up to the helo deck then brought by fork truck to the main deck. The SKs break down the pallets and have the Petty Officer of the Watch call the departments to the main deck to sign for and pick up their supplies. After that, they carry the remaining boxes down to GSK.

Suppo makes a surprise visit and chats with SKC, which means that the SKs can't just stack the boxes in the back and go on liberty, they'll need to keep working for as long as Suppo is in GSK. By the time he finally leaves, most everything has been unpacked and stowed away. The packing material is placed into one of the giant paper bags and taped shut for Trevion to take off of the ship before he can go on liberty. The bag isn't too heavy and Trevion is feeling strong after the workout of humping boxes down to the storeroom.

He gets to the Quarterdeck and can see the large garbage bin about a hundred yards away. It sits a few yards off of the path that runs down the middle of the gravel-covered ground. As he walks towards it, he imagines all of the sailors who had to carry trash from the ship all the way down there. He steps through the gravel and looks up at the garbage bin, wondering if he could shot put the paper bag up there. "Yeah, no," he laughs to himself and begins to climb the metal stairway welded to the side of the bin.

He gets halfway up and decides to throw the bag into the bin, in one motion he heaves the large bag over the side and spins around to walk down the stairs. When the bag hits, Trevion hears loud, frightening screams coming from inside of the bin. He runs down the stairs and away from the bin, looking back to see dozens of monkeys jumping out of it. He stands there looking at the monkeys as they sit on the gravel looking back at him; in the distance there is laughter coming from the Quarterdeck.

"You little fuckers scared the crap out of me!" he says as he turns to walk away, only for the monkeys to follow him. He stops and turns around and the monkeys stop, he turns to walk back to the ship and the monkeys begin following him again. Trevion looks up at the Quarterdeck and can see that they're all watching him and laughing. After walking a few yards, he turns to see that the monkeys are still following him.

He picks up a handful of gravel and throws it at them. "Go back to the trash, you dirty little pests!" The monkeys all grab handfuls of gravel and look at Trevion, who quickly turns and makes a break for it back to the ship. Rocks fly by Trevion as he makes a dash for the gangplank, he looks back and can see that the monkeys are running the same speed as he is and reloading by grabbing more rocks as they chase him.

As Trevion reaches the pier, the monkeys all stop and begin to return to the garbage bin. Trevion spends the entire port visit being teased about the incident, which the crew began calling Operation Dumpster Storm.

The base in Olongapo has a phone center where servicemen can call home with a calling card sold at the center. Trevion buys a card and calls home to speak with his parents and let them know the date that the ship will be returning to home port. A ship returning from a long deployment is an event as family and friends are allowed onto the base to welcome the returning sailors.

This particular deployment was a war, so there will be an additional amount of fanfare for their return. Trevion wants to make sure that he has someone on the pier when he returns to port, but his parents inform him that they won't be able to make it.

Trevion's mom is speaking in a slightly cryptic manner, like she's trying to hide something from him. She keeps asking if he's met anyone other than the girl from the picture. "Mom, I was at war. I didn't have time to meet anyone. Plus, I was in the Middle East, where they cut your eyes out if you look at one of their women. Why are you so interested in my love life all of a sudden?" She gives him the classic Because I'm your mother speech then hands phone over to Trevion's father who thanks him for the leather hats that he sent, then asks if he was able to get his hands on any Cuban cigars.

Trevion says No but he actually does have a couple of them that he's trying to smuggle back home. Phone lines on a military base; no question that they're being tapped and every conversation is being recorded, so Trevion chooses his words carefully and doesn't reveal what he's bringing home with him on the ship. "Tell Big Mamma that I said thanks for the gumbo. I'll be able to take leave once we get back, so I'll call and let you know when I'll be home. Kiss Mom for me. Love you, Dad. Bye."

Last night in the Philippines, and perhaps the last time ever if the rumors of the base being turned over to the Philippine government are true. Trevion relaxes in his room at the hotel built up the side of a mountain; several officers and Squad members are staying there because he tipped them off to the beautiful hotel.

He can hear the music coming from the restaurant area, so he decides to go and investigate. People are dancing and have a good time. Someone walks up behind Trevion and covers his eyes. "Um... Young Pam Grier? Hallie Berry? The curly-haired girl from A Different World?" Trevion receives a slap on the back of the neck. "No, boy!" Daisy says as she hugs then kisses him.

"You're not here with anyone are you?" she asks. Trevion says no and the two begin dancing. "What did I tell you!" a voice bellows from the entrance. "Didn't I tell you that my apprentice knew what he was talking about? Pay up, sucka!"

Suave hands Monster three dollars and says, "Whatever, it was still a long-ass ride to get here!" The guys from the clique walk up and greet Trevion then find a booth towards the back to set up their club base.

Daisy asks if Trevion wants to hang out with his friends then find her later on. Trevion looks the buxom young woman up and down. "Um, no. I'm just a boot camp to those guys, they even still call me Boot even though I'm not the juniorest guy in the berthing. You're finer than anything that they're going to pull out here tonight so I want you with me, making me look good."

Daisy smiles very brightly and hugs Trevion again, "Fine by me, I'll be your arm candy tonight if you'll be my farewell fling later."

10. Dues Owed

Hawaii is beautiful, especially to the sailors onboard the Mt. Wilson because Hawaii is a US State, which means they're home; or at least one step closer to home. The base at Pearl Harbor is offering a liberty package to the ships for two days and two nights in Maui, everyone in the clique jumps on the very inexpensive trip which includes meals, a shared bungalow on the beach with two bedrooms, and transportation to and from the base. Trevion looks at his budget and wonders if he should spend money on this trip. Most of his funds have been mailed home, and he's left with enough to buy the liberty package and not much else.

"Hey, Boot!" Trevion looks over as Big Boats pokes his head into Supply berthing. "Come here for a minute." Trevion walks out of the berthing and finds Big Boats standing there with a small group of people. "Boot, I mean, Trey; this is my mom and pops, and this is my baby sister, Niqua." Trevion says hello to Big Boats' family and answers a few questions about what he does on the ship. Big Boats isn't the only person with family on the ship, the Mt. Wilson offers a Return Cruise for family members of sailors on-board.

They sail with the ship from Hawaii to the home port, sleeping up in the Officers' staterooms. The cruise is rather pricey so not too many crew members take advantage of the offer. "Ok, Trey, I'm about to finish showing them around, then I'll be back to pick you up." Trevion says that *it's a pleasure to meet you* to Big Boats' family then walks back into the berthing, then stops and thinks for a moment. Why did Big

Boats say that he was coming back to pick him up? He looks over at Monster who is trying very hard to contain his laughter.

"Hey, what just happened?" Trevion asks, which sparks a roaring round of laughter from everyone there. "Big Boats got you, now you have to have dinner with him and his chubby little sister." Trevion is not amused. He runs out of the berthing to try and catch Big Boats and let him know that he's not going to join them, but he can't find them.

There are lots of civilians on the ship so walking around takes a bit of time, nothing like watching as granny tries to navigate the steep, narrow, metal stairwell for the first time. Trevion gives up and heads back to the berthing where Big Boats sits waiting for him.

Before Trevion can speak, Big Boats pulls him out into the passageway. "Look here, young fella. It's time for you to pay some dues to the clique, this may be my last shot at going to Maui. My dad is retired Navy and retired fireman, and he spends that double-pension like its fucking water. He paid for him, moms, and Neek to fly out here and ride the ship back; and he paid for the Maui trip. A room for him and moms and a room for me and Neek."

Trevion shrugs his shoulders. "What the problem is?" Big Boats threatens to slap him. "The problem is I ain't trying to be in the bungalow with my nineteen-year-old sister. Her in one room listening to me banging some skirt in the next. I already bought the package so, here's what's going to happen; I'm going to give you my packet, then when we get out there, you're going to give me the key to that room and you can crash in the bungalow with my sister." Trevion gasps and begs Big Boats to think about what he's just said. "That's your sister, bro!"

Big Boats hits Trevion in the chest. "She cute too, if you play your cards right you might get some third base action." Trevion asks what happens if he meets a girl out there and wants to bring her back to the room. Big Boats shrugs his shoulders. "Better you knocking some pussy in there than me, stop acting like a punk and go get dressed."

Trevion leans against the rail of the catamaran taking them from Honolulu to Maui, thinking about all of the ribbing that he received from the guys in Supply berthing about having to entertain 'Neek the Geek'. Looking at her, Trevion can see what she must have looked like when she was seventeen and chunky with braces and nappy hair, as the guys kept describing her.

But, now she's nineteen, slimmed down, no braces, long braids and the confidence of a popular college Junior. Trevion isn't impressed. Although he's glad that he's on the early boat over to the island, which means less time on the ship and more time on the beach, he's not at all happy about Big Boats and his parents practically throwing Niqua at him.

As the landing comes into view, Niqua walks over to Trevion. "Hey. I am so sorry about them, I'm sure you're feeling pretty uncomfortable."

Trevion smiles. "No, weird and awkward situations are what I live for." The two laugh and begin to chat. Trevion learns that the reason why her family is pushing so hard is because Niqua is bisexual, but leans more towards the ladies. "I'll make you a deal," she whispers as Big Boats walks up grinning, "if I end up bringing a girl back to the room, we can share her. But you can't touch me, deal?"

Trevion's eyes get very big, which makes Niqua burst out in laughter. "Alright, I see you two are getting along. That's good. Put your stuff away quick because we're going sight-seeing as soon as we get there. If we do this right, we can be done and headed to the beach by around 3 o'clock when they get tired and want to sleep. Are we in?"

Big Boats puts his hand out and looks at the two, who chuckle at his corniness but puts their hands in. "Do the damn thing on three, one-two-three... Do the damn thing! What happened? Fuck y'all."

Trevion and Niqua laugh hysterically as Big Boats waves them off and walks away. "Is he that corny around the guys?"

Trevion shakes his head no. "I've never seen him like this before."

Niqua gives a sigh. "I grew up with him acting like that so..."

The weather couldn't have been better for a morning of sightseeing, Big Boats made sure to take the tours which contained a fair amount of walking so as to tire out his parents. Trevion spent the entire time fielding a barrage of questions from the couple and pretending to be attracted to Niqua.

Awkwardness actually turned into amusement as he and Niqua toyed with her parents by looking as if they were getting along, then ignoring each other, then acting close again. Each shift in attitudes brought on a reaction from her parents and coaching from Big Boats.

As predicted, by 3pm the parents were looking to go to their room and lay down. As they walk towards their bungalows, Niqua thanks Trevion for being such a gentleman then gives him a big hug and a kiss on the cheek before walking into her room. Her parents also thank Trevion before heading into their bungalow, and he and Big Boats walks down the beach talking.

"I think this goes a little beyond dues, Big Boats, you may need to shoot me some cash for this one."

Big Boats laughs loudly. "What? You got further today than any kid ever has with Neek and with my folks. Hell, Neek even kissed you! I can't remember her ever liking a dude so much."

Trevion considers his next few words carefully, trying to imagine the multiple possible outcomes from what he wants to say. "I mean…" he says hesitantly.

"What?" Big Boats asks. Trevion looks over at the large, muscular sailor and wishes Monster were there to keep Big Boats from killing him.

"You do know that she's gay, right?"

Big Boats explodes, yelling at Trevion and daring him to repeat himself. "It's alright, she's still your sister. She's still in college, still has a bright future ahead of her…"

Big Boats interrupts, "But she won't be having any kids though, will she? There won't be babies popping out of that coochie if another girl is licking on it, it don't work that way, Boot!"

Big Boats explains how he's not planning on having any kids, ever in life. His sister is the one who was supposed to give his parents grandchildren. But if she's gay then it'll be up to him. Trevion tries to keep a concerned face as Big Boats pours out his emotions to him, but can't help but burst into laughter as soon as Big Boats stops talking.

"This shit ain't funny, Boot! I'm supposed to sail the seven seas for twenty-five or so years, then take a couple of years off before starting my second career; just like my dad did. Only I won't be getting married and having kids at the end of my life like him. Now he's worried that he won't ever see his grandchildren because he chose to have us so late."

Trevion tries to contain his laughter and asks why he doesn't just give them a grandchild. "Nigga please, I'm not going to be yet another statistic. Another absentee dad to point at from some ivory tower of righteousness, I'm going to enjoy my life. Neek is supposed to be dropping babies on the family, not me!"

Trevion looks at his friend, who is visibly shaken, and tries to calm him down. "Look, she told me that she was bisexual. That she likes boys and girls so, you actually still have a shot here. But you can't tell her that I told you that, alright? Just be cool, and love her regardless of what she decides."

Big Boats looks over at Trevion for a moment, then cracks a big smile "She likes you, don't she? That's why she told you she liked boys too!" This isn't exactly true, but Trevion will take it as an exit from this extremely uncomfortable conversation.

Big Boats hugs Trevion so hard that he can't breathe. "You might end up being my brother-in-law, Boot! Welcome to the fambam!"

11. Island Girls Forever

One more night in Hawaii and the USS Mt. Wilson will be returning to its home port. The guys all sit on the mess decks eating breakfast and discussing their final port visit of the war. They all want to go back to their favorite bar to shoot pool and throw darts.

Moorish and Suave keep taking shots at Trevion for having to babysit Niqua for Big Boats; until she shows up at the table with her tray of food. "Where can I sit, Peanut?" she asks, prompting Big Boats to make Franky vacate the seat next to Trevion. Both of the 4-man tables that the guys occupy are silent as they look at the suddenly sexy little sister.

"Hey, Moe," she says to Moorish who fumbles out a reply. Big Boats looks over at Niqua and asks what she and Trevion have planned for the evening, which makes Trevion kick him under the table. Big Boats looks at Trevion and says, "Steel toes, mothafucka!"

Niqua giggles then says, "Mom and Dad want to go to this luau that Trey told them about, so we're going to go shopping and then do that.

Trey has been nice for long enough; he deserves a night out with his boys. He's going to have to put up with me from here to California anyway."

She and Trevion go back and forth with mild insults and threats of boxing matches, then Franky says, "So, you're telling me that I'm the only one who heard her call this guy Peanut?" The group gives a collective cringe as Big Boats stops laughing at Trevion and Niqua's bickering and focuses on Franky. Franky looks around at everyone, Moorish is shaking his head NO at him with a horrified look on his face.

"Family thing, I get it, my bad. I never said it, will never say it again," Franky says as he nervously finishes his breakfast.

Big Boats looks over at Trevion who is looking away and trying not to laugh. "What the hell is so funny, Boot?"

Trevion looks over at him, "That big-ass vein in your forehead makes you look like a Klingon." Big Boats tries unsuccessfully to contain his own laughter and everyone laughs the incident off.

That night, the clique all take turns giving sometimes funny and sometimes heavy and heartfelt toasts as they hang out at the bar; vowing to stay there until the bar kicks everyone out when it closes at 5am. The guys are playing cards and invite Trevion to join in. As they play, Suave looks over at Big Boats and Moorish and gives a wink. "I got a bet for you, Boot. If I win this hand, you have to go and give the bar owner a great big kiss." Trevion looks behind the bar and sees the 70ish bar owner, nicknamed Mamma, taking orders.

She's very round and very wrinkled with a grizzled voice and is chain smoking behind the bar. "But, if anyone aside from me wins this hand, I'll hand over this beautiful gold necklace around my neck; anchor medallion and all. Is it a bet?" Trevion looks at his hand then over at Moorish who gives him a yes nod.

"We can do that, it's a bet." Trevion was unaware that when he turned back to look at the bar owner, the guys swapped cards behind his back. Trevion puts his cards down, full house. Suave puts down a straight flush then demands that Trevion goes and fulfills his bet.

The guys begin chanting 'Boot! Boot! Boot!' Trevion takes another look at the bar owner then takes another shot of whiskey.

"Fuck you guys!" he says as he walks over to the bar. The guys watch as he explains to the bar owner the terms of the bet and that he owes her a big kiss. Mamma laughs and goes through a door behind the bar. "Maybe she went to brush her teeth!" Fernandez yells, bringing everyone to laughter.

Mamma comes back through the door followed by a stunning Hawaiian woman who jumps over the bar and gives Trevion a passionate kiss. The two chat for a short while then Trevion returns. "The fuck was that horse shit?" Suave asks as Trevion takes his seat.

"Mamma doesn't own the bar, her granddaughter does." The waitress begins bringing Trevion free beer, then free food; much to the chagrin of Suave and the guys. The bar owner returns and says that she's done with all of her paperwork and invites Trevion to go upstairs with her to play video games.

The next morning, the guys are shooting pool and swapping stories when Trevion comes walking in from the back with the female bar owner. He's shocked to see the guys still there. "Hey guys!?!?" They all respond with Boooot!

Trevion looks at his watch, "You guys do know that it's like, 0630, right? Last boat back to the ship leaves at 0700." The guys all freeze in their spots with looks of shock and horror on their faces.

Big Boats looks at his watch. "I thought this place closes at five?" Trevion looks at the bar owner who says that she let them stay since they were with him.

Big Boats drops his beer "Oh shit!! Fuck me!!" They all run out and begin sprinting through the streets towards the landing, which is about mile and a half away. Big Boats is in front, then veers over to the side to throw up.

Monster yells "Man Down!" but Fernandez says, "Fuck that, I'm not stopping!" But five steps later he veers to the side to throw up as well. One by one they all take pit stops to empty their stomachs as they dash through the street.

When they finally reach the landing, they're all sweaty and out of breath. They see Trevion there, leaning against a motorcycle and making out with the sexy bar owner. *All aboard!* The guys stumble onto the small ferry and collapse into their seats, Trevion gives a final kiss to the bar owner before climbing aboard.

"Suave, I gotta thank you, man. I think she was the hottest girl that I've ever been with and you set the whole thing up." Trevion holds out his hand to give Suave five, but Suave slaps his hand down.

"You can keep that five, Boot!" he says, still trying to catch his breath. "Oh, and by the way, fuck you."

Trevion laughs, "No thanks, she took care of that for me last night. And, once again this morning."

Chapter Six

1. Davy's Boys

The ship is scheduled to set sail at 1500 hours, one hour before Trevion is finished with the Rover watch. Him standing the 12 to 16 watch didn't go over too well with the other SKs since it left them one man down when last-minute supplies arrived on the pier. Trevion knows that he'll have to pay for that somehow once he gets down to GSK, but he's happy that when the supplies showed up at 10, he only had to help for just under two hours because he needed to relieve the watch at 1145.

The engines have been vibrating the ship since earlier and the civilian friends and family members are all excited to steam back to the Home Port aboard a real Navy ship, some are already wearing the pussy patch behind their ears. By the time Trevion's watch is over and he heads down to GSK, the place is a mess with boxes stacked everywhere. Rolling up his sleeves, Trevion jumps in and begins helping the SKs with the supplies.

He ignores the passive-aggressive comments that are being tossed around about him not being there to help bring all of the boxes down to the warehouse and keeps Middleton from chiming in on his behalf. Before they can get a real rhythm going, Trevion and the others hear an announcement over the 1-MC; *SKSN Carson, report to the Executive Office*. Everyone stops and looks at Trevion, SK2 yells, "Move your ass,

Boot Camp! And hurry back, we have a lot of work to do." Trevion runs out of GSK and to Supply berthing to change out of the dusty coveralls that he was wearing, then hustles up to the Executive Office.

When he gets there, he sees the XO standing in front of the office talking to a civilian. "Carson!" the XO calls out. "I'd like you to meet someone. This is retired Admiral John Byrd; sir, this is Seaman Carson." Trevion shakes the man's hand and the three quickly walk into the XO's office, closing the door behind them.

"So, this is the new prospect?" the retired officer asks. "Recommended by Francois and seconded by Dan himself; Color Company in boot camp, top 2% of his class in A-School, got a wartime name buzz on the circuit and is already a trusty Shellback; how old are you, son?" When Trevion says that he's only nineteen, the man looks over at the XO then both men burst into laughter.

"Well, looks like the only thing that you need now is to stop whoring around and get yourself a steady girl. But, until then, I'm here with an extension of the Limited Duty Officer, or LDO program. My team is here to give three men an exam tomorrow as part of their petition to be selected as LDOs, but I'm here to administer a test to you to see if you qualify for the Officer Candidate School. I understand that you've actually picked up a few college credits during the summer in high school, correct?"

Trevion is shocked to hear this man mention the summer courses that he took in order to not work at his dad's store, but nods his head yes at the question. "Well, it's not enough to qualify for the program; unless, of course, you take and pass an assessment exam given by a certified member of the Board of Directors which, coincidentally, I just so happen to be. So, you have one night to study; take this." He hands Trevion a very thick binder. "At 0900 meet in the Chief Petty Officers' Lounge for the exam, any questions?"

Trevion nods his head "Who is Francois?"

The XO says, "He would be, The Honorable Judge Francois Boudreaux. He's also one of Davy Jones' Boys." Trevion looks at the book then promises to study hard tonight, opening the book and reading from it as he exits the XO's office. Once he had went down two levels, he closes the book and looks around. His heart is beating quickly and his thoughts are dominated by the suddenness of this exam and the sheer breadth of this secret organization that he's being recruited into.

Judge Boudreaux? He's the judge that allowed Trevion to come to the military rather than stand trial with the others who were in the courtroom. John said that he was the one who nominated him and Dan only seconded the nomination. Trevion thinks back to the day he walked into the bungalow in Hawaii with the morning McDonald's order; he was the only one who raised his hand when asked who had a license, and the sailor already knew Trevion's name after it happened. That whole thing felt like a setup then but makes a bit more sense now. He isn't sure that he wants to be a part of this, but these guys seem to know more about him than he knows about himself.

Trevion begins making his way back to GSK. He stops in Supply berthing to put the book in his locker and slide back into his coveralls before walking down to finish working. He no longer needs to ignore the comments that are coming from his coworkers because they're simply going over his head now. All he can think about are the moments between the court date and today, wondering how many of those moments were due to Davy's Boys invisible assistance.

The rest of the day was like a blur as he and the SKs worked on the supplies until well after 1800 hours. Trevion takes a quick shower then lays in his rack reading the book given to him by the retired officer. He skims through the book quickly in order to get a feel for the exam, putting makeshift bookmarks on whichever areas were not his strong suit.

"Yo, what's up Trey? You looking up at Big Boats' little sis or what?" Trevion opens his rack curtains to look across at Stafford "No, but I do have one of the owner of the Coconut Cup."

Stafford lets out a disgusted, "Eww, blood! The hell you got her picture up there for?"

Trevion laughs as he pulls down the picture and hands it over. Stafford looks at the photo of the bar owner laying naked atop Trevion. "The bartender is the owner's grandma. She took that picture with her camera so, I only got to keep two of them; that one and a wilder one."

Stafford hands the picture back "Wilder than that?"

Trevion puts the picture back in its place amongst his growing collection then, in a low voice, tells Stafford about the surprise exam happening in the morning and how he's not sure if he's going to go through with the exam or just go and give them their book back and say no thanks, so he's studying just in case.

"Why you?" Stafford asks. Trevion makes up a story about applying for the test back at the recruiter's office before he even went to boot camp. He wants to tell Stafford everything, he wants to tell someone everything so that he can at least hear the words aloud and analyze the situation on a deeper level. He was hoping to tell everything to his dad once the ship returned to its home port, but his dad has a gun show to go to.

The store makes just enough money to pay for itself but the gun shows are where Trevion's dad makes the majority of his income. Trevion knows that, so he's not hurt that his dad can't cancel. His mother, on the other hand, should drop everything in order to be on the pier waving at Trevion as he pulls into port; at least, in his opinion she should. Stafford buys the story and agrees that Trevion should be studying instead of shooting the shit with him. "Get your head in that book, boy. Get some bars on those collars so I can have a powerful connect."

2. No Escape

Trevion didn't fall asleep until after midnight, the book was full of leadership questions that he kept getting the wrong answers for. According to this book, the leader always makes the hard-line choice while Trevion tends to choose the compromise option. He decides to mentally begin each leadership question with the words 'If you were an asshole dictator...' so that he'd make the rigid decision. Sadly, this worked, and he picked the correct answer every time. He went over every leadership question in the book trying to prove the theory wrong, which is why he went to sleep so late.

He does his normal morning routine then eats breakfast with the guys as usual. He and Monster chat as they make their way to Quarters, but as soon as Suppo sees Trevion he yells, "Carson! What... the... hell are you doing here? Get your ass upstairs and get ready, now!"

Everyone looks back at Trevion, "Yes, sir" he says as he turns around and heads to the berthing area to grab his book then back upstairs to the CPO's Lounge where the tests are being given. Trevion sees two Chiefs and the ship's Boatswain, who is a Chief Warrant Officer, waiting in the hallway.

"Hey, Carson," LT Cruz yells from across the passageway. "San Diego State has a great program, not trying to pull you to my alma mater or anything like that; I'm just saying." Trevion gives him a nervous smile and a thumbs up, to which LT Cruz motions for him to walk over. He tells Trevion not to worry "You uttered a complete walk-through when I gave you the Rover exam. Hell, you answered all of my follow-up questions before I could even ask them. Do your best, that will be more than enough. That's an order." Trevion salutes the Lieutenant then walks back over to the now four-man line.

"You must be taking a different test," the Boatswain says to Trevion who affirms his guess. John walks out with two uniformed officers who instruct the four to take seats in the area that they've prepared. They direct Trevion to the back, separate from the others.

"Good morning, gentlemen, my name is John and I'm a retired Admiral working for the United States Department of Defense in the Navy Examination and Certification Division. Today, you will be taking a competency exam with the exception of Seaman Carson back there who will be taking an entry exam. This test has a ninety-minute time limit; except for Carson who will be taking a six-part test starting with a ninety-minute section."

Trevion's heart begins beating quickly as he takes in what John just said about the exam he'll be taking. "Do you three gentlemen have your binders?" The two chiefs and the Boatswain say yes and pull out their blue binders. "And Carson, do you have your DJ-7C?" Trevion holds up the binder that John had given him yesterday. "Good, because this will be an open-book exam, but only open to those binders. No other materials are allowed. This young lady and her able partner will be your proctors, please follow their instructions."

Trevion listens to the two LTJGs as they explain the test and the rules. The exam begins and Trevion opens his test packet to the first question; and immediately begins sweating. The first question of the exam is the first example in his binder, word for word. He looks at the next question in the exam and it's the same thing. Trevion looks up at John, who is staring hard back at him. If Trevion hadn't realized it before, now he's absolutely certain that he's been on a carefully laid out path that began as early as Hawaii, perhaps even A-School or as far back as boot camp.

"Not to add any pressure to any of you," John suddenly says, "but you would want to do your very best on this exam; aim for perfection. Remember, you're not the only ones in the Navy taking these tests, but you want to be the best in the Navy taking these tests." Trevion turns back to the first question and begins.

In the Cook's office, Suppo meets with SKC regarding the influx of new sailors who will be coming aboard soon as well as the high number of sailors leaving the ship which will include the both of them. Suppo was able to take enough credit for Trevion's performance to warrant a transfer to Pac Fleet while SKC is simply at the end of this tour and has received his next orders. They'll both have around two more weeks aboard the ship and are meeting to discuss the turnover.

Stafford overhears their conversation then hurries down to GSK to tell Trevion. When he gets there, Monster reminds him about the exam. "Damn, that was this morning! He's still up there?"

Monster nods his head. "Yeah, he didn't even come down for lunch. Why, what's up?" Stafford looks around at the other SKs then leans in to whisper to Monster.

Monster isn't pleased with the news about SKC but can't wait for Suppo to leave. SK2 suddenly yells, "It's about time, Boot Camp! Did they have to hold your hand while you took the test or what?" Trevion walks in and gives SK2 a thumbs-up, then walks back to his desk with Stafford and Monster following him. They fill him in on what Suppo and SKC were discussing.

Trevion sighs, "That's not all. SK1 is leaving too, which would make SK2 in charge down here until the new chief shows up."

Monster's eyes grow wide "What? How do you know that?"

"I just do, it's going to be stupid here in GSK for at least a few months until the new chief gets here; the new Suppo will be here next week when we pull in, but the new chief is going to take a while because they're still interviewing candidates." Stafford looks over at Trevion and asks how the test went. "It was a super-long exam but that book helped a lot, glad I studied."

SKC returns to GSK and Stafford slips out. SKC calls everyone together and gives his instructions for the return-to-port coming up in a few days, informing everyone that they're required to wear their dress white uniforms and stand in a pre-assigned area as the ship pulls in. There will be family members and loved ones on the pier waiting for them and that as soon as liberty is called, everyone not on duty can leave the ship.

SKC advises everyone to get their uniforms out and take them to the SHs as soon as possible because the rest of the ship's crew will be doing the same. He ends the meeting by telling SK2 that he will begin training on the OPTAR, which is the budget, due to him and SK1 receiving their orders.

Monster looks over at Trevion with a sad expression on his face at that announcement. As they return to work, Trevion returns to his desk and begins going through his mail which Middleton had collected and distributed while he was testing. He opens a letter from the Department of the Navy, telling him that his application was accepted and detailing the amount that the grant will pay per semester. Trevion looks at the envelop and notices the post date was weeks ago.

How can this be when he just took the entry exam, literally minutes ago? He puts the letter to the side and continues opening mail, a letter from San Diego State University saying something about his sponsorship status. "What the hell is going on?" he asks himself aloud. He puts that letter with the one from the Department of the Navy then and finally gets to a letter from his mother.

My beautiful son, Sorry for the short letter but your father is watching me write this and wants me to make it quick. He says 'hi'. Your father and I have taken care of everything and your room will be waiting for you once you come home. I will be with your grandmother and your father will be out of town working at a show, we'll both be back that Saturday so you'll have the house to yourself for two days. Your father says that your money orders are in his safe but he left you some cash behind the picture of your honey. See you soon! Love, Mom and Dad.

Trevion laughs, "Behind my honey!" When Trevion put the picture of Diwata in his room, his dad called her a *Full-Blown Honey Dip*, so he must have put some cash inside of the picture frame. "I love those guys." He says with a sigh, then looks over at the two frightening envelops to his right. Davy's Boys seem to wield quite a bit of influence, and not just in the Navy. LT Cruz suggested SD State this morning and suddenly an envelope from SD State shows up.

College entry exam this morning and now a letter saying that a grant has been approved; a grant that Trevion hadn't even applied for. It isn't that they're giving Trevion the option to do this, they seem to be doing it for him. He wasn't given a book to study; he was given the actual exam book. Only, it was the teacher's edition with all the correct answers. There is no way that he's not going to Officer Candidate School at SD State. "Damn, am I really up to this?"

3.   Headed Home

In the days leading up to the return of the USS Mt. Wilson, the ship's crew has been suffering from Channel Fever and the anticipation has everyone working together and getting along. SK2, however, has been even more of a tool towards Trevion. SK2 is feeling the power that he's about to wield, and it has already gone to his head; he walks around GSK with a smirk and finds any reason to visit Trevion in the back of the storeroom to pick at him. But SK2 is the least of Trevion's worries, number one on his stress list is the invisible hand of Davy Jones' Boys and the apparent ease in which they exercise their will.

Trevion studied the Officer Candidate School up in the secret library and read that it takes up to a year for a candidate to be accepted into the program after taking the entry exam, but Trevion already has letters confirming sponsorships and grants; how? The only positive about all of this is that he won't be around when SK2 takes over GSK with no SKC, no SK1, and reporting to a new Suppo.

Trevion thinks about all of this as he sits in the Armory waiting for the final Security Squad meeting before returning home to begin. He suddenly notices something, one of the Squad members has a small tattoo on the inside of his right ring finger. Trevion tries to get a good look at it without raising suspicions, but notices that another guy has one too. It's a small, blue anchor just below the second joint between the ring finger and pinky.

LT Cruz begins the meeting and Trevion notices that he has one of the anchor tattoos as well, so does the XO. Looking around, Trevion counts six of the twenty men in the room who have the tattoo. He assumes that the ones without one, himself included, are either not one of Davy's Boys or are still under consideration.

The XO wraps the meeting up by thanking everyone for a stellar job and reminding the Squad that they have Priority Leave status, which means that their leave will be approved regardless of the needs of their departments. Trevion has already taken advantage of that privilege by beginning his leave the day after the ship pulls in; which is one of the reasons why SK2 is picking on him so much.

After the meeting, Trevion chats with LT Cruz about the upcoming trip to Canada when the XO walks up, "Carson, I saw you looking around during the meeting. Anything you'd like to ask me?"

Trevion's body gets weak, but he puts on a confident face then looks around to see who is within earshot. "Just noticed some interesting body art, sir. I've never considered getting any myself, but I've seen a few interesting designs recently."

The XO smiles and looks at LT Cruz, "This guy just keeps pushing forward, doesn't he?" He pats Trevion on his shoulder then walks away saying, "All in due time, Carson, all in due time."

LT Cruz nods at Trevion then walks out as well, as do the rest of the sailors until only Martin and Trevion are left. "Guys, I need to lock up so shove off." They give fist-bumps to the Gunner's Mate in charge of the space as they head up to Supply berthing where the finals of a Spades tournament is at its conclusion. The berthing area is crowded with spectators as Monster and Big Boats take on a team from Engineering.

It's not looking good for the guys as the Engineering team is close to reaching their goal. One final hand and it will be over. The cards are shuffled and dealt by one of the engineers and the two teams call out their books. "How many are you looking at over there, Boats?"

Big Boats looks carefully at his hand, "I swear I see six and a possible!"

Monster's eyes get big, "If you're for real, we can run this right now! Call it!" Big Boats looks at his hand again and bids twelve books. The Engineering team bids set, or the bare minimum amount of books.

The game begins and the crowd cheers as the Engineering team begins losing every book. When each player only has four cards left in their hands, Big Boats lays his cards down face-up. "That's game, y'all!!" The berthing erupts with cheers and applause. The Engineering team collects their second place prize and heads out as Monster and Big Boats fan out their prize money and wave it at their faces.

"Nothing cools you down like cold hard cash!" Monster says as he smells the money in his hands.

The berthing begins to empty and the clique talks and compares leave periods to see when they'll all be together again. The last guys going on leave won't be back to the ship for at least eight weeks. "Cool, just in time for Canada." Martin says.

Everyone stops and looks over at him, Trevion closes his eyes and shakes his head. "Canada? What about Canada?" Martin realizes that he wasn't supposed to tell anyone about the upcoming trip up to Victoria where, along the way, the Mt. Wilson will be UnReping with several ships.

"Guys, I'm trusting you with this. We might be going to Canada in two months, but it's not for sure yet. Please, please don't leak that out, ok?" The guys all agree to keep it under wraps but Trevion knows that simply won't happen. Martin makes up an excuse and bolts out of the berthing, the guys begin to discuss Canada but Trevion quickly changes the subject back to the come-from-behind victory that just happened. Big Boats begins giving a play-by-play of his and Monster's win, and everyone forgets about Canada, for the moment.

4. Let There Be Enlightenment

Trevion maintains a cool confidence and matches his shipmates' enthusiasm over finally going home, but on the inside, he's a total mess of paranoia and mistrust. Everyone seems as if they could be a spy for Davy's Boys, which makes him guard every word that escapes his lips. SK2 and his ever-growing power boner are a secondary concern to Trevion as he tries to figure out how he can jump from this fast-moving train if he needs to. Channel Fever doesn't even begin to describe the night before pulling in as almost no one can sleep.

Trevion lays in his rack looking up at the blank, gray bottom of the middle rack where his collection of pictures used to hang. All that's left is the slight residue from the tape. Trevion looks up and can remember the XO's voice ordering him to "Police your rack, Carson. As impressive as it may be, I need that situation of yours squared away before we pull in!" All of the pictures were taken down and are now in an envelope hidden in Trevion's desk down in GSK. In the morning, the ship pulls in and there will be mail delivered to the ship; Trevion is very interested in any additional mail that would explain what's going on.

"Psst!" Stafford is trying to get Trevion's attention.

"What's up?" Trevion whispers as he pulls his rack curtains open to reveal his face.

"So, I can't sleep and you can't sleep. There's some sleeping aide down in the refer leftover from Bahrain." The two grab Monster and Fernandez then head down to the cold storage area where the bottle of Hennessey has been hidden. The four friends take shots of the expensive cognac and talk about all of the free meals and discounts that they're about to enjoy as the first war veterans that the United States has had in a while. They stumble back to Supply berthing just before midnight and have no trouble falling asleep.

Three tugboats come out to meet the USS Mt. Wilson as it makes it's slow approach to the naval base. The crew is already in their dress white uniforms and are falling into their predetermined positions along the port side of the ship. Flags are flying and the ship sounds its horn as it is taxied to pier, where a crowd of people wave and cheer their homecoming heroes.

There is a military band on the pier playing God Bless America which makes the whole thing seem so surreal to Trevion as the ship gets close enough to see the faces of the cheering loved ones. Stafford is standing next to Trevion and is joking about the wives who may be four months pregnant even though the ship has been gone for six months.

The two crack jokes for a while until Trevion suddenly stops laughing, "No way, that guy looks just like…" Trevion squints his eyes and focuses.

"Looks just like who?" Stafford asks.

Trevion suddenly starts smiling, "It is him, that's my dad right there! Look to the left of the band, he's standing right next to that…" Trevion's heart begins beating very fast and sweat begins peeking from his pores.

"Right next to that what? Damn, blood, finish a fucking sentence!" Trevion focuses on the young lady standing next to his dad; then she sees him and begins pointing while frantically tapping his dad's arm. His dad holds up a fist, something that he used to do from the bleachers during Trevion's high school basketball days. Trevion holds up a fist and the young woman begins jumping up and down.

"How is that even possible?" Trevion says aloud.

"How is what possible? What's going on? Who's down there?" Stafford's questions fall on deaf ears as Trevion is transfixed on a brightly smiling Diwata standing next to his father on the pier. Every muscle in his body does a hard twitch as the XO slaps him on the shoulder.

"Carson, reporters from the USO and the Pac Fleet Newsletter are on the pier and they need to interview you so, smile real big because they're taking pictures of you right now since I've just pointed you out. After this, I need you to head up to the War Room, so we can brief you before they come aboard."

The XO motions to a specific point on the pier, Trevion can see the cameraman pointing at him then follows the XO's lead and begins to wave. When the XO walks away, Stafford asks Trevion what that was all about. Trevion reminds him of the Canadian officer, "I guess that was a big enough deal to where they want to brag about it or something."

"Oh, they taking pictures?" Suave says from the other side of Trevion, then adjusts his hat, licks his fingertips to smooth his eyebrows and mustache then begins to pose. Trevion looks down at the pier and still can't believe Diwata is there with his dad.

The ship finishes its docking routine and the Quarterdeck is established. Trevion stands in the War Room hoping that this will be very brief so that he can see... "Diwata?" The beautiful young woman walks in with Trevion's dad, then runs into Trevion's arms, and the two hug very tightly. Before he can ask any questions, she showers him with kisses which are caught by the photographers in the room.

The XO is calling for Trevion to come over and sit in the area that has been prepared for the interview. "Sir, with respect, may I please have five minutes with my father and my sweetheart? I just need to talk to them very briefly."

The XO chuckles, "You have three minutes, make them count."

The three walk over to the other side of the room, Trevion hugs his dad then asks, "I thought you had a show today; how is she here with you; where's Mom?"

Trevion's dad laughs, "Here's the skinny, son; I flat-out lied about the show so that I could surprise you today, the show starts day after tomorrow and it's out here in the Bay Area. Also, you know that I go through any paperwork that shows up for you, especially once you went to war. Dee applied for sponsorship while she works on getting her citizenship; and since it's my house and I'd need to fill most of it out anyway, I went ahead and submitted all of the forms. It pretty much crushed your savings but, I figured you'd approve of the move. And your mother is with your grandmother, she was the only one telling the truth."

Trevion looks over at Diwata who still has tears in her eyes. "So, you've been living with my parents?" She says yes, on the weekends. With the sponsorship, she was able to transfer to SD State and live on campus during the week.

A rush comes over Trevion as he suddenly feels very foolish. "Oh, sponsorship, school grants, San Diego State; right, right! Ok, I get it now."

The interview was long and involved several crew members. Diwata was described as Trevion's *Soulmate who is currently attending SD State's Nursing Program.* Half of the questions that the interviewer asked Trevion were about the war and his outstanding duty, while the other half were about his plans with Diwata whose smile and energy stole the spotlight. She tells the story of how Trevion paid for her to finish school back home and how her outstanding grades earned her the opportunity to transfer to the top-rated nursing academy at SD State. The interviewers eat it all up and spend lots of time on the fairy tale couple.

When it's over, the ship's Captain comes over and introduces himself to Trevion's dad then says, "I know that your leave begins tomorrow, Carson, but I'm granting you seventy-two hours for making us look good just now. Take twenty-four right now then put the rest on the tail-end of your leave; you've earned it." The Captain salutes Trevion who pops to attention and returns the salute. He quickly runs down to Supply berthing to grab his already-packed bags; never bothering to change out of his white uniform. He wants to leave the ship as quickly as possible.

The XO is standing on the Quarterdeck when Trevion arrives, he pulls him to the side. "Carson, Davy Jones himself must be smiling on you. The Boys all chipped in to help with your engagement ring." He hands Trevion an envelope filled with cash. "I'm not supposed to flat-out tell you this but, you getting engaged is the final requirement. Once you put a ring on that girl's finger you'll qualify for the initiation. You have the ship's main phone number; the moment she's wearing a ring, you give my office a call to let me know; am I understood?"

Trevion closes the envelop and stuffs it into his pocket. "You are understood, sir. And please pass on my undying gratitude." The XO pats Trevion on the shoulder then stands back for a salute.

As they drive off of the base, Trevion's dad asks, "So, tell me Son, how were you sending home so much money and so many expensive things? I mean, don't get me wrong, I love everything that you pushed at me, but I know what your salary is and the math is way off."

Trevion explains slushing to his dad, then mentions the little crew that he ran for a few months. "But I got word that they were about to start cracking all the slushers so we got out while the getting was good. I still have my connections but, better safe than sorry, right?"

His dad smiles and says, "Damn right, that's my boy." Suspiciously quiet in the back seat was Diwata, who somehow looks even more beautiful than Trevion remembers.

"Dad, can we stop and eat before we get to the hotel?" They pull into a small diner. Trevion asks his dad to get their table while he speaks to Diwata. "Why didn't you write and tell me any of this? We went back to the Philippines twice and I couldn't find you anywhere." Diwata grabs and kisses him, telling him that she thought that he wouldn't pay the fee to bring her to the U.S.

"I returned to school and realized that I only had one course remaining for my degree. For me to go to America would cost so much money, but my school had a sponsorship program if you knew anyone living in America. I only knew you. After two months of hearing nothing, I thought that you didn't want me anymore. Then my packet arrived, it had plane tickets and food coupons for my trip. Your mother picked me up from the airport, I love her so much. I wanted to speak to you when you called home but your father always said no, that you were busy with war and shouldn't be thinking of these things."

Trevion looks into her eyes and sees something that he's never noticed in any other woman; love. Not desire or excitement, but this woman looking at him actually loves him. His mind goes back to the various flings that he's had over the past few months and he feels a bit guilty "I really wish you would have, like, wrote me or something because... I went out on a few dates while I was gone."

Diwata just smiles. "You're a sailor but you're a good man, I know that if I told you to be true to me then you would have. But I didn't." Trevion holds her very tightly and gives her a sweet kiss.

"Plenty of time for all of that, come and eat!" his dad yells from the diner door.

Trevion spends the rest of the day and half of the next playing tour guide to his father and Diwata, showing them around the Bay Area, then he and Diwata take the train down to Beach City. His dad asks him why he didn't take the quicker and less expensive bus, Trevion smiles at his father and says, "Because we will be on a romantic train ride rather than a stinky, crowded bus."

His father laughs and mentions, "You know, you don't need to do anything to impress that one. Money saved now can be spent later."
Trevion bursts into laughter and asks how such a beautiful woman like his mother could have fallen for such a tightwad. "I can think of a few reasons..."

Trevion stops him, "No, eww, not trying to hear that! I'll call Mom when we get home. And, thank you, Dad! I really do appreciate what you do for me, I see your fingerprints on everything that I achieve."

As Trevion hugs his dad, he says, "More than you know, Son." Trevion and Diwata board the train. His father quickly leaves the station so that he doesn't show how deeply his son's words had moved him, all the way to tears.

5.   Cheaper to Keep Her

Two days alone with Diwata was like a honeymoon for Trevion. Going around to all of his old hangouts and showing her off, taking her to Hollywood so that she could see all of the things that she's heard about, and going to hot spots to take her dancing. They talked and talked, revealing deep thoughts and inner secrets about one another that neither had ever shared before. Trevion learns that Diwata, who now wants to be called the more American-sounding 'Dee', was indeed the product of her mother's encounter with an African-American sailor. Her father had sent a bit of money to her for years, but eventually stopped.

Her mother saved the money and used it to pay for Dee's schooling, but when it finally ran out it forced Dee to drop out and either return home to inescapable poverty or try to get a job that pays enough to live on. "I was at disaster's door!" she keeps reminding him, I prayed and prayed for you to help me and sponsor my trip here. God answered my prayers and brought me here; then brought you home from war safe."

By the time his parents return, Trevion is completely in love with Dee and asks his father for advice. The two go ring shopping and Trevion listens to his father's wisdom as he explains how he's kept the family together through the good and bad times. "And it was all worth it," he says as he grabs Trevion's shoulder. "I look at you and see a young man with options, good options. You've been an overachiever your whole life; and even when you're reluctant to do what I need you to do, you still get it done. Your girl is a sweetheart. My house has never been cleaner than since she moved in. Hell, your mother has someone to talk to that's not me and the food tastes even better; on the weekends, anyway."

Trevion uses most of the gifted money to buy the wedding set and the rest to rent a car so that he can drive Dee back to school and himself back to Vallejo. He takes his family to dinner at his mother's favorite seafood restaurant; one that they've been going to since he was in elementary school, but he is a nervous wreck the entire time. His father keeps giving him reassuring looks as he tries to keep a confident expression on his face. The waiter brings over a bottle of champagne, which is the cue for Trevion to pop the question.

He looks over at Dee, who is laughing with his mother, and imagines her saying no. She does nothing but express her love and appreciation, but the thought that she's just using him keeps entering his mind; which was implanted by the clique. The waiter pours the champagne then walks away; Trevion's dad is staring at him with raised eyebrows. With a deep breath, Trevion clears his throat "Diwata, I know that we've not been together for very long and we're both really young but..."

Trevion stands and then kneels in front of Diwata's seat, pulling out the ring. Before he can ask the question, Dee squeals and exclaims, "Yes! The answer is yes! Oh my God, yes!" Trevion stands and puts the ring on her finger and the entire restaurant begins cheering. The ride home consisted of Trevion and Dee kissing in the back seat and Trevion's parents making plans in the front. With Dee's parents across the ocean, everything will fall on them to throw the wedding.

Trevion's mom wouldn't have it any other way. She's already

planning on whom from her church she's going to call to help her with the arrangements. "Mom, we just got engaged. Let us enjoy being engaged for a while, ok?" Trevion's father gives an 'Amen' to that request which earns him a slap on the arm.

"You are my only baby, you went to the Navy and came home a man; and you found yourself a good, respectful woman. This wedding is the last thing that I'll be able to do for my baby and neither you nor your smart-ass dad is going to take this from me. Ain't that right, Dee?"

"Yes, momma," Dee answers, then before Trevion can say anything, Dee grabs his face and kisses him.

6.   Property of Davy Jones

Early the next morning, Trevion drives Dee back to school then takes the long trek from Southern to Northern California; arriving at the rental car drop-off point at close to midnight. When he finally gets to the ship's Quarterdeck he's exhausted. LTJG Brown is standing the OOD watch. "Carson! Welcome back son, and congrats!" Trevion salutes and says thanks, then walks down to Supply berthing to jump into his rack. He lies in bed thinking about Mr. Brown's comment and realizes that the Davy's Boys all must know about his engagement because of the call that he gave to the XO. He thinks about how cool it was for them to take up a collection to help pay for the rings as he drifts off to sleep.

Roughly two hours later, he's awakened and pulled out of the berthing by masked men. A hood is put over his head and his hands are tied. "Davy Jones requires your presence" is whispered into his ear. They lead him a few feet then make him lay on a mat on the floor, but he quickly realizes that the mat is actually a body bag as he's zipped into it.

Trevion feels himself being carried up flights of stairs and then down the gangplank before being loaded into a vehicle. "I advise you to grab some shut-eye!" he hears, followed by laughter. Falling asleep won't be too difficult, Trevion was trying hard to stay awake during his transport off of the ship so, sleep comes quickly.

"Let's get these corpses to their watery grave!" The loud exclamation jars Trevion from a deep sleep. He can hear what sounds like other body bags being slid out of the van, then feels his own bag being pulled out then carried. After a short walk, he's dropped to the ground. The bag is unzipped and a sailor dressed in a weird uniform unties Trevion's hands and instructs him to stand in the forming line.

There are seven others who emerged from the body bags like Trevion and thirty others standing around them. Trevion looks around and wonders how long did he sleep; it's daylight and they're all in the middle of a wooded area. Everyone is dressed like pirates, some in colonial sailor outfits, and they are standing around the eight kidnapped men in what appears to Trevion to be specific places and with a certain number of men in each group. Trevion recognizes the XO standing to the side wearing a white British Navy uniform, complete with a frilly taco-hat.

A boatswain whistle is blown and they all stand at attention. "All hands come to order! From the grimy and vile surface come these filth-covered sailors whom the Most Exalted Davy Jones has deemed worthy to dwell amongst us and share in the gifts of King Neptune. As with any gift, it can be refused. You may choose now to refuse the initiation, return to your body bag and re-enter the surface world with the rest of the land lovers. If you decide, instead, to become one of Davy Jones' Boys, then you must remove those putrid clothes and stand on the plank!"

Trevion looks to where the man was pointing, a long, wooden board supported by two-foot metal crates. Trevion thinks to himself

So, these guys want me to strip naked and stand on a board with these other naked guys. Or, I can lay back down in that body bag and avoid whatever homoerotic initiation these kooks have dreamed up. I think I'm going to tell them 'No thanks' and go lay my ass down in that bag! He looks down at his naked body in disappointment then begins walking towards the 'plank'. As he climbs up on to the plank, he begs his penis to stay asleep.

"Hear this, you still have the stink of land on you so, before you are allowed to walk the plank and jump into the deep blue sea you must be cleansed. Before you jump, you are to say these words; 'I renounce the land and all that creepeth upon it! I give myself to Neptune and I serve the Most Exalted Davy Jones!" Now, repeat what I just said until you have it memorized."

Trevion and the others begin reciting the two sentences but are being heckled by everyone present. They're saying alternate versions of the sentences, changing some of the words or just yelling random insults; all in an attempt to prevent the sailors from saying it correctly. Trevion can hear that, as a group, they've distorted the original statement so he raises his voice and recites it correctly.

The others follow his lead and after a few times of saying it correctly a boatswain's pipe is heard. "Left Face!" the guys all turn to their left, making Trevion first in line. He's instructed to walk to the end of the plank and recite the statement, which he does flawlessly. As soon as he does though, he's doused with several buckets of ice-cold water. "Now, walk the plank and enter the sea! Enter the depths and begin your quest to receive your rewards direct from Davy Jones' Locker!"

Trevion hops off the end of the plank and drops the short distance, the two 'pirates' standing near bring him a large towel and wraps it around him. They lead him to the four officers standing next in the circle who give him clothes to put on. Trevion takes another look around at the group of men and their arrangement becomes more obvious. He notices that some groups have things behind them, like tables with covered objects on them, or benches with restraints tied to them.

He thinks to himself, *There is the other side of all this, just like Shellback Day, I've just got to get to the other side.* Trevion puts on the clothes then is led to the next group of men where he waits for the next guy as this trial requires two initiates. It was already pretty cold in these woods, but the buckets of ice water that doused Trevion has him shivering uncontrollably. "Don't worry about it, shipmate," one of the men tell Trevion, "I promise you'll warm up shortly."

7. Just One of The Guys

The ride back to the ship was filled with chatter as the new members asked a barrage of questions to the seasoned members. Trevion only listened to it all and didn't participate in the Q&A that took place. All he wanted to know was when he would get back to his ship so that he could process what had just happened to him.

He looks down at his finger and the fresh tattoo that he now has and realizes that its placed there so that it can be either seen or hidden during a salute. As the bus enters the base in Vallejo, Trevion is the only one left and the bus is pretty quiet. "Here we are, shipmate, home at last!" Trevion laughs then gives the salute given by Davy's Boys when no one else is around.

Trevion gets to the Quarterdeck which normally would be cause for reprimand because he doesn't have his ID card. But the XO had already left word that he'd be coming aboard without one. He makes it down to his locker in Supply berthing and begins to change into his uniform, hoping to catch lunch before it's over.

"Yo, what's up, Tre? How was home?" Stafford asks from inside of the galley.

"You won't believe it when I tell you, cuzz," Trevion answers as he receives whatever is left from the lunch menu.

"What, did you get married or something?"

Trevion laughs, "I took the first step, I'll let you know when the bachelor party is gonna jump off."

Stafford drops the baking pan that he was carrying and runs out of the galley. "Say what?" he demands. "You got engaged in less than two weeks? The fuck is wrong with you, blood?" Stafford stands there with his arms crossed waiting for an answer, but Trevion just chews his food and looks at him with a pleased expression. When he finishes chewing, he tells Stafford that he's engaged to Diwata, then explains the whole sponsorship and college package that brought her from the Philippines.

Stafford looks at Trevion in amazement. "Damn, you brought some beautiful, young pussy from overseas and the government paid for it? And, your momma is cool with it? You have to be the luckiest asshole breathing!" Trevion wanted desperately to tell Stafford what he had just gone through; what he's now a part of, and how much influence they have. How the Gunner's Mate that died of heat stroke didn't really die of heat stroke but was actually killed for trying to expose them.

They talk for a short while, then SK2 walks onto the mess decks. "Boot Camp! Welcome back! Suppo said that you'd be back sometime today. When you get down to GSK I'll fill you in on the new structure since, you know, SKC left and SK1 is leaving next week." SK2 smiles then turns to leave, maintaining his smile and keeping eye contact with Trevion until he walks out.

"Alright, I take that lucky shit back! But, you're still an asshole. Welcome back to the bullshit, asshole," Stafford says as he punches Trevion on the shoulder then walks back into the galley.

No SKC to act as a buffer between him and SK2; the thought removes Trevion's appetite. He walks over to the tray station and hands over his tray to the mess crank working inside. Monster is in Supply berthing when Trevion walks in. "Yo, what's crackin' Boot? How was home?" They make small talk until SK2 walks in and interrupts the conversation.

"Guys, I'm trying to shut it down by 1600 but if you want to stay late that's fine with me, I have duty anyway so I'm not going anywhere. Boot Camp, start working on that pile on your desk. Monster, I need the rest of those receipts logged. Let's go."

Monster smiles at Trevion once SK2 walks away. "Little does baby Napoleon know; our new Chief will be here in two weeks. His reign will be over before it even begins!"

After work, Trevion hangs out in Supply berthing with the clique. It feels very different to him now. He never really felt like he was a part of them before, but now he's clearly not one of them. But he slips into his normal routine and cracks jokes and tosses insults with the guys. Monster looks around and says, "So, me and Boot got duty tomorrow so we'll be off on Friday night. Who else is off on Friday?" Fernandez and Stafford say that they're off, which brings a bunch of groans from everyone else who must stand actual duty. Franky and Suave are off but Big Boats and Moorish are still away on leave.

"I count six," Monster says with a smile. "All we need is five to go out."

8.   Trevion Vs. SK2 – Round 2

Two weeks under SK2's rule felt much more like two years in Leavenworth to Trevion. SK2 took full advantage of his rank by assigning Trevion to every menial task that he could think of while insisting that Trevion's regular duties be completed. The other SKs jumped onto the SK2 bandwagon and kissed up to him daily; with the exception of Monster who has begun to feel some of the wrath directed at Trevion.

Friday morning and the clique sits at breakfast discussing the weekend when Martin walks up and whispers something in Trevion's ear. "Yes, finally!!" Trevion exclaims which makes Martin laugh on his way out.

"Finally, what?" Monster asks.

"Finally, I can see the light at the end of this dumb-ass tunnel we've been in. Come on, let's get to quarters."

Half-way through quarters, the new Suppo walks up accompanied by a Chief who she introduces as the new SKC. Trevion and Monster take great delight in looking at the expression on SK2's face as he hands over the clipboard. After quarters, the SKs meet in GSK with the new Chief. "I'm looking forward to meeting with each of you individually and discussing whatever you'd like to talk about. For now, I'll just be observing your current procedures and bringing them up to standard. Except for the R/R stuff, I know that Carson is on the cutting edge of Returnables because my last post was with Nav-Logistics and his name has come up a few times."

Trevion should be feeling proud of those words, but he's fixated on the small, blue anchor tattooed on SKC's right ring finger. A mixture of fear and relief is swimming around inside of him; he's glad that SK2 won't be bullying him as much anymore, but isn't sure if the new SKC is going to protect him or put him through more trials.

"Carson, I need you to make photocopies of your log book, and I want pictures taken of your secured area so that I can submit them to Nav-Log. Your procedure is a bit different than regulation but, we might be changing that if your technique proves to be more efficient.

Alright, everyone please finish up whatever you're working on and make sure that your desks are organized. I'm letting everyone go at lunch today. I'm on duty, so me and the duty section will finish up. I've got Carson, Middleton, and Patterson with me, right? So then, the rest of you need to square away your work so you can get out of here by noon."

SKC ends the meeting and everyone gets to work. Trevion gives the new SKC a tour of his R/R cage and the two discuss what it took to turn the area around. "I was actually on the inspection team that came to this ship and gave the R/R log a failing grade. So, when I heard that this ship was the one that's going to change procedures, I was ready to call bullshit. However, when I heard that one of the Boys was the sailor responsible, I accepted the offer to take over down here. How many of us are on the ship?"

Trevion thinks hard "I think that I'm ten and you're eleven, the skipper isn't marked so the XO is the highest-ranking shipmate."

SKC is shocked and whispers, "The XO? That's bitchin'! I guess that explains how quickly my transfer went through. And here I thought that I actually had some pull, ha! Tell me, why is the office area and everyone's desks way over there, then the rows of supply cabinets, then the warehouse area, and then your desk?"

Trevion tells him that the desk hadn't been used in years so he cleaned it up and moved into it to be next to the R/R cage. "Plus, it's kind of like my own little office." SKC laughs and agrees as he looks around.

"Well, good to meet you, shipmate; keep up the excellent work." SKC looks towards the front to see if anyone is watching then gives the salute, which Trevion returns.

"Well, I need to get ready, I'm standing with the OOD for the 12 to 16 watch. Come down after dinner so we can talk."

Noon approaches and Trevion knows, not because he looked at his watch, but because SK2 bellows "Boot Camp, give me some sweepers!" *With pleasure,* Trevion whispers because sweeping up the office area signals SK2's departure from GSK for the rest of the day. Halfway done and SK2 teases, "There you go, Golden Boy; you're even the best at cleaning up."

Trevion chuckles "You mean, like how I cleaned up that huge mess of an R/R locker? Or how I cleaned up that fraudulent log book? Naw, you mean like how I cleaned up my desk and found three R/R items that someone boneheadedly left there for weeks instead of processing."

There is a deafening silence in GSK but Monster can no longer contain himself and bursts into hysterical laughter, "Oh shit, I smell smoke... 'cause somebody just got BURNED!! HAHAHAHA!!" SK2 looks around the office and sees that most of the SKs are also struggling to contain their laughter. Trevion just continues sweeping up the area as if he hadn't said a thing.

"Don't think that since we have a new SKC that things are changing around here, I'm still the next highest-ranking Storekeeper and it's Chain-of-Command! That goes for everyone! Whoever isn't on duty can go, Boot Camp will take care of the trash when he's done sweeping." SK2 walks out, stepping in Trevion's dirt piles and tracking it all the way to the stairwell.

The other SKs wait until he's out of range so that they can laugh and crack jokes. But Monster is having no parts of it. "Yawl pussies need to shut up and leave! I didn't hear any of that shit when SK2 was down here. Beat feet!" Monster points a finger at the door and holds it there until the SKs all leave. Trevion returns to sweeping. Monster looks over at Middleton who is quietly processing invoices. "This ain't the cool duty section no more, is it Middleton?" She ignores his comment and continues working. Trevion looks over at Monster and silently tells him to lay off.

Middleton sided with SK2 when he was in command of GSK, which caused problems in her already turbulent relationship with Stafford. During an argument she called everything off, which has happened a dozen times before, but this time Stafford is refusing to reconcile. She blames Trevion for the whole thing and enjoyed the two weeks of bullying that he was receiving, cracking jokes in the background along with most of the other SKs.

In one day, all of that has changed and she's now standing duty with Trevion and the new Chief who obviously likes Trevion on reputation alone. Monster wants to rub that in as much as he can, but Trevion feels sorry for her. Especially since Stafford had been just waiting for her to lose her temper and break up with him so that he can be single again.

"How was home, Boot?" Monster asks as he goes around and sweeps up the dirt piles.

"I got engaged."

"Say what!?" Monster says as he drops the dust pan.

Trevion looks down at the dirt on the floor. "For real, big homie?"

Monster apologizes and begins cleaning the mess, but demands an explanation from Trevion. "She goes to college down in San Diego but she stays at my folk's place on the weekends." Monster puts away the dust pan and dry mops and asks for more details.

Trevion tells him that he's seen her before. "So, remember the girl that got us kicked out of your favorite bar?"

Monster pauses then frowns and shakes his head. "Not the bar in Hawaii because we didn't get kicked out of there. Can't be the bar in

PI…"

Trevion smiles and asks "Why can't it be?"

Monster erupts when Trevion pulls a picture from his wallet of the two posing in front of Mann's Chinese Theater. "How in the hell is this picture even possible? So, wait, I'm saying… Wow, she really used your money to go to college? How did she end up in San Dog?"

Trevion tells him that her grades earned her a transfer opportunity. "She lives with my parents on the weekends and on campus Monday through Thursday. So, we can all still go out and party or whatever but, I'm pretty much off the market." Middleton suddenly slams the paperwork down onto her desk and storms out of GSK. She goes up to the mess decks and looks inside of the galley to see if Stafford is there. When she doesn't see him, she walks around to the Cook's office where Stafford and Bubba are eating lunch.

"Can I speak to you for a minute?" she asks. Stafford doesn't look up from his tray, he just shakes his head 'no'. "Did you know that Trey got engaged while he was on leave?" Again, Stafford doesn't make eye contact but nods his head 'yes'.

Bubba stops eating. "Carson got engaged? That boy ain't even twenty-one yet!"

Stafford looks over at Bubba. "She fine as fuck, though."

Bubba thinks for a moment, looking up into the air. "Nope, I'll take a bunch of pretty girls over one fine as fuck girl any day." The two laugh and make jokes, but Middleton stands there with her arms folded repeatedly asking if she could have a moment with Stafford.

"Damn girl," Bubba says with a mouth full of food, "the man obviously ain't even much trying to deal with you no more. It's a whole, big-ass world out there full of nappy-headed little boys just like this one. Pick up your dignity and slide on." As she storms away, she has a few choice words for Stafford, who stays quiet. "Damn, you gonna take that?" Bubba asks.

Stafford looks up and says, "If I engage, if I make eye contact, if I make any sound at all, any motion other than nodding my head yes or shaking my head no… it'll be a launchpad into more bullshit. So, to answer your question, hell yes I'm gonna take that, and like it!"

9. Birth of the Hook-Up Guy

Trevion bags up all of the trash and packs it into a large, paper bag, then uses the staple gun to shut it. "Yo, Monster! I'm about to dump the trash!" he yells as he carries the huge bag out of GSK and up to the Quarterdeck.

SKC is standing there next to Mr. Brown, both in their white uniforms. "Carson," SKC asks as Trevion walks towards him, "isn't there an SKSR on duty today? Why are you taking the trash down, aren't you an E-3?"

Mr. Brown chuckles. "Carson is either being a gentleman since the SKSR is a lady or, and this is the one that I'll put money on, SK2 ordered him to dump the trash."

Trevion walks across the quarterdeck and says, "Ladies and gentlemen, we have a winner!" which makes Mr. Brown laugh but SKC doesn't understand. Trevion goes down the gangplank and carries the bag of trash to the dumpster. When he returns, SKC asks what's going on between him and SK2, but Mr. Brown answers, "Shipmate over here came on-board and kicked ass, earning a spot on the Security Squad. SK2 has been trying to make the Squad for over two years now and this guy made the Squad without even trying. And I haven't even mentioned the R/R stuff and the cleaning gear; both were

217

clusterfuckingly mismanaged by SK2, and both were perfected by this guy."

The cleaning gear? Trevion didn't even realize that SK2 was upset about that. He does remember the former SKC spending an unusual amount of time talking about how the cleaning gear disbursal was so 'seamless' but didn't know that SK2 had that job before him.

SKC looks at Trevion. "Well, I saw that you're standing the Mid-Watch tonight so after dinner we'll meet for a few then I'll let you grab some shut-eye. We need to figure out what we're going to do about this SK2 situation."

Trevion agrees, but Mr. Brown looks around then clears his throat and says, "Um, too late."

The two SKs look over at Mr. Brown who is looking over at the other two sailors standing watch. "It's on the radar so, we'll fill you guys in when the Boys meet."

Trevion heads back down to GSK. Big Boats is there talking with Monster about something that happened at a club recently. "What's the word, Boot?" he says while giving dap to Trevion. "I just heard that you managed to pluck a flower out of PI before it got pissed on, now you got yourself a ball of clay that you can mold into whatever you want!"

Trevion gives him a weird look and says, "I want her to be herself, people always make the mistake of getting with somebody for their potential rather than for who they already are." Monster and Big Boats erupt into laughter, along with Middleton who is sitting at the computer station processing invoices.

"We'll see, young fella." Monster says with a smile. The phone rings and it's SKC calling from the Quarterdeck, he heard from Mr. Brown about Trevion's connection at the surplus depot in Oakland and wants him to go and look for a nicer office chair.

Grabbing two of the blank forms that Pete gave him, Trevion heads up to the Quarterdeck where SKC signs the blank forms. "And, see about more of those nice foul-weather jackets that the old Suppo used to flaunt at us," Mr. Brown says as Trevion leaves the ship.

Pete is very happy to see Trevion. "Hot damn, you made it back! Welcome home, Trey!" The two embrace and chat about the war. Pete suddenly stops talking then looks around to see if anyone is close to them. "Are you a shipmate?" he asks with a smile. "Yo-Ho" Trevion is shocked by the question. Pete takes off his gloves and shows Trevion a small, blue anchor tattooed on his finger. Trevion gives the salute.

Pete returns the salute the slaps Trevion on the chest, "Damn, I knew there was a reason I liked you. Welcome aboard, son. And, welcome to the real surplus depot; let's go." Pete walks with Trevion to a door next to the restrooms and unlocks it, the door is a freight elevator leading down to the basement where the very best items are kept. "Your new chief signed the blank forms?" Trevion says yes, but is taken aback at the items that he's walking past. The place looks like a fancy department store, with everything placed into sections rather than just thrown wherever like upstairs.

Pete takes him to the furniture section and tells him to pick out a chair for his chief. "Take these tags, fill out the top and the bottom, then tie the tops to the merch, pop off the bottoms and bring them to me. Delivery will be Monday before noon for anything that you can't carry out. Let me know if you need more tags, shipmate." Pete turns and leaves while Trevion looks for a chair that will fit SKC's desk. Having wheels is pretty much standard on office chairs, but while underway the chair needs to be tethered to the desk in case of rough seas.

He finds one that is sturdy enough and has the headrest that SKC asked for and tags it. "I know we walked past an electronics section," he says aloud as he backtracks to an area with printers, computers, and other electronics. He sees a stack of boxes that contain brand-new computers with large, color monitors. "Are you kidding me? These just came out, what are they doing down here?" Trevion contemplates tagging the very expensive computers, wondering if he's allowed to; then he decides to just try, and he tags three of them.

Trevion returns to the ship just before 1700 and the Messenger helps him bring down the five boxes that he has with him. SKC sits at his desk waiting as the last box makes it to GSK. "Is my chair in one of those boxes?" he asks.

"No, Chief, the chair will get here Monday morning. But you'll like what I have in here." Trevion opens one of the boxes and pulls out an unpacked computer and puts it on SKC's desk. "I have three of these; one for you, one for me, and one for LT Cruz who will have his guys come down here and install them on our desks."

SKC looks at the box then looks at his very old-model computer on his desk and picks up his phone and calls LT Cruz who rushes down to GSK. He begins reading off various specs from the side of the box, "Where did you get these, Carson? This is top-of-the-line equipment!" SKC tells LT Cruz that one of the new computers is his if he gets his crew to replace his old computer and install the other one at Trevion's desk.

"I have some guys on duty right now doing a whole bunch of nothing. Somebody will need to stay down here while they work, but they'll be installed before taps. I'll have tomorrow's guys upload all of the programs and the encryption systems."

SKC volunteers since Trevion needed to sleep for the Mid-Watch. LT Cruz leaves with one of the boxes and Trevion pulls out the jacket that LTJG Brown wanted. "I'm going to bring this up to Mr. Brown then rack out before my watch, Chief. Is there anything that you needed me to do?" SKC begins questioning Trevion about his relationship with SK2. It's clear Mr. Brown's comments earlier has the Chief curious about what's going on.

After a bit of prodding and finally a light threat, Trevion tells SKC about the things that SK2 has been doing to him and how he's been treated. "I could tell that there was something going on; he has a bunch of backhanded compliments and passive aggressiveness going on towards you, but I thought that you all spoke to each other that way down here. Go ahead and bring Mr. Brown his jacket, and I should never have to work so hard to get information from you; no shipmate should. We always tell each other the full story, understood?" Trevion nods and apologizes before heading up to the Officers' Staterooms to deliver the jacket and then back down to Supply berthing to try and sleep before he's awakened for his watch.

10. Testing, Testing S-K-2

The next morning, Trevion drags himself out of his rack and puts on his coveralls to stand Quarters. He plans to go right back to his rack afterward since it's Saturday and he'll be off duty and off work. The Duty Section Lead makes a few announcements then thanks everyone for a smooth day of duty, then dismisses everyone E-4 and above.

Trevion turns to leave then realizes that he's only an E-3 so must stay behind. The Duty Section Lead gathers everyone closer then informs them that on their next duty day, there'll be fewer E-3 and below available so there will be lots of double watch days. "We're about to get another big wave of sailors coming aboard in the next few months, but in the meantime we'll have to just make it work."

As he leaves, Trevion wonders if that announcement applies to him since he's on the Rover watch bill. He gets back to his rack and pulls off his coveralls; but before he can crawl into bed, Monster calls him over to the opposite side of the berthing area and begins asking him questions about how he organized Smoove Criminal. He and Big Boats listen as Trevion explained some of the things that his father had taught him about organizing a business and who not to hire. Big Boats laughs, "Shit, then we can't hire anybody from the ship except for Boot over here. What you think, Monster, should we bring him in on this?"

Trevion interrupts and politely declines the offer. "I've got way too much on my plate right now, and they're watching me ever since that Canadian General thing so all I'd do is attract attention." Monster agrees and thanks Trevion, who heads for his pillow. Trevion's face is finally reunited with his pillow as he gets comfortable and tries to doze off.

"Attention on deck!" Big Boats announces as the Captain walks into the berthing area. Trevion rolls out of his bed and stands at attention. The Captain turns the corner then laughs when he sees Trevion standing there in his skivvies. "Carry on, everyone. Carson, get dressed. I need to have a word with you."

The CO walks out and Trevion begins putting on his working blue uniform. Big Boats walks back and asks what the CO wanted. "The hell if I know, maybe he wants me to find him a foul-weather jacket or something." Trevion gets dressed and walks out of the berthing, only to come right back in and open his locker. Big Boats asks what's going on. "He told me to take off my fleet cap and wear my Dixie cup." Trevion puts on his white hat and rushes out of the berthing.

The Captain hands Trevion a suitcase and tells him to carry it down to his car. Along the way he explains that he's a member of the Benicia Yachting Society and that they're hosting the Benicia High School prom next month. "I'm going to need you and a few others from the ship to be color guards. That means escorting some of the students and taking pictures. Which reminds me..." CO reaches into his car and pulls out a camera. He tells Trevion to stand with the ocean at his back and takes a few pictures.

"You're going to be my daughter's escort, she's on the Queen's Court and will be featured in lots of photos; so I want one of my best guys standing next to her in those photos. Plus, I kind of want to poke at some of the more racists members of the club, which means you're going to have a bunch of heat on you. I just needed to know if you're up for the task."

Trevion looks at the CO with a bit of surprise on his face, which makes the Captain break his normally stoic demeanor and actually crack a smile. "I'm sure that you can handle yourself, you're a pretty big kid, in great shape, and relatively handsome; plus, you have a few accolades which I'll make sure they announce when they introduce you and my Betty. Pick two more guys from the ship to come with you; but no white guys and no one over the age of nineteen, understood?"

Trevion agrees as he loads the CO's suitcase into the trunk of his car. "This conversation never happened, I'll owe you one for this, Carson." With speed, Trevion makes a bee-line back to the berthing and is almost undressed before he even reaches his rack. The feeling of his face collapsing onto the wonderful, goose down pillow that he bought in Hawaii almost gives Trevion an erection; and with a deep breath he finally drifts off to sleep.

11. The Clique

Saturday night and it's pretty much the same routine; head to the Palladium to have a beer and get stamped, off to another club which turned out to be dead, so Plan-B to the bowling alley, then back to the Palladium. This time, though, there are two long lines. One for newcomers and one for those with stamps. "The hell is this?" exclaims Suave as he looks at the amount of people standing outside of the club.

Rissa Gold is doing an impromptu performance inside and the local urban radio station is there covering it. "You should see if you're on the list, Boot," Monster suggests as they take their places at the end of the stamped line. Trevion walks up to the front and speaks to the bouncer, then waves the guys over. "I have seven guys with me tonight, am I good or do a few of them need to stand in line? They're all stamped already."

The bouncer says, "Naw, go ahead." And the guys walk in with Monster yelling, "What I tell y'all? My young apprentice got pull wherever we go!"

The guys all fan out throughout the club with Monster and Big Boats sticking close to Trevion. Big Boats suggests that Trevion go over to the VIP area and see if he can get in. "We'll act like we're your security, see if you can get us back there." The three walk over to the VIP area and the guard stops them.

"Let Rissa know that Trey Boogie is out here." The guard looks at Trevion for a moment then speaks into his radio. After a few moments he tells Trevion to go in, but his friends need to stay. "They're my security. Are you telling me that I'll be safe in there?" The guard looks over at Monster and Big Boats who stand there silently, then allows the three to enter the restricted area.

As the guys enter the VIP area, Rissa screams, "Trey Boogie! Oh my God, please tell me you're dressed to perform tonight!" She runs up and gives Trevion a big hug and a kiss on the cheek.

"Cool, that means I didn't miss the show." Trevion answers. Rissa wants him to be in the front during her six-song set so that she can pull him onstage for the last two songs to dance with her. "I tried in three separate shows to bring a guy onstage to dance with me, and every time they sucked! I got my old dance partner tonight so we're going to turn this set out!"

Franky and Moorish are lapping the club trying to find the three missing clique members. "Damn, I've never seen it this packed in here," Franky remarks. "I don't think we're going to be able to find these fools." The music fades and a man makes the announcement that Rissa Gold is about to perform and that the dance floor needs to be cleared.

Several security guards begin herding people off of the dance floor and setting up parameters. Moorish suddenly sees Big Boats. "There they go! What they hell are they doing?" Big Boats and Monster are helping put up the waist-high barriers that surround the dance floor and DJ stage. Several people are allowed onto the dance floor, including Trevion.

Moorish and Franky push their way to the guarded entrance to the dance floor, Moorish is trying to get Trevion's attention, but the DJ is playing music and everyone is excited to see Rissa Gold perform, so the noise level is very high. "Yo! Malcolm X Jr.!" Moorish recognizes Picasso's voice coming from the dance floor. He gives the 'What's up' signal to Picasso who moves over to the security guard, pointing out Moorish and Franky.

The DJ breaks the music down and introduces Rissa Gold and the club goes nuts for their local, home-grown star. Franky shoves his way to Trevion, followed closely by Moorish, then slaps him on the shoulder. "Thanks for grabbing us, dick!" Trevion tries to explain that it all happened too fast for him to grab anybody, but Franky just shines him on.

Rissa's performance has improved dramatically since the last time that Trevion saw her. Her background dancers are the same girls as before, just with the addition of much better performers doing a different routine. After two songs, she performs a duet with a rapper that Trevion has heard of; Spicy A, a Korean underground rapper from his hometown of Beach City.

After that song, the DJ stops the music and Rissa gives a heartfelt thanks to everyone who supported her on her road to success. She then says, "Now, the last time I performed this next song out here was on Picasso's show, and I danced with a guy that I met right here in this club! So, it's only fitting that I drag him back up here with me so we can get this party jumping! Trey Boogie! Get your tall, dark, and sexy ass up here, right now!!"

Trevion walks onto the stage as Monster and Big Boats urges the club to begin chanting 'Trey Boogie! Trey Boogie! Trey Boogie!' Rissa hugs Trevion and the music starts. Their hug turns into the beginnings of their dance routine as the two put on a rousing show; completely improvised. Rissa and Trevion have a mutual rhythm which seems to make them know what the other wants to do. This makes their routine seem choreographed.

After the show, Rissa invites Trevion and his friends to a party being thrown by a bunch of record execs at a hotel, "I want to introduce you to my husband, Frank. Frank, this is Trey, the one that I told you about."

Frank shakes Trevion's hand and laughs, "So, you're the reason for all of the temper tantrums that this girl throws? I feel like punching you in the stomach because you set a bar that nobody can even come close to; and she's been giving me hell ever since."

Rissa slaps Frank on the arm and tells him to be nice. "But, come on! You saw us up there tonight, tell me that wasn't the best segment you've seen! And we didn't rehearse, we haven't seen each other in ages…"

Frank concedes and tells her that she's right, then looks over at Trevion, "And now it's forever because we got it on film; thanks sport!"

12. Crash Course

Monday morning and the XO calls down to Supply berthing, instructing Trevion to come to his office. When he gets there, Mr. Brown is standing outside of the door. "Superstar has arrived! Don't disappoint me, young brotha." He gives a distinct knock on the door then opens it for Trevion, who steps in and takes a seat. The XO is standing next to his desk while another man sits there. Also seated in the office are LT Cruz and four other officers who Trevion has never seen before. The man at the desk introduces himself as Captain Aaron Palmer, Commander of the Sworn Officers Guild.

The XO calls the meeting to order by having everyone swear in "Repeat after me; I, state your name... By the will of King Neptune and by the order of the Great Davy Jones... Do hereby swear... To not repeat nor report... The happenings in this meeting... By penalty of death." Everyone swears in and is told to sit as Cpt. Palmer reads announcements and gives orders. Trevion is amazed at the scope of these men's responsibilities as one officer is instructed to meet with the Vice President.

"Carson, our Master of Logistics retired some time ago and we haven't found a suitable replacement. Aside from the fact that you've already gone through and excelled in SK school, are the coauthor of the new R/R procedure which will be taught at that school, were featured on the AFN and on various news outlets across the country and in Canada, and you've already built a positive relationship with Piccolo Pete over at the Oakland Supply Base; we're going to put you in the position on an interim basis.

"It'll still be a few years before you can officially take the position, which is good because you've got a lot to learn. Once you finish school and get your commission, we'll have a full ceremony for you. By the look on your face, you're pretty-much wondering why you're up here with us, am I right?" Trevion takes a breath to speak but nothing comes from his mouth; which brings a chuckle to the group.

"Think you can handle all of this, Carson?" asks the XO.

Trevion clears his throat and says, "I'm honored to be sitting up here. I do feel like I've kind of buffooned my way here so, I'm going to make damn sure to perform my duties at the highest possible level going forward."

The XO looks down at Cpt. Palmer with a confident smile. "And he's not at all cocky about the whole thing, you know as well as I do that he's going to bust his ass for us."

Cpt. Palmer nods and tells Trevion that he's about to be in charge of making sure that anything that one of the Boys need, they get. "Over the next few months, we're going to be sending you around to meet your network and build relationships with them. If you do half as well as you've done so far then it'll be a walk in the park for you."

As Cpt. Palmer moves on to the next person, Trevion has a moment to think about what's just happened. He was afraid that this little, secret boy's club was more like a powerful secret society and that, if he got involved, he'd be nothing more than one of their drones; and it has just happened. Trevion's life is no longer his own. After the meeting, everyone mingles for a while, introducing themselves and discussing the Sworn Officers Guild which exists within Davy's Boys. Trevion wonders if his eyes are giving away the terror in his heart as he talks and jokes with the officers.

One of them mentions the pending commission and reminds Trevion not to tell anyone. "In a year or so, you're going to go on leave for a few months to do your Mid-Shipman time. When you come back, you'll be an Ensign. Right now is the time to pay close attention to the sailors on-board and how they treat you." The XO agrees and adds that he shouldn't even tell any of the Boys on the ship. Secrets on top of secrets! Trevion is relieved when they finally begin exiting the office.

Instead of returning to GSK, he heads straight to his bunk and puts his face in his pillow. Towards the end of his panic attack, he hears "You good, blood?" Stafford's voice pulls Trevion back from the edge.

"Yeah... yeah, man, I'm good. Just got some bad news and needed a minute to get back right."

Stafford exhales deeply. "Trust that I know exactly what you mean, why do you think I'm lying in my bunk in the middle of the morning?" Trevion wants so badly to tell Stafford what he's going through, but knows that he would be putting Stafford in danger if he did.

Stafford asks if it's about his girl in college and the thought of Diwata immediately calms him down. "Naw, that's actually one of the only things that's going perfectly right." Trevion exits his rack. "Let me get my ass back to work, I'll holler at you later." The walk from Supply berthing to GSK isn't very long at all. But, in that brief trip, Trevion has time to consider that maybe the reason Diwata was able to transfer so quickly is because the Boys made it happen. Maybe she's their insurance policy against him if he messes up or starts talking to anyone. Is that why they insist that you have a wife or fiancé?

13. Ripple Effect

Trevion makes a beeline to his desk, trying to avoid SKC, when Monster calls him over. "You're never going to guess what just happened! Somebody that SK2 knew back on his last ship called and offered him a shore-duty spot... in PI, but he had to leave immediately.

He packed up his shit and bounced!"

Trevion looks around at the office as everyone laughs and talks about how abruptly SK2 left, then looks over at SKC who flashes him a low-key sign then says, "Alright, everyone, enough being tacky and petty. Finish up so we can go get lunch."

Trevion heads back to his desk, passing Monster who is doing the Cabbage Patch dance and chanting "Ding-dong, the witch is dead!" Trevion logs onto his computer and is about to go to his inventory spreadsheet when he notices a new icon on his desktop display. It looks like a… gym locker. He clicks on it and a program opens with a calendar and several documents. On the calendar, today's date shows the meeting that Trevion had just attended scheduled for 0700 and another at 1800 located at a restaurant in Benicia.

There's an RSVP button below the address, Trevion clicks it and a message pops up which reads *Thank you, Master of Logistics, your response has been noted.* Master of Logistics. The title sends chills down the spine. He silently suffers from anxiety for the rest of the day, the clique helps to take his mind off of it by bringing up the historic time they all had partying with Rissa Gold and all of the celebrities over the weekend, each telling the same stories from different perspectives.

At 1430, Trevion begins logging out of his computer when he notices that the icon has a little star on it. He clicks it and receives a message telling him to wear his dress blue uniform and to be in the parking lot by 1700. The anxiety returns as Trevion stares at the message, but is snapped out of it when he hears footsteps headed back to his desk. He closes the message and exits the program just as SKC arrives. "Carson, give me some sweepers back here then you can go. Suppo gave me her wish list, and I added a few things to the bottom. Start chipping away at this ASAP."

Trevion takes the list and looks it over; he's sure that some of these items are in the basement storage area back in Oakland. "You got it, Chief."

Trevion stands with Mr. Brown on the Quarterdeck waiting for the XO to arrive. The Officer-of-the-Deck asks Mr. Brown where they're going all uniformed up. "XO has a thing to go to and we pulled background duty, XO and the two Pips." They all laugh as the XO arrives, leading them down to a waiting car sitting in the parking lot. Mr. Brown gives Trevion instructions along the way on how to carry himself and what's expected of him. His words are actually calming as Trevion begins to feel as if he can actually do what's being asked of him.

They pull up to the Benicia Yachting Society and Trevion says, "Cool, I can scope the place out before I come to the prom party." Mr. Brown and the XO look at each other in shock. The XO asks how he knew about the event. "Well, the Skipper recruited me to be his daughter's escort and told me to pick two other guys from the ship as long as they're under twenty and not white."

Mr. Brown bursts into laughter but the XO isn't amused. "Glad you told me that, shipmate."

Inside at the bar, Trevion meets other Sworn members and they all chat. The age difference is striking as the youngest one of them is the XO, who is around forty-five years old. They all ask Trevion what feels like character questions; to which he does exactly what Mr. Brown advised him to do, which is "answer every question with all honesty, even if you don't think they'll like the response." Over dinner, Trevion is relieved to learn that he won't have very much responsibility for the next few years.

Instead, he'll be traveling and meeting the people within the supply network and getting a feel for the system. Cpt. Palmer tells him,

"Square away everything on your ship tomorrow because we're going to pull you for a week or so to work out of the Long Beach base. Ivan, grease the wheels back on your ship to make sure he's traveling to Long Beach by Wednesday morning."

The XO nods and says, "Won't be a problem." Dessert is served which signals the end of the meeting as the conversation turns to family and personal issues.

The XO announces Trevion's engagement and Cpt. Palmer orders another round so that they can toast. "Here's to our newest Sworn Officer and to his future wife; may their engagement be long and their marriage eternal!" Cpt. Palmer toasts Trevion's mug as everyone at the table says Here, here! Afterward, on the ride back to the ship, the XO commends Trevion on his mannerisms and responses in the restaurant. Mr. Brown echoes the praise and reminds Trevion to keep what's discussed by the Sworn Officers extremely private.

14. Quicksand

The flight from Oakland to Long Beach was very pleasant and Trevion garnered quite a bit of attention dressed in his working blue uniform. The war was a surprisingly popular one and most of the country celebrated the returning servicemen and women, so Trevion enjoyed the hero treatment the entire time. This did very little to quiet his anxiety which was boiling just beneath the surface, threatening to erupt at any moment. Trevion grabs his bag from the overhead storage area and makes his way down the jet bridge.

As he enters the airport, he drops his bag and runs forward, lifting Diwata and spinning her in the air the moment the two running lovers met. Her kisses are extinguishing any fear, doubt or anxiety that plagued him moments earlier. Trevion's dad walks over and grabs his bag then walks over to the two "Yeah, so... Think we can stop acting like it's been years since you've seen each other and get out of this crowded-ass airport, please?"

Trevion fields questions from both his father and Diwata as they drove from the airport to the Navy base. Trevion will be working in the neighboring city until next Friday and will be able to go home every night. "I'm not sure about the weekends but, I'll definitely be sleeping at the house every night." Trevion is dropped off at the front gate where Diwata kisses him and promises a surprise when he comes home for dinner. Home for dinner. The very thought of his mother's cooking has Trevion floating as he checks in and is shown to his quarters.

After a quick tour around the logistics area, Trevion is dismissed and told to report at the main Supply Office by 0800. Trevion takes the bus home and has time to sit and reflect as he stares out the window watching one city turn into another. The bus lets him off about three bus stops from home so he decides to walk rather than wait for the connecting bus. Trevion hasn't been gone very long but the city has changed quite a bit.

He's taken aback by how many of the small mom and pop shops are either gone or closing. When he turns onto his street, he notices the For-Sale sign in his neighbor's yard. "Hey, baby!" Diwata yells from the porch as she sees Trevion walking up. She runs over and hugs him, but he's a bit distracted by his neighbor's house being empty. They walk back home, and Trevion asks his mom what happened to the Taylors who lived next door.

"Child, Mr. Taylor got a promotion out of state and they packed up and left. Didn't even say goodbye either, I saw the moving trucks outside and went to be nosy. Hazel told me that her dad got offered a management position but he had to go immediately, so they packed up, called the movers and the realtor, and left."

"You should buy it!" Trevion's dad yells from the kitchen. "It's bigger than this one, in better shape, pool in the back that your father can fall asleep floating in during the summer…"

15. Light

Everyone jokes around about Trevion buying the house, but with an undertone of genuine possibility. Trevion remembers something that Mr. Brown told him a few nights ago at dinner; "When you're ready to buy a house, call me. I have connections who understand that you're just starting out and don't have a bunch of money." Trevion says that he'd like to call someone and walks into the kitchen to use the phone. He calls the ship and asks to speak to Mr. Brown. "Hey there, youngblood! How's that home cooking treating you?"

Trevion chuckles, "Pretty great, actually. Sorry to bother you sir, but I have a question about buying a house."

Mr. Brown compliments Trevion on calling him first, then asks for the address of the house that he's thinking about. Trevion is about to give the address when Mr. Brown says, "I'm just kidding, I know the address. It's 1045 Olive Avenue, right next to your parent's place. Recently vacated by your long-time neighbor whose job took him out of state a few weeks ago, right? I'll have the realtors out there tomorrow at 1600 sharp to get your John Hancock on the paperwork. I can hear you hyperventilating, compose yourself. You have a lot to learn, kid. Thank me with some of that home-cooked food you got over there, shipmate."

Trevion takes a deep breath and ends the call with a "Yes sir, thank you sir." He hangs up the phone then sits at the table with his dad, who breaks into one of his stories as a way to calm his son. He talks about when he was fresh out of high school and how he joined the Merchant Marines, a story which Trevion has never heard.

"You joined the what now?" His dad continues with brief but crazy stories about his time out to sea, none of which Trevion had ever known. He ends the stories by pulling off his class ring, revealing a small anchor.

"And this was the craziest thing that I've ever done. And I see that crazy is genetic because my son has one too."

Trevion looks at his own anchor tattoo and wonders if his father is as afraid of them as he is, but he doesn't wonder long because the pride on his dad's face shows that he's embraced being one of the Boys; and is thrilled that his son is one too. "Finally, I have somebody to talk to, you have no idea how hard it is to keep this from your mother. She's nosy as hell!" Trevion laughs with his dad, then admits that it's all pretty overwhelming. His dad reassures him and says, "Just go with it, we're nothing more than a bunch of really great guys who look out for each other."

Trevion's dad goes on about the Boys until Diwata walks in. "So, are you ready for my surprise, baby?" Trevion just received two surprises that pretty much changed his world; he now questions his entire childhood with the realization that his father is, and has been, one of Davy's Boys. Has he been priming Trevion this whole time? Training him to one day be a member of this frightening little club? Nothing that Diwata can say will come close to any of this.

"What's you're surprise, beautiful?" Diwata sits on Trevion's lap then pulls out a picture and hands it to him. "This is a picture of my mom from before I was born. The man standing next to her is my father. When she found out that I was coming to the US, she went to my granny's village and sent me some of her old pictures and letters."

Trevion's hand becomes weak as he looks at the picture that he's holding. "His name is Chuck. My mom said that he lived somewhere in California, so I looked him up. He's still in the Navy, stationed up

North, I talked to him yesterday. He's coming down here to see me and to meet you this weekend. Isn't that incredible?"

Trevion stares at the picture of a young LTJG Charles 'Chuck' Brown standing next to Diwata's mother and wearing the uniform of an E-4. He looks up at Dee and can suddenly see the resemblance; along with the delight in her eyes at the prospect of meeting her father for the first time. Trevion looks at the picture again, then over at his dad who still has the proud smile on his face. With a deep breath he says, "This will be one hell of a weekend.".